continued . . .

Killing Thyme

LESLIE BUDEWITZ

BERKLEY PRIME CRIME
New York

BERKLEY PRIME CRIME
Published by Berkley
An imprint of Penguin Random House LLC
375 Hudson Street, New York, New York 10014

Copyright © 2016 by Leslie Ann Budewitz
Penguin Random House supports copyright. Copyright fuels creativity, encourages
diverse voices, promotes free speech, and creates a vibrant culture. Thank you for buying
an authorized edition of this book and for complying with copyright laws by not
reproducing, scanning, or distributing any part of it in any form without permission.
You are supporting writers and allowing Penguin Random House to continue to
publish books for every reader.

BERKLEY is a registered trademark and BERKLEY PRIME CRIME and the B colophon
are trademarks of Penguin Random House LLC.

ISBN: 9780425271803

First Edition: October 2016

Printed in the United States of America

Cover art by Ben Perini
Cover design by Colleen Reinhart
Book design by Kelly Lipovich

For the readers, who let me keep them up too late

Acknowledgments and Historical Note

The Emerald City, aka Seattle, is never the same place twice, nor the same to every visitor or reader. That's part of its magic.

In the early 1990s, I volunteered at the Family Kitchen, a daily meals program at St. James Cathedral in Seattle run by Pacem in Terris, a Catholic Worker community. (Now the Cathedral Kitchen, operated by the parish, it continues to serve those in need.) While that program and the social justice advocates who started it inspired my fictional Grace House and Jimmy's Pantry, the people and events here are completely my invention.

For an understanding of the Vietnam-era protests in Seattle, I drew on *Rites of Passage: A Memoir of the Sixties in Seattle*, by Walt Crowley, and the HistoryLink online archives. Although the "Catholic left" did engage in public protests in the early 1980s, the events that set in motion the present-day conflicts here are fictitious. Any resemblance to actual history is proof that even a writer's imagination has its limits.

Pepper's hibiscus flower and sea salt rub was inspired by a tin of Paradise Flower Salt rub given to me by Karyn Schwartz, proprietor of Sugarpill, a "culinary mercantile and apothecary" in Seattle's Pike-Pine corridor.

Pepper consults *The Complete Idiot's Guide to Private Investigating* by Steven Kerry Brown. What she does with the information in that highly useful book is entirely my fault.

Thanks to all the booksellers and specialty retailers who have put the Spice Shop Mysteries in readers' hands across the country. Seattle Mystery Bookshop has been a great partner in crime, even letting me borrow the shop on these pages. At home, Derek Vandeberg of Frame of Reference and Marlys Anderson-Hisaw of Roma's Kitchen Shop continue to give my books a local boost. Amanda Bevill, owner of World Spice Merchants on Western Avenue in Seattle, offered insider knowledge of the spice business with a hearty dash of enthusiasm. Market staff, merchants, and vendors shared their time and knowledge with me. Like most writers, I'm an eavesdropper and a sponge, soaking up tales and tidbits that have wriggled their way, often much scrambled, into my stories. Thank you all for helping season the story stew.

I could not set a book in Seattle without the help and hospitality of Lita Artis and Ken Gollersrud. Thanks also to Debbie Burke for years of literary friendship and sharp eyes. I would not be a published writer without Sisters in Crime, and my pals in the Guppy chapter. Hugs and thanks to you all.

Thanks to my agent, Paige Wheeler of Creative Media Agency, Inc., my editors, Robin Barletta and Tom Colgan, and all the staff—editorial, art, marketing, production, and more—at Berkley Prime Crime for shepherding my words into print and pixels, and into your hands.

Readers often ask who does my covers. Ben Perini brings the Spice Shop of my imagination to such delightful life. And, the dog.

My husband, Don Beans, aka Mr. Right, happily chops, stirs, and tastes every recipe, listens when I need an ear, and dives in when I need an idea. Plus, having an in-house doctor is every mystery writer's dream.

The Market Roll Call

Your lineup for a tasty mystery!

THE SEATTLE SPICE SHOP STAFF

Pepper Reece—owner, ex–law firm HR manager
Sandra Piniella—assistant manager and mix master
Reed Locke—part-time salesclerk, full-time college student
Kristen Gardiner—part-time salesclerk, Pepper's oldest friend
Cayenne Cooper—salesclerk, the spicy new hire
Matt Kemp—salesclerk, an experienced retail hand
Arf the Dog

THE FLICK CHICKS

Pepper—her real name is her secret, for now
Kristen—she knows, but she knows enough to keep her mouth shut
Laurel Halloran—deli owner, caterer, houseboat dweller
Seetha Sharma—still a bit of a mystery

MARKET MERCHANTS, RESIDENTS, AND FRIENDS

Glenn Abbott—Pepper's next-door neighbor, a city council member
Jen the Bookseller and Callie the Librarian—Pepper's former law firm employees
Mary Jean—the chatty chocolatier

Hot Dog—man about town
Vinny Delgado—the wine merchant
Ben Bradley—ace reporter, Pepper's boyfriend

THE PAST MEETS THE PRESENT:

Lena Reece—Pepper's mom, still the Earth Mother
Bonnie Clay—aka Bonnie Pretty Pots aka Peggy Manning
Terry Stinson—war protestor turned Uncle Sam and family man
Sharon Stinson—his loyal wife, dance mom
Brian Strasburg—not the best advertisement for the legal
   profession
Hannah Hart—displaced artist

SEATTLE'S FINEST

Officer Tag Buhner—aka Bike Boy and Officer Hot Wheels,
   Pepper's former husband
Detective Cheryl Spencer—homicide
Detective Michael Tracy—homicide
Detective John Washington—cold case detective

One

To everything—turn, turn, turn
There is a season—turn, turn, turn
And a time to every purpose under heaven.

—Pete Seeger, "Turn! Turn! Turn!" adapted from
Ecclesiastes 3:1–8

"WHY IS IT CALLED A SALT PIG?" MATT SAID. "IS THAT LIKE salt pork?"

"No, silly. Salt pork is pork belly that's cured by salting instead of smoking. Think bacon. My grandmother used it to flavor her Sunday pork and beans." Cayenne's dark eyes flickered open and shut in remembered rapture, long lashes brushing her high cheekbones.

The banter between the Spice Shop's newest employees put a smile in my heart. No last-minute desperation hires this time. He knows retail; she knows food. And as their boss, I knew within days of hiring them that they would be great additions to the Pike Place Market, Seattle's heart, soul, and stomach.

But Matt's cocked head and half squint said her explanation hadn't cleared up the muddle over the classic salt container.

"Some sources say it looks like a pig's back end if you

stand it sideways on its head." Cayenne used a particularly porcine model—smooth, glossy, and pinky-beige—to demonstrate. "But I've also heard that pig is an ancient Scottish word for a clay pot."

"That works for me." Roundish, sixtyish, sporting the short, dark hair of an Italian pixie, Sandra lifted the lid off a celadon green oval jar and mimed scooping out salt with two fingers. "This one's good. Lets you get a grip on the stuff."

"That's another thing I don't get," Matt said. He slid into the mixing nook beside the rest of us. Seeing the crew gathered for our Wednesday morning staff meeting, each sipping coffee or our custom-blended spice tea, a box of pastries open before us, gave me the satisfaction of a mother hen.

After all that upheaval . . . I perished the thought. As if he read my mind from where he lay under the table, Arf rested his muzzle on my knee. I rubbed a thumb on the magic spot on his forehead.

"A pinch is really a guess. Why not measure?" Matt continued. "And what about hygiene?"

"You measure with your eyes and your mouth," Sandra said. "A recipe may look precise, but it's a guideline. You can't know how much salt your soup needs until you taste it. Is your broth salty? Are your carrots and onions on the sweet side? You taste, and balance."

"Except when you're baking," I said, raising a finger. "Then you're talking chemical reactions. But with herbs and spices, you have more freedom."

"And cooks are trained to wash their hands a *lot*." Cayenne set the salt pig back in the weathered wooden box and withdrew a rounded container. The lower half was glazed a rich, blue-streaked mahogany, the upper a cinnamon-speckled oatmeal. A hand-carved wooden spoon poked out of the almond-shaped opening in front. "Isn't this wonderful, Pepper? The potter's new to the Market."

She handed me the earthenware pig. The opening allows easy access while keeping the salt free of kitchen dirt and drips. Salt is hydrophilic, so an unglazed interior absorbs moisture and keeps the salt from clumping. Nice, in Seattle's damp clime.

"It's food safe, obviously, and dishwasher safe," Cayenne said.

"Are you her new sales rep?" Matt gibed.

"No. I just love her work, and I think we should carry it."

"Wish we could. But if she sells through us, she'll lose her Market permit. And the artists' tables are a huge draw—she'll do better on her own." Cayenne opened her mouth to protest, but I cut her off. "Hey, I don't make the rules." I set down the pig and reached for the potter's card. "*Bonnie Clay—Potter—Functional Sculpture*. Oh, too funny."

Blank faces stared at me. "Continuing the Scottish theme," I said, "'bonnie' means pretty or attractive. So, her name translates to Pretty Pots."

"Maybe she named herself," Reed ventured. "Because of her work."

Sandra snorted. "Ya think?"

She and Reed had come with the shop when I bought it nearly two years ago, and despite their differences in age and temperament, she treats him like a favorite puppy. Most days. Now, she ignored the wounded look on his gentle features, and he hunched over his tea, a lock of black hair flopping onto his forehead.

"Sorry, Cayenne," I said. "Good find, but no go. I'll take the samples back and talk to her." We turned our attention to the long list of daily tasks. We'd all pitched in to train the newcomers while unpacking shipments, refilling hundreds of jars and canisters holding spices from around the world, making deliveries to restaurants, yada yada. Plus blending our own tea and spice mixes fresh every week. After years working all variety of retail, Matt had grasped our customer-first philosophy from the get-go. Cayenne oozes natural charm and has an encyclopedic knowledge of food. But she occasionally needs a reminder that no matter how busy she is sweeping up spilled thyme, the customer is never an interruption.

"Were you able to solve that glitch in the wedding registry software?" I asked Reed.

He opened his mouth, but Sandra spoke first. "There was no glitch. The bride has the same personality as her mother. The registry shows no gifts purchased because she has no friends."

I suppressed a smile. The bridal mother had stomped in yesterday afternoon spewing complaints. We had wrongfully delayed sending her beloved daughter any gifts; our system bordered on false advertising, if not fraud; and we were not fit to kiss the hem of the most beautiful bride in Seattle's pearl-encrusted train. "Send the bride our thyme gift box as a thank-you for registering."

A perennial best seller, thyme was also our featured Spice of the Month. By mid-June, most Seattle gardeners are deep into maintenance mode, so we'd arranged the last few seedlings in the center of our main display table. The slightest movement of air sent pleasant grassy notes swirling through the shop.

"Anything else?" Three bright-eyed heads shook "no." "Great. Let's have a spicy day."

The fourth head stayed bowed, and its owner stayed put. I waited until the others had slid out of the booth and started their morning routine. "What's up?"

A long silence. "I hate women who bawl at work."

Sandra, my assistant manager, on the verge of tears? About as likely as Momzilla sending me roses to apologize for her hissy fit. But thirteen years working HR in a law firm, managing legal secretaries, assistants, and receptionists, had taught me to keep my mouth shut and leave room for her to speak in her own good time.

Sometimes you have to sit a little longer than your backside wants.

She wrapped her arms around her ample midsection and gripped her elbows, eyes damp and unfocused. "I—I can't talk it about it, Pepper. Not yet."

My mouth went dry. *Was she ill?* Selfishly, I worried about the shop—how could we manage without her?

The citrus-and-spice smell of our signature tea filled the air as Matt poured an extra-strength batch of hot brew into the giant cooler, the ice in the bottom crackling.

I touched her arm. "We're here for you. Whatever you need." Sometimes the clichés are true.

At ten o'clock, I sent Arf to his bed behind the front counter and unlocked the door. Two minutes later, Kristen swept in, a bubbly blond cloud.

My lifelong BFF and part-time staffer, she'd skipped this week's huddle for a plotting session with her landscaper, arranging the final floral touches in her backyard. Two days till her annual shindig—a joint birthday party for the two of us, born two weeks apart. It was also a celebration that her family's long-running remodel was finally finished and a chance to welcome my mother home for a visit from Costa Rica.

"What a pretty day! We are going to be swamped, even midweek. Pepper, the house looks so fabulous. And the garden. Ohmygosh." She disappeared from view long enough to stash her purse in back, then emerged, tugging her black Spice Shop apron over her head. Our white logo—a saltshaker sprinkling salt into the sea—bobbed as she wound the strings around her narrow waist and tied them in a floppy bow.

"Is this Cayenne's new potter? How fabulous." She

picked up a card and read the name. Tossed it aside. "I can't wait for you and Lena to see my surprise! You won't believe what we found in the basement."

"What? You never said a word." The year we were born, Kristen's parents and mine established a communal household in the four-story Capitol Hill house her mother had inherited. I'd helped her with design work and shopping, but knew nothing of a basement discovery.

She wiggled her brows and lifted one shoulder. "A girl's got to have some secrets."

The bell on the front door jangled, and a gaggle of women surged in. "Don't be nervous," she said before rushing off to welcome the customers and offer samples of tea.

I headed for my office to return a few phone calls and follow a lead on a Portuguese whole black mustard seed I'd been trying to import for months. A cell phone is an unreliable mirror, but in that fleeting second between powering on and lighting up, the screen reflected my raggedy-on-purpose hair, and I fluffed it instinctively. My mother had not been surprised when I'd left my police officer husband, after catching him and a meter maid—I can't bring myself to say "parking enforcement officer"—practically plugging each other at a back table in a posh new restaurant when he was supposed to be working overtime for a buddy. She had not been fazed when, thirty days later, I plunked down every penny I had on an unfinished loft in a century-old warehouse above the waterfront. She barely blinked when the law firm imploded in scandal and I lost the job I loved. And she kept her mouth shut when I responded by buying the Seattle Spice Shop, a forty-year-old institution mired in the past.

But cutting my sleek, dark, city-styled hair to a two-inch mass that resembled an old-fashioned dust mop, made of twisted yarn and electric with static—that gave her major heartburn.

She wouldn't say a word until we were alone, but I'd know the moment she walked in whether she'd forgiven me.

And Kristen wondered why I was nervous.

Back out front, I surveyed my domain. Behind the counter, Sandra measured and bagged a large order, while Cayenne rang it up.

"I need a hostess gift," a customer said. "I love your tea, but she's a coffee drinker."

"A lot of those around." I gestured toward a display of gift boxes. "Does she grill? This set features our Cajun blend and a Southwest rub. If she prefers a milder touch, we've got another combo that's high on flavor and low on heat. Or we can put together a custom box."

"She loves Indian food."

"We've got just the thing." I handed her a tester. "Four custom blends: two curries, a garam masala, and a vindaloo cranked up with an extra dose of cayenne. All in an easy-to-ship gift box."

She passed the open jar under her nose, her eyelids fluttering shut as she took in the aroma of our mildest curry. Her face softened, and she crossed the line from skeptical to satisfied.

Spice does that.

After a late-morning rush, we skidded to a pre-lunch lull. My predecessor had carried a handful of spice guides and ethnic cookbooks, but I'd spotted the sales potential right off the bat. We'd brought in two long, double-sided shelf units and added tons of cookbooks, essay collections, chef lit, and even fiction.

I sat on the floor to straighten the foodie mysteries. Whether it's spice jars or books, I find alphabetizing a soothing task. "A for Albert and *Rosemary Remembered*, C for Laura Childs and *Gunpowder Green*. Gotta order her new one." My friend Jen works in the Mystery Bookshop in

Pioneer Square and alerts me to authors my customers might enjoy. "What is *The Diva Runs Out of Thyme* doing way down there? That belongs in the Ds for Davis."

"Are you talking to the books or yourself?"

"Mom!" I stood and embraced a smaller version of myself, her well-tanned face breaking into a grin. Behind her, looking like an echo of my father—except that I hadn't seen my father in a suit since my wedding day—towered my brother, Carl.

He leaned in and kissed my cheek. "Can't stay—I'm double-parked. Mom, I'll pick you up around five thirty."

She waved a hand. "You go play with money or whatever it is you do. Pepper and I need girl time."

My brother manages the city's bond portfolio, thrusting him into debates over construction projects, interest rates, and investment doodah that brings glazed looks to the faces of our parents—a Vietnam vet turned history teacher and a barely reformed hippie chick.

He kissed her and strode off, waving to the staff on his way out.

Kristen finished helping a customer and joined us. "Lena," she said, and my mother took her face in her hands.

"So like your mother. I miss her." They hugged, and Kristen dabbed at her eye.

My mother walked slowly around the shop, taking in the changes. "That apothecary is exactly right for the tea things. And to think Tag wanted you to leave it for the junkman."

Actually, my ex had called *me* the neighborhood junkman. Not that he was wrong.

She paused in front of the registry and gift display, a video of brides, grooms, and idyllic settings looping across the computer screen. "I can't believe what the wedding business has become. Brilliant of you to find a niche of your own within it."

"Any new thing takes time, but it's starting to pay off."
Behind my back, I crossed my fingers.

She took my arm. "Lunch at the Pink Door? I'm desperate to drink the city in."

The dog and I made a quick trip to the alley, then Mom and I headed out. My tote over my shoulder and the box of borrowed pottery in my arms, we wove through the crowds of tourists and downtown workers who'd dashed to the Market to grab a quick lunch and shop for dinner. Pike Place is the main thoroughfare, a curious L-shaped street paved in ancient cobblestones. Only the brave or the lost drive down it after opening bell. And a late delivery van or two. We cut between two idling trucks, my mother's hand on my shoulder, the hot diesel-y exhaust from a tailpipe whipping the leg of my black yoga pants.

On the other side of the street, we stepped into the North Arcade, a covered walkway lined with two long rows of wooden tables painted green. To our left, where the farmers and other growers cluster, early-summer produce filled the four-foot allotments, and flowers burst out of buckets. My mother kissed Angie and Sylvie Martinez, aka the orchard sisters, and asked about their grandmother, an old friend from the farm boycotts and protest lines.

"Down this way." We took a right and headed north-ish—directions are iffy in the Market. The box of pottery was awkward, and I had to be careful in the crowd. Finally, we stopped at a display of hand-thrown bowls, vases, and crocks. Behind the table, a wiry woman bent over a box, her graying blond ponytail falling forward to hide her face.

"You must be Bonnie Clay," I said. "I'm Pepper Reece, owner of the Spice Shop, and this is my mother." The woman straightened and turned to face us.

The Market is not a quiet place. Thousands of people stroll the streets and sidewalks, chattering and calling to each other. Trucks and delivery carts rattle across the cobbles. Bicycles whiz by, and motorcycles zoom up the hills. Street musicians sing and play guitars, violins, cellos, even a piano on wheels. Vendors proclaim their wares, and customers barter for better prices on beans and broccoli. Traffic rumbles down First Ave, and out on Elliott Bay, ferries sound their horns.

For one long moment, it all stopped, sucked up by my mother's sharp intake of breath.

"Peggy Manning," she said. "I thought you were dead."

Two

The human brain can differentiate hundreds of odors, far more than it can verbally identify.

—psychologist Frank Schab, in *Memory for Odors*

THE DARK RIMS AROUND THE WOMAN'S PALE BLUE IRISES seemed to flash and flare. They reminded me of the cobalt-streaked glaze on her salt pig.

They reminded me of something else, too. But what—and where?

My mother glanced from the woman to the pots to the name on the hanging sign. "A nom de kiln? How clever." She held out a slim hand, the nails neatly trimmed. The potter hesitated, then wiped a hand on her apron and extended it. A dark vein throbbed against her rough skin.

Something unspoken filled the air between them as they touched, something thick and impenetrable. As though a private history was written in the dust motes and could never be fully read, or understood, by anyone else.

"Lena Reece. Good God. I thought you'd moved to Guatemala." Her voice was low and a little creaky, as if it didn't get used much.

"Costa Rica. Just home for a quick visit. Peggy—Bonnie—you remember my daughter, Pepper. She was a kid the last time you saw her, back in the Grace House days."

That must have been where I'd seen those eyes. Around the communal table, or in the third-floor yoga and meditation room.

I set the box down. "So nice to meet you. Your work is terrific. But you're new—you may not have known that daystallers can't also sell through the shops. I'm sorry."

Her eyebrows rose, and she lifted her chin a fraction, her head tilting a few degrees. "This place sure does have a lot of rules."

The Market is a city within a city—three hundred shops and restaurants, two hundred vendors renting daystalls, and more than three hundred residents. Not to mention ten million visitors a year, all in nine acres. "The rules" had rubbed me the wrong way a few times, mostly over updated signage, but we need them. Some, like the rule against dogs in shops, are honored in the breach. But much as I liked this woman's work, I wasn't about to cross the line separating the shops from the daystalls.

"I can put a few pieces in our display case and send customers to you. If you expect to be around for a while. Meanwhile, I'll take the pig, for myself. Your blue glaze is spectacular."

Her lips twitched. She shot my mother the briefest of looks. "Oh, I'm here to stay."

My mother's shoulders stiffened.

Bonnie wrapped the pig in brown paper. "Grace House. I bet it hasn't changed in thirty years."

"Oh, but it has," I said. "Kristen and her husband own it now. You won't believe the place, Mom. That reminds me, she's got a surprise for us. Something they found in the basement."

Bonnie-Peggy handed me the pig and took my cash, her

eyes hooded, her lips unsmiling. "Kristen? The little blonde? You two ran around like each other's shadows."

"We still do. She works in my shop." I felt my mother tugging at me, though she hadn't touched me.

Next to me, a woman reached for a vase, the same pale green as the lidded salt jar Sandra had admired.

"Porcelain," the potter told her. "Fired at a very high heat. Nonporous—it won't leak."

"It's so light," the woman said.

"Why don't you choose three pieces to display," I told the potter. "And give me a stack of your cards."

She nodded, wordless, but those extraordinary eyes were on my mother.

"Good to see you, Peggy," my mother said, her tone steady and kind.

"And you, Lena."

I didn't believe either one of them.

THE door really is pink. Not a bold raspberry pink, but the pink of a young girl's ballet slippers, or her first lip gloss.

The door is the only understated thing about the place. For years, there was no sign, and even now, people miss it. In good weather, they spot the rooftop deck, ripe with food and drink, Puget Sound sparkling beyond, and stop anyone strolling by for directions.

It's worth the effort. Our waiter poured the Prosecco and vanished like the mist that had hung over the Sound this morning.

"Ahhh." My mother leaned back. A touch more gray— she calls it sparkle—shone in her hair than when we'd last seen each other, and when her face relaxed, lips upturned, eyes closed, I saw a few more fine wrinkles. "How I have missed Seattle."

"Tell me about Bonnie. Or Peggy. I don't remember her." I reached for the bread basket.

"Some other time, sweet pea. Your hair's cute, by the way. Now that I'm used to it. I want to hear about the shop. And your love life."

I felt my cheeks warm and hoped the awning kept my embarrassment in shadow.

"Shop's great," I said. "Matt and Cayenne fit in well. It's a relief to have a solid crew in place again."

"You were worried about losing customers over the last— incident." She avoided the word "murder." I'd be happy to avoid it for a good long while myself.

"Yesterday's news. When the connection to the shop hit the paper, people came in all wide-eyed. 'Oh, you're that Pepper.' But the talk faded fast, and we didn't lose any commercial accounts over it."

"Good. You've infused the shop with such a positive spirit. Jane's a dear, but her vibration's been slowing the last few years, and the energy had drained out of the place. I'm looking forward to meeting your young man. Although he's probably not so young, is he?"

I snatched up my glass so the waiter could set the Italian chopped salad in front of me. She meant to point out that I was no longer so young myself, but it was funny. Both Ben and I are blessed—or cursed—with youthful faces, and we'd hesitated over our mutual attraction, unsure about dating someone so much younger. Then we'd discovered that wasn't the case. "We're two years apart—he turned forty-one in March. You'll like him."

My mother pointed her flute at me. "The question is, do you like him? What's his sign?"

I picked up my fork and speared a chickpea, described on the menu as raised on the wild grasslands of the Palouse country in eastern Washington. "I'm not sure. I'm so glad you're here. And I can hardly wait to see Dad." My father had flown to Vancouver to meet Kristen's dad for their annual sailing trip up the Canadian coast. They'd be back in Seattle in a few weeks.

"You don't know the man's birthday, let alone his moon and rising signs? Pepper, what are you thinking?"

I was thinking that I didn't want to have this conversation. After the debacle that had been my previous relationship, I'd plunged into the tidewater of timidity and the cesspool of self-doubt. Kristen had urged me to flirt, have fun, go bowling, and stop worrying about my judgment in men. Ben fit the bill. Reading the stars too closely meant investing too much in the future.

I'd told him I wanted to take things slowly, and he'd agreed. I got the impression his last relationship had been pretty volatile, one of those off-and-on things that can take a while to recover from.

She sighed. "Remember, you're a Gemini, but you have strong grounding influences. That's why you manage to accomplish so much. You need someone who can complement that."

"Is that the secret to your happy marriage?" Forty-five years of true love, far as I could tell.

"Hmmm." Her eyelids drifted shut, then opened, and she fingered the bright floral tablecloth where it draped and formed a soft pleat. Vinyl, the modern substitute for oilcloth. "I think so. Along with honesty and flexibility. And trust in the other to make choices for the well-being of all."

"To the well-being of all." I raised my glass. For the next hour, we ate, chatted, and sipped, the sun dancing on the waves, our food fresh and well seasoned. My mother seemed to relish the very air, to be invigorated by the chit and chat around us. But I sensed something pensive about her, something guarded.

"Mom, why did you think Peggy Manning was dead?"

She pushed her empty salad bowl away. "Not now, Pepper. This has been the perfect afternoon."

Put off the topic twice in one conversation. Why? My jaw twitched. I gripped the edge of my chair, to keep my fingers from rubbing the tight spot, and resisted the urge to fidget.

Amazing how your mother's arrival can make you feel four years old again.

We paid the bill, and as we headed into the dining room, its elegant tables off-limits until the next rainy day, I excused myself to visit with the chef. I like to let customers know when I've been in the house, that I put my mouth where my money came from. And sometimes I walk out with a spur-of-the-moment order.

When I emerged from the kitchen, my mother had disappeared. Figuring she'd already headed up the stairs to Upper Post Alley, I followed suit. One step out the door, I found myself face-to-face with a bewildered middle-aged man.

"Is this how you get there?" he said, pointing to the deck. In answer, I held the door and made a welcoming gesture while he called to his wife.

And that's when I heard my mother, out of sight but not out of earshot. "I can't believe you're telling me not to worry," she said. No reply—she had to be on her phone. "I've got to run—my daughter doesn't know anything about this. But she won't like it."

Right on both counts, Mom.

"YOU'VE got work to do, so I'll wander around a bit," my mother said when we returned to the shop. "See what's new."

"You must have riotously good farmers' markets in Costa Rica," Sandra said.

"The *feria*. We go every Saturday morning. We've learned to eat fish and tropical fruit we'd never heard of up here. Yuca, mangostino, guanabana. But this place is part of me."

"It's changed a lot." Sandra's words held a note of regret.

"More tourists. Fewer services, more gifts. Not so many locals doing their weekly shopping."

"Shopping's changed," I said. "Every suburb has its own farmers' market. Grocery stores sell arugula now." The sped-up pace of modern life was another factor. The Market had responded by creating weekly pop-ups in public plazas downtown, taking the farmers' bounty to the office workers. Great idea, though it didn't help the merchants—the "stores with doors."

"We can't let ourselves get stuck in the past," my mother said.

"Never thought we'd be the older generation," Sandra replied. She and my mother were kindred spirits—Seattle natives, of an age, who love food and taking care of people. When I bought the shop, they'd quickly discovered shared memories of shopping here with their immigrant parents in the 1950s. Historians may call that an ebb tide in the Market's chronicles, but not if they heard these two women recall the aromas of fresh fish and fried chicken, playing games on the cracked floor tiles, and the sounds of a dozen mother tongues clucking.

Was my mother considering coming home?

"Do you think your sister-in-law will mind if I pick up a few groceries?" she said.

"I think if you mess with her menu planning, you'll be living dangerously, but if you bring treats for Carl and the kids, they'll rally 'round you." My sister-in-law is a lovely woman who firmly believes in the well-planned life. She is also a card-carrying member of the food police.

Mom had barely cleared the door when I pulled Kristen into the nook. "The weirdest thing happened. Do you remember a woman named Peggy Manning? She's got crazy blue eyes."

Kristen's own eyes widened. "Go on."

"On our way to lunch, we detoured through the Arcade

to drop off the pottery Cayenne brought in. And the potter, Bonnie Clay? She and Mom recognized each other in a flash."

I described the encounter and my mother's refusal to tell me anything about Peggy, now Bonnie. The phone conversation in the alley I kept to myself. Something about it nagged at me, and I wasn't ready to spill. Being each other's shadows much of our lives didn't mean Kristen and I didn't keep a few things to ourselves.

People assume Kristen is an airhead because she's blond, pretty, and gets a weekly manicure. And because she lives in a great house in an old neighborhood and doesn't need to work. I knew better. I watched her turn thoughtful.

"That was a challenging time."

"You mean during the war? When our parents met?"

"No. Later." Kristen folded one arm across her body and rubbed her chin between her left thumb and forefinger.

I didn't remember any of that. Or rather, I didn't remember anything out of the ordinary. Talk about principles and commitments, intention, and deliberate action was commonplace in Grace House. "Was there something specific—?"

The door chimes rattled.

"Oh, good, you're both here." Laurel Halloran headed toward us, her gray-brown curls trailing like a veil. "Don't forget about tonight," she said to me. And to Kristen, "Lemon thyme shortbread."

"Ohmygosh," I said as Kristen asked, "What's tonight?"

"Chef's dinner at Changing Courses," Laurel said. "Pepper's first class is graduating."

A longtime Seattle chef, Laurel had cajoled me into volunteering with a project that trains homeless and disadvantaged adults to work in the food service industry. Every week, I teach a new group of students about herbs and spices. Every Wednesday, a local chef coordinates a three-course dinner, open to the public, the students serving as sous chefs. The opening ceremony honors that week's graduates. Even with my mother in town, I wouldn't miss it. Besides, she was staying at my brother's house, to spoil the grandchildren.

"We need to finalize this menu," Laurel told Kristen as she slid into the nook. "After that wet spring, the herbs are exploding, and I've got more thyme than I know what to do with."

"You're the only woman in the world who can say that," I said.

"I found a recipe for thyme-flavored lemonade. For the adults, add tequila or gin."

Kristen shot me an over-the-shoulder look I couldn't read. Did it say our conversation wasn't finished, or that she was relieved to be cut off? She didn't need to worry about the interruption—I give my staff leeway when personal stuff pops up during the day. And when your two best friends are planning a party together, that's inevitable.

Besides, the party was partly for me.

"Too many choices," I heard Kristen say, from the nook.

"That's the problem," Laurel replied. "Time to choose."

Always the problem, isn't it? I picked up where Kristen had left off, filling shallow wicker baskets with darling silicone tea infusers shaped like owls, gingerbread men, and musical notes. Talk about choices. (I'd passed on the sea creatures, doubting that my customers would find a green octopus floating in their tea as appetizing as the manufacturer hoped.)

My pals finished their kibitz in time for Kristen to dash off and for Laurel to head back to Ripe, her deli, or home to her houseboat.

"C'mon, Arf," I said. "Let's go stretch your legs." He sat to let me click on his leash. I tucked a plastic bag into my apron pocket, and we headed north on Pike Place to Victor Steinbrueck Park, a haven of green named for the visionary architect who saved the Market from the ravages of progress in the early '70s. Near one of the two totem poles commemorating the region's Native heritage, Arf pooped and I scooped. Then we meandered over to the wrought iron railing to take in the view of Puget Sound.

"'Lo, Miz Pepper."

I turned to see Hot Dog, a fortyish ex-boxer who spent most of his days enjoying the Great Outdoors, ranging from the Market to the waterfront to Pioneer Square and back again. A few weeks ago, he'd let slip that as a young man, he'd earned money for boxing lessons as a short-order cook in his uncle's café, and I'd suggested he consider enrolling in Changing Courses.

It was unusual to see him without his buddy Jim, and I said so.

One shoulder rose and fell, his blue Seahawks jersey flopping loosely. "I got some thinking to do." He rubbed Arf's ear and fell in beside me as we headed back to Pike Place. "Miz Pepper, you honestly think that cooking school you and Miz Laurel work at would take me?"

"I don't know why not."

"You know I haven't always been a Boy Scout," he said.

"Doesn't matter," I said. "Drop in and check it out."

We'd reached the arts and crafts tables, and I glanced over at Bonnie Clay. She held up a large platter for a customer to inspect, muscles straining against her thin T-shirt.

"Be seeing you, Miz Pepper," Hot Dog said, and he gave Arf a final pat on the head.

Between the tourists and the regulars, the shop buzzed all afternoon. Sunshine in Seattle is a glorious thing, in more ways than one.

The after-five mini rush wound down, and I stepped outside, iced spice tea in hand, for a quick breather before my closing chores. The farm tents in the street had come down, giving me a clear view. A riot of color spilled from the flower boxes mounted on the edge of the Arcade roof. The three men who sing in front of the original Starbucks, a block north of my shop, paraded by in the middle of the street, their voices in perfect harmony, and the last-minute shoppers slowed to drink it all in.

This is why I love the Market.

Shouts drew my attention to the North Arcade and the artists' stalls. Heads turned. The singers blocked my view, and I couldn't see the ruckus.

The clamor stopped, and a moment later, a small figure emerged from the gap between the tables and marched diagonally across the cobbles toward my shop.

Holy marjaroly, Mom. What's up now?

Three

Araucaria araucana, *the Chilean pine, got its common name when a nineteenth-century wit observed that "it would puzzle a monkey to climb that." Now endangered, the living fossil and source of Victorian jet does well on the North American West Coast, and a few older Seattle homes still boast monkey puzzle trees in their yards.*

"SOMETHING WEIRD'S GOING ON," I TOLD CARL FIVE MIN-utes later after he closed Mom's car door. "But she won't talk about it."

"Five-two and a hundred pounds, Pep, but she can take care of herself." He took Mom's shopping bag from me and headed around the back of his white SUV. "See you this weekend."

Family. Where would we be without them?

We closed up the shop, and Arf and I dashed back to the loft, he to settle in for a nap in front of the big west windows and me to swap my uniform of stretchy black pants and a black T-shirt for a fun pink-and-yellow tunic dress and my lucky pink T-strap shoes.

The dress had been a good choice—festive, with no both-ersome waistband. Three hours later, Laurel and I waddled out of the Changing Courses dining room, the flavors of North Africa rolling around on our tongues.

"If I'd eaten one more bite, I would have exploded," I said.

"You practically licked your plate," she said. "Me, too. That spicy lamb tagine was heavenly. You should create a harissa blend for the store."

"Chiles, caraway, coriander—what else?"

"A touch of mint, a dash of salt. Add olive oil and lemon juice, and hello, Morocco! No passport needed."

"And no jet lag. Have I said thanks for roping me into this project? The food inspiration alone is worth every moment, not to mention seeing the changes in the students' lives."

"You can never say thanks too often."

We hugged good night—gingerly, careful of our full stomachs—and she found her car. I declined her offer of a ride—after that feast, I needed the short walk home. All downhill, thank goodness.

I hadn't wanted to spoil the night sharing my doubts about my mother and her old friend. Besides, Laurel's advice would only echo Carl's.

After another quick clothing change and a dog walk, I poured a glass of a crisp Italian white—a Bastianich Sauvignon Blanc from Venice, by way of Vinny—and settled onto the caramel chenille couch in my living room. The Viaduct, the elevated highway above the waterfront, blocked most of my view, its long-slated removal delayed yet again by problems boring the tunnel that would replace it. Still, the last rays filled the loft with an orange-pink westerly glow. No place I had ever lived had felt so much like home.

I reached for *The Reeve's Tale* by Margaret Frazer, from her series featuring Sister Frevisse, fifteenth-century nun and amateur sleuth. Fifteen minutes later, I was dreaming of giant jars of preserved lemons, cinnamon-scented couscous dotted with dates, apricots, and almonds, pigs made of salt, and a potter with startling blue eyes in her weathered face.

"THEY want *me* to teach a class on chocolate?" Mary Jean practically squealed at the news.

At the Changing Courses dinner, the director of volunteers had said the regular instructor had a family emergency and did Laurel or I know who might step in on short notice. So first thing Thursday morning, I headed Down Under—the name for the Market's lower levels—to twist an arm. Turned out, the chatty chocolatier needed no cajoling.

"One hour. Monday at ten." I handed her the outline the director had given me. "Keep it simple: types of chocolate, their uses, a few basic cooking methods. Your experience makes you a natural."

Plus her shop was new and, despite her blissful truffles, struggling. Heresy though it might be, I wondered if there wasn't a limit on how much high-end chocolate one city could eat.

And the HR pro in me can't stop searching for solutions to problems.

"Oh, Pepper! Thank you!" The petite redhead threw her arms around me, and I hoped I wasn't sending a lamb to slaughter.

MIDMORNING, Kristen and Cayenne returned to the shop with the potter's display models.

"She almost didn't let us take them," Cayenne said. "She said maybe doing business with you wasn't a good idea."

After what I'd witnessed the day before, she might be right. "Did she say why?"

"Too much time, water under the bridge. I didn't catch it

all." Cayenne handed me a lidded salt cellar, a black herringbone pattern on white porcelain. "Isn't this fabulous?"

"Mm-hmm." I held the lid in place with two fingers and flipped it over. Two small diamonds had been scratched into the bottom. A fragment of memory gnawed at the back of my brain.

"But then she asked about the house," Kristen said, "so I invited her to the party. She hedged a bit—I could tell she wanted to go, but she's a little shy. So I said you'd give her a ride."

No doubt I resembled a salt pig myself, my mouth hanging open. "But if there's some tension between her and Mom . . ."

"We're throwing this party to honor the history of the house, and both Bonnie and your mother are part of it." The door opened, and one of Kristen's regular customers entered, a woman who counts on us to spice up her weekly dinner parties. "Be right there," Kristen called to her. And to me, "Time for bygones to be bygones."

What bygones were we talking about?

Cayenne and I arranged the crockery on a shelf, next to our favorite sea salts. We tucked Bonnie's cards in an open jar, and Cayenne headed to the office to make a small sign.

And then it was business as usual. We sold spice and served samples of tea. I told myself that Kristen was right and that whatever the old tensions were, Mom and Bonnie could work them out. Despite the shouts I—and everyone else on the street—had heard, no punches had been thrown. My mother had always advocated airing disagreements sooner rather than later, "so they can blow over."

And by a certain point in life, we all learn a few things about water and bridges.

As if to prove the point, a set of bicycle wheels whizzed by the open door and screeched to a halt. The presence of a uniformed officer inside the shop can create a stir, so I marched to the door and met my ex on the sidewalk.

"Hey, Tag. What brings you here?"

"Just making my rounds, keeping the peace." He adjusted his Ray-Bans. The shades hid his baby blues, but I knew they were teasing me.

I spread my hands in a "what could be wrong" gesture. "The sun is shining, people are shopping."

"And your mother's in town."

He knew me well. "I'm thrilled to see her, Tag, you know that. It's just—well, I'm not entirely sure why she's here. Yeah, she misses the family, especially the kids. But I get the sense there's more going on."

"If you need an ear, or a shoulder, you know where to find me."

Even the sight of Tag's backside in his regulation black bike shorts wasn't enough for that.

AND then, after a whirlwind of tourists, a late-night restocking, and all the daily dramas and traumas of retail life, it was Friday.

Time to party.

"Champagne?" The angled hem of Kristen's gauzy blue dress swung as she grabbed two glasses from the tray her fourteen-year-old carried. Mother and daughter both wore flat black ankle-strap sandals, and their blue toenail polish matched. "No worries—the flutes are plastic."

"Wow." Bonnie eyed the deep couches and rich mahogany woodwork. The once-drab room, home to a hodgepodge of mismatched furniture and lamps with perpetually crooked shades on wobbly tables, had been transformed into a warm, tasteful gathering spot. "This sure isn't how I remember it."

Kristen laughed. "My parents were too busy saving the world to care about cracked plaster or that the living room only had one working outlet."

I raised my glass. "A toast, to a piece of Seattle's history—and our own."

An arm slid around my waist, and I leaned into Ben's embrace. He'd had his hair freshly trimmed, close on the sides, longer on top. A bit of gel darkened it—a wet look I found both appealing and a little silly. We were in Seattle, after all—why fake the wet look when it comes naturally so often?

I'd warned my mother that we were bringing Bonnie, but she'd only said it would be good to catch up. And I couldn't wait to be a fly on the wall.

"These windows weren't here, were they?" Bonnie asked of two stained glass windows, classic Victorian medallions with tulip edging and a shimmering blue border. Each stood above a bookcase, flanking the original tile fireplace.

"No. My uncle put a baseball through one when he was a kid, and my grandparents replaced them with clear glass. We found one in the basement and had it fixed, and a twin made for the other side." Kristen pointed.

But Bonnie's gaze was no longer on the windows. She was staring at Kristen's wrist. Or rather, her bracelet, diamonds and sapphires set between twisted strands of silver and gold.

Kristen held out her arm. "Isn't it stunning?"

"That's what you found in the remodel? My best score was a 1918 silver dollar." But then, I'd redone a century-old warehouse, not a semi-posh private home.

"A family piece, I guess, though I don't remember ever hearing about it. 'The Case of the Missing Sapphires.' Too grand for a casual summer party, but how could I not wear it today?"

Beside me, Bonnie tensed. Did all this splendor give her revolutionary heart an attack? Had she been one of those angry hippies, declaring war on the middle class? Part of the faction that viewed home repair and decorating as signs of hopeless middle-class bourgeoisie, an evil to be avoided like locusts and Buick station wagons? I'd racked my brain last night, trying to place her or recall the name Peggy Manning, but while I could feel those eyes burning into my young soul, I remembered nothing more about her.

"I'll show you the house later." Kristen's freshly polished fingertips brushed Bonnie's ropy arm. "Old friends are waiting for you out back."

"Show-and-tell time," I said to Ben. "Got your Mom shield up?"

Bless the man—he winked.

The glorious summer day had become a stellar summer evening. As we made our way to the backyard, I stopped to hug Kristen's sisters, Raine and Aja, whose kids were playing bocce ball with Carl's two. Then it was on to more of my parents' old friends, their names run together—TimandGina, LarryandKaye, DaveandJanet. Now it was GinaandKaye, and Tim had a new wife.

The Spice Shop crew had come—sans Sandra and Mr. Right—and the Senior Señoras, a group our mothers had started to improve their Spanish. They'd continued meeting, despite my mother's move and Kristen's mother's death. I only hoped our foursome, the Tuesday Night Flick Chicks, had half the staying power.

"Uncle Sam," I called. A counselor who worked with veterans, Terry Stinson often rode around on a moped, wearing an Uncle Sam costume, the pointed white beard his own. He gave me a hug, then greeted the woman beside me.

"Hello, Peggy. So good to see you," Terry said in his gentle, throaty bass. In my childhood, he'd been the fun single adult who played hide-and-seek with the kids and often stayed for dinners around the big, battered table. He hadn't visited much after we moved to our own house, but I ran into him downtown every few months.

I couldn't tell whether Bonnie was about to hug him or cry. Clearly, she had not expected to see him.

Or had she feared it?

"My wife, Sharon," he said, a hand on his wife's back. "My old friend Peggy Manning."

Sharon's lips thinned, her muscular shoulders tensing visibly in her sleeveless dress. She tugged at one diamond ear stud, about the size of an oyster cracker.

The two women were cast from the same mold—there are a lot of those slender, blue-eyed blond, Scandinavian genes floating around the Pacific Northwest. Bonnie had twenty years on Sharon, but age difference aside, it was clear that life had treated the potter more roughly.

Terry coughed gruffly and turned aside, his hand a fist in front of his mouth. Sharon turned, too, her hand on his shoulder, her face close to his. "It's nothing," he said.

I felt my mother's presence at my side before I saw her.

"Mom, this is Ben. Ben Bradley. My mother, Lena Istvanffy Reece."

She ignored his outstretched hand and went up on tiptoes to kiss his cheek. "Come tell me all the things my daughter won't."

Two blond, blue-eyed girls approached. "Meet my ballerinas," Terry said, recovered from his coughing fit. "This is Peggy."

"Call me Bonnie," the potter said. Sharon stretched out an arm to draw her older daughter close.

"Do you go to the PNB school?" I asked. The famed Pacific Northwest Ballet, at Seattle Center.

She arched her long neck. "Next year, I hope. We're at Beacon Hill Ballet."

"Oh, in the basement of Wedding Row. Isn't that near your studio, Bonnie? I saw the address on your card. Love those old brick buildings."

Bonnie's gaze flicked toward Terry, then Sharon, and she took a step back.

"Time for a drink." Kristen looped an arm through mine and led me to the bar. The scent of thyme, newly planted between the pavers, perfumed the air. I glanced over my shoulder at Bonnie, standing on the edge of the circle that had gathered around Terry and his family. He the social butterfly, she the observant artist.

Across the yard, my mother had cornered Ben at a table for two. Other mothers might quiz their daughters' dates about jobs and family, assessing security and suitability for marriage. My mother would be asking when and where he was born, looking to the stars for signs of trust and trouble. Or she might ask his Myers-Briggs personality type, or his number on the Enneagram.

I had no fear. Ben was sweet and solid, and I was less concerned about his intentions than figuring out my own. And he was laughing, a good sign.

But as long as my mother was focused on Ben, I'd have no chance to suss out the tensions between her and Bonnie.

Kristen handed me a glass of tequila-thyme lemonade.

"Oh my. Can I get this in an IV? And the yard—wow."

We sipped our drinks. Tiny white lights sparkled in the trees, and a double strand wound its way up the thick trunk of the monkey puzzle tree. Finds from what Kristen likes to call our antiquing trips dotted the yard. Most days, it was charitable to call our excursions junking. But we had hit the mother lode a few months ago in Anacortes, including a washtub that now held bottled water and pop on ice, and a raft of Japanese glass floats we'd scattered in her flower beds. The real treasure had been a replacement samovar for the shop. With Arf along, the Mustang had already been overfull. We'd had to send Eric, Kristen's husband, and the girls up to fetch the stuff in a borrowed truck.

Across the yard, Bonnie sat on the stone wall.

"What is up with Mom and Bonnie?" I asked Kristen.

Beside me, Kristen breathed in sharply. "Remember the old saying, Pepper. Don't ask a question unless you're prepared for the answer."

And with that, she marched off to greet a new arrival.

I chalked her reaction up to nervous tension, and grabbed a plate. A few minutes later, I joined Laurel and Seetha, seated near the rose garden. "Good job," I told Laurel, my mouth full. "Love the black bean pasta salad. And I can't believe you put my cucumber cantaloupe salad on skewers."

"Old catering trick," she said. "Serve as much fork-free food as possible."

"I'd like to share your lemon thyme cookie recipe at the shop."

Beside her, Seetha's face lit up. "You two should write a cookbook. Recipes from Ripe and the Seattle Spice Shop."

Before I could ask when she imagined we would find the time, Cayenne bubbled up in front of us, her hair gathered in a magnificent red-and-black lobster roll. "House tour. Wanta come?"

I'd seen it through every phase of the remodel. I'd helped pick paint colors. I'd even stumbled across the stone lions that now guard the front door, in a weed-infested lot behind a secondhand shop where Kristen had refused to venture in her white linen pants. And she didn't need any more of us clomping around the house than absolutely necessary. "You go. You'll love it."

Ben sat beside me, and we watched my mother take Kristen's arm and move inside. To my surprise, Bonnie and Sharon brought up the rear.

I scanned him, tip to toe. "No visible grill marks."

He grinned. "Your mother is lovely. Smart, funny—a lot like you. She's very proud of what you've done with the shop. Although she did ask me my intentions."

"What did you say?"

"I said I intended to drink another beer."

We mingled and chatted. I wrapped a few cookies in a napkin, for later. The summer solstice was approaching rapidly, and sunset was hours away, but a few shadows had begun to appear. Kristen's oldest pranced around the yard in a tank top and shimmery skirt, lighting candle lanterns on the tables. Give her wings and she could have been a garden fairy.

Tour over, a group of women appeared in the open French doors.

"Lovely, simply lovely," my mother gushed to Kristen. "Who knew this old Seattle Box had so much potential? Your mother would be so pleased. So sorry your father isn't here for the party."

"Oh, you know him. Happier on a boat than anywhere else, since Mom died. The house is kind of a memory magnet."

"Next time, I want to see the theater in the basement," Cayenne said. In her heeled sandals, she stood about a foot taller than Bonnie née Peggy. I was about to tell Bonnie we needed to head out—Friday night isn't Friday night when you work retail—when she spoke.

"You kids had a playroom downstairs, and there was a guest room."

"And a cold cellar," I said. "We locked Carl in there once."

"I don't think anyone ever cleaned out the storerooms. All those little pack rat nooks and cubbies." Kristen shuddered.

"Hey, did you show Mom the bracelet?" I said.

"I took it off—too heavy. Another time."

An old neighbor approached, and it was a good fifteen minutes before I could drag myself away to find Ben.

"We'd better go. The Market will be crazy-busy tomorrow."

But no sign of Bonnie. Sharon stood alone near the monkey puzzle tree, its weird, wiry green branches eerily human in the fading light. A flush covered her cheeks, and if she'd been gripping her champagne flute any harder, it would have cracked in her hand.

"So nice to see you again, Sharon," I said, and she jumped, snapping her head toward me.

"Pepper. Sorry. Daydreaming."

Nightmaring, from the looks of it.

"Great kids you've got there."

Her chin rose, and she drew her shoulders back, worry turning to pride. "They're everything to us. Oh, Terry. There you are."

I followed her gaze. A stone path alongside the house led to a gate, open under a rounded arch. Terry ducked under the arch, his long face weary, and held out his hand to his wife.

"I meant to tell you, Sharon," I said, "those are gorgeous earrings. Your husband's gift?"

"She's the kind of woman a man gives jewelry to," he said, sounding tired but tender.

"That's because you're the kind of man who gives a woman jewelry," she replied, her shoulders softening.

We found our passenger sitting on the front steps, arms clasped around her bent knees, her faded blue-and-white paisley skirt spread around her. Bonnie rose quickly, shoving her hands in her pockets, ready to make a getaway.

And I found myself trying to recall that old line— Shakespeare, or was it Faulkner? "The past is never dead. It isn't even past."

Four

It was just my imagination, runnin' away with me.

—Norman J. Whitfield and Barrett Strong, "Just My
Imagination"

"HAVEN'T SEEN HER," THE JEWELER WHO REPURPOSES
guitar strings and bits of painted car skin told me.

I'd have scratched my head if my hands hadn't been full
of coffee, croissants, and Arf's leash. When we'd left the
party last night, Bonnie had been all too ready to get home
and get a good night's sleep before a busy summer Saturday
in the Market.

The doll maker, the satchel seller, and the bookbinder
who creates stunning leather-bound journals all agreed:
Bonnie Clay had missed the mandatory roll call, and now,
minutes after the opening bell, had still not shown.

"You work weekdays to be sure of a table on Saturday."
The T-shirt designer (THERE'S NO NOOKIE LIKE CHINOOKIE)
frowned. "Nobody skips Saturday."

*Don't let last night's under-the-surface tension spill into
today.* If I'd learned anything working here, it was that life
in the Market is as unpredictable as the Szechuan pepper-
corn supply.

On the drive back to the Market where she'd left her big blue van, Ben and I had insisted Bonnie sit up front, and I'd watched from the back as she stared, wordlessly, out the window. All evening, I'd kept an eye—and ear—out for another confrontation with my mother, but the two women had barely exchanged a word.

Back on my side of the street, a customer juggled her shopping bag and sample teacup to hold the door for me, and I thanked her. The shop smelled like a pizzeria. Sounds charming, but the scents of basil, thyme, and oregano were left over from a bag of Italian blend that broke yesterday afternoon.

Spice happens.

Sandra hustled out of the back room, tying her apron strings as she walked, and I gave her the latte and croissant I'd intended for Bonnie. She said nothing about being late, and the set of her jaw said "don't ask." So I didn't.

Midmorning, I stood on the sidewalk and scanned the artists' stalls across Pike Place, but the shoppers and sightseers blocked my view. I stepped into the street and wound my way north, past the delivery vans and trucks. Daystall locations are never guaranteed, so I stretched and peered the full length of the North Arcade.

Still no sign of her. The pricks of curiosity sharpened into worry. If Bonnie's encounter with the old crowd had thrown her off, I wanted to know. And undo the damage.

Back inside, I found her card and called her number. Voice mail.

Made another call, fingers crossed that I was fretting over nothing.

"Now that you mention it, I didn't see her this morning. She usually stops in before she heads to the Market on Saturday. But weekends are crazy here." Josh Gibson had run the takeout for the Italian grocer in the Market until leaving last winter to start his own place down on Beacon Hill. "I'll run down and check."

He called back five minutes later, when I was helping a customer choose a salt grinder. "You were right, Pepper." His voice wobbled. "911 is on the way."

THE row of 1930s redbrick storefronts had become a destination, nicknamed "Wedding Row." I'd met all the shopkeepers at a spring bridal fair. A florist anchored one end. One dress shop catered to the bride and bridesmaids, a second to mothers and men. Two sisters offered wedding planning, stationery, and funky gifts. And on the north, Josh's bakery–deli–catering company kept them all well-fed. Apartments occupied the second floor, and artists' studios and the ballet school filled out the basement.

I saw the police car angled across the road from a block away and circled around to approach from the other direction. Left Arf in the car and dashed across the street. (And no, convertibles aren't the safest places for dogs, but he loves it, and I always make him lie down on the backseat while I'm driving.)

In the wedding planner's front window, a display of picnic-themed gifts with an old mint green Dr Pepper cooler in the center caught my eye. I'd wanted one for ages, but it seemed beyond trivial now.

The street address I'd seen on Bonnie's card was etched in gold on a half-round window above a glass door next to Beacon Hill Bakery. But I didn't need the numbers to know this was the place. A shiny red Medic One ambulance idled in front of the building entrance, its back doors open. Maybe there was hope . . .

I stepped around the police barricade, then through the bakery door.

Inside, the hiss of the espresso machine greeted me. Half a dozen tween girls in practice leotards and stretchy shorts, their hair in ballerina buns, sipped rainbow-colored frappés and bubble teas as they chatted. Young couples tended strollers, and the barista and counter clerk spun around each other as smoothly as tango dancers. Alt-rock ebbed and flowed.

Other than a few nervous peeks out the window and the occasional loud bleep from a police radio, the Saturday routine went on.

"Oh, I'm sorry. No more truffles," the woman behind the counter explained to a woman staring hungrily at the pastry case. "Our chocolatier quit."

A pass-through divided the front of the house from the kitchen. In the bakery's prior incarnation, heavy white plates piled high with Reubens or BLTs had sat on its counter until white-clad waitresses grabbed them, three and four at a time.

His customary blue bandanna wrapped around his head, Josh stood at a stainless steel table, piping the final curlicues on a small round cake. Two larger layers sat close by. He straightened and noticed my approach.

"Pepper. My God, can you believe it?"

"I can't believe you can ice a fancy cake at a time like this."

He glanced at the clock on the wall, then back at the project on the lazy Susan. "We're catering a wedding this afternoon."

Yikes. "I'll get out of your way, but tell me quick, what happened? And where?"

"The building door was locked—I have a key—but the door to her studio was open. It's the big one on the north end, down below. I called her name—" He rubbed his left eye and drew his fingers down his cheek. "I thought maybe she'd run upstairs to her apartment, but then—then I heard a noise. I went in. She was lying on the floor. Someone smashed—"

"Hey, Josh." A young man poked his head around the corner of a tall rolling rack. "Where's the salad dressing for the job?"

"It's in—oh, I'll get it." Josh turned back to me, wiping

a hand on his zebra-striped pants. "Thank God you called, Pepper. I don't know what happened or who did this, but if she lives, it's because of you."

I didn't trust my throat to let me speak. He disappeared into the recesses of the kitchen. I walked out past the babies and ballerinas and the long row of bakery cases. For once, the cookies and cupcakes didn't tempt me.

Outside, I searched the street for Bonnie's van. No sign of it, but she might have parked farther down the block. Another group of dance students had gathered on the corner. One familiar profile—Terry and Sharon's older daughter?

My breath deep and shaky, I sent the Universe a silent message to let Bonnie live. There was no one to ask how she was. The ambulance idled, the EMTs still inside. The only cop in sight was leaning against his cruiser, arms crossed, radiating "don't come anywhere near me" signals as he surveyed the scene.

But I'm not much for standing around, and I didn't see any reason why I couldn't slip down the hill and take a peek. The police hadn't blocked it off. And if I was quick about it, Officer Don't You Dare wouldn't notice.

I rounded the corner of the building and made my way through the urban bramble, glad I'd worn climbers today. Despite their thick rubber soles, I slipped on a damp rock and landed on my bottom, scraping the back of my hand on the brick wall as I reached out to break my fall.

"Whose bright idea was this?" I muttered, staggering to my feet.

Tall windows faced west, ideal for artists. One window had been cracked open, but the hillside sloped away, and I wasn't tall enough to peer inside. I spotted an old tire in the brambles and yanked it free. Rolled it up the incline. Shoved it against the brick wall, where it rocked, then settled into place. Stepped on it and peered in, hands cupped around my eyes.

In the dim light, shadows took shape: shelves of unfired

pots, rows of creamy clay pieces. Two large worktables. In the far corner, a kiln.

I made out a potter's wheel. A stool, lying on its side. And then, two uniformed medics, crouching, shoulders and upper backs visible. I craned my neck for a better view.

No luck.

One medic stood. Fragments of their exchange drifted through the open window. ". . . ME," the standing medic said. ". . . pack the gear," the other replied, and his partner stepped to the door, speaking into his radio.

My hand flew to my mouth. "Bonnie," I heard myself say. On the floor lay Bonnie-Peggy Pretty Pots, in her blue paisley skirt, her long gray-blond hair splayed out, amid fragments of a thick clay platter and a dark red liquid I knew wasn't glaze.

WHEN I finally scrabbled my way to the top of the hill and brushed the dirt and broken weeds off my black pants, one EMT chatted with an officer while the other closed the ambulance doors. The red lights were off now, the urgency gone.

I stood on the sidewalk, stunned.

A white van backed into view, maneuvering its way around the ambulance, BEACON HILL BAKERY AND CATERING painted on its side. An apron-clad woman emerged from the bakery, pushing a cart filled with trays of macarons, éclairs, and mini sandwiches.

From out of nowhere, a deep voice accosted me. "What do you think you're doing, interfering with a crime scene?"

Five

What if you knew her
And found her dead on the ground?
How can you run when you know?

—Neil Young, "Ohio"

THERE ARE COOL JUNE DAYS IN SEATTLE. THIS WAS NOT one of them, and if the bakery had AC, it wasn't keeping up. My chill came from what I'd seen in the studio. The triple shot I'd drunk earlier meant the one the barista had pressed into my hands would put me way over my limit—I'd have the shakes by noon. A new medical phenomenon—*caffeinum tremens.*

What I needed was a cold glass of water, to wash the sour taste of vomit out of my mouth.

Before I could answer him, Detective Tracy had been called down to the crime scene, leaving me with the beat cop, Officer Don't You Dare. He worked out of the South Precinct. He didn't know me, and his face barely registered when I mentioned Officer Tag Buhner of the West Precinct Bicycle Patrol. He flipped to a new page in his notebook. "Now, who are you, and why are you snooping around?"

"I *told* you. I'm a friend of Bonnie Clay. The victim.

When she didn't show up for work in the Market this morning, I got worried. I knew she lived below the bakery, and I know the owner—"

"Well, aren't you the social butterfly?"

"So I called Josh, and he found her and called you. 911. I came right down. I . . ." My words trailed off, stretched thin by adrenaline.

"Now why would you do that?"

"Because she's a big-hearted woman who drops everything when a friend's in danger."

Our heads turned, and Officer Don't stood. "You know this woman, Detective?"

"We go way back," Detective Cheryl Spencer said.

All the way back to last fall and a series of unfortunate incidents in the Market. Actually, we'd been acquainted before that, through Tag and the annual police officers' picnic, but we'd forged our own relationship in recent months.

"A chai latte, please," she told the hovering barista, then pulled a chair up to our table. The budding ballerinas had dispersed, picked up by parents anxious over the police fleet blocking off the street and the barricade keeping looky-loos away. Now that the word was out—"dead," "murdered"—I imagined thumbs were flying on Twitter or whatever social media site drew the tutu set.

"Pepper, I'm so sorry. Was she a friend?"

"Yes. Old family friend." I gripped my rapidly cooling cup. That much I could say for sure.

Rare to see Spencer without Tracy. (They won't arrest you for making the joke, but they won't laugh, either.) The tall, cool blonde and her short, stocky black partner were Mutt and Jeff, salt and pepper, opposites who complemented each other.

He and I were oil and water.

"Now, fill me in."

Outside the plate glass window, another patrol officer

directed the CSU investigators and the ME's crew to the basement.

"Victim was a tenant. Bonnie Clay, age unknown, reportedly a potter." Officer Don't read his notes with no trace of amusement, but Spencer's lips twitched. I turned away, staring at the blank white walls. The upbeat music made my skin itch.

"According to the baker, Josh Gibson, who is also—"

The front door opened, and said baker entered, trailed by Detective Tracy. "And I'm telling *you*," Josh said over his shoulder, "this wedding is at two o'clock, in the Arboretum, and if you don't let me leave in the next five minutes, thousands of dollars' worth of food will be ruined. Along with my business and my reputation."

"Sir, you are a witness to a major felony."

"I didn't witness anything. All I did was find her." Josh pivoted and held his arms open wide, palms out. Pleading.

Spencer's highlighted bob barely swayed as she shifted focus to her partner. "Seriously, Mike? Do you want to tell that bride and her mother why they have no cake?" A petrified look replaced Tracy's usual smugness, and Spencer took over. "Mr. Gibson, give us the names of all the staff working today, and make sure everyone you take to the job comes back to the bakery with you, so we can get full statements. And give the happy couple our best."

I'd never seen her contradict her partner. A new side of Detective Cool.

She turned back to the beat cop as if we hadn't been interrupted. The officer cleared his throat. "According to the baker, who also owns the building, there are five retail spaces, all on street level. Six apartments upstairs, four linked to a corresponding art studio downstairs. Studios one and two have been combined into a ballet school and rehearsal space, with a separate entrance."

"What about the other two apartments?" I hadn't known

Josh owned the building. Either there's big money in maca-rons, or he had a major mortgage.

"The owner lives in one, and another is vacant. We have not located all the tenants yet."

His chilly tone made it sound like their absence was suspicious. Like they might not simply be out grocery shop-ping or taking a Saturday morning bike ride.

"We talked to the employees here and in the other shops," he continued. "No one heard or saw anything suspicious, except for Ms. Reece rushing down and prowling around a crime scene, demanding to know what happened."

Prowling and demanding? It hadn't been that way at all. I raised both hands in a "hey, I'm innocent" gesture.

Spencer didn't flinch. "Get names and contact info for all the dance teachers, and find out who worked yesterday or today. And all the students, both days, and their parents."

When he'd gone, she leaned back in her chair, her manner gentle as she asked me to tell her about the victim.

I cradled my espresso, now cold comfort. What did I really know? "Potter. New to the Market. My mother knew her years ago. Back then, she was called Peggy Manning. She came to a party at Kristen's house last night. Ben and I dropped her off downtown around nine, and she said she'd see me in the morning."

I'd expected to see her alive. To chat about the present, and the past. Truth be told, I'd intended to poke around a bit to see why her reappearance made so many people I knew uncomfortable.

But now she was dead, and I didn't want to say any of that. Because it had all been conjecture. Hunch. Intuition. Sixth sense. All traits much valued in the community of my childhood, and in HR circles, but not high on your typical cop's list of Reliable Sources of Information.

Although Cheryl Spencer isn't your typical cop.

"So you sensed trouble and decided to track it down. Figures." Detective Tracy's camel-hair jacket—practically a uniform for him—fit better than the last time I'd seen him.

The barista set Spencer's chai latte on the table and turned to Tracy. "Just coffee. Black," he said, fingers reflexively touching his stomach.

So, he was slimming. Or, judging by the arch of his eyebrows as he glanced around, slumming. Seattle coffee shops tend to fall along two lines: sleek, modern cafés boasting tall tables, shiny surfaces, and colored glass pendant lights, or the coffeehouse look, a collection of mismatched furniture and accessories deliberately styled to seem serendipitous. This one fit neither mold. It was pure vintage, a 1950s coffee shop with 1950s linoleum on the floor, 1950s chips in the Formica tabletops, and 1950s rips in the vinyl chair seats. At least the music was up-to-date, and the plain white walls had been refreshed in the current century. Who needs atmosphere, the space seemed to say, when your food and drink are this good?

"ME's pronounced," Tracy said to his partner, not saying the actual word. "Now we wait for the official manner and cause."

But I didn't need to hear it from anyone official. Marriage to a cop had taught me the terminology. "Homicide, from blunt-force head trauma, and an intra-cranial bleed. No one smashes herself with a platter," I said. It appeared to have been a finished piece. Could they get fingerprints?

Officer Don't had stepped outside when Tracy arrived. Now he returned and whispered into Spencer's ear.

"Pepper, will you excuse us?" She didn't wait for my reply, and the two detectives followed the uniform outside. He gestured up the street, then down, no doubt reporting that they had not yet found the potter's van I'd described.

I wasn't hungry, but I finished my cranberry-orange

scone anyway. Maybe it would soak up the excess caffeine. I needed to call my mother, out of earshot of the customers, who chattered wide-eyed as they funneled in through a lane formed by yellow tape and those orange traffic-stick things.

I stepped outside and crossed the street to check on Arf, napping in the Mustang's backseat. Leaned against the stone retaining wall next to the sidewalk and punched in my mother's number, half hoping she wouldn't answer. I'd delivered plenty of bad news when I worked in HR, but it never got easy. And telling my mother her old friend was dead was way worse than telling a secretary we were letting her go.

But I got my selfish wish—voice mail—and struggled to keep my tone level. "Hey, Mom. Call me as soon as you get a chance. It's—important." Same result on Carl's home line.

Kristen didn't work weekends, didn't know I'd rushed away from the shop worried about our new-old friend. I got ready to poke the phone again.

"That one of them—what are they called? Some kinda terrier."

Was someone talking to me?

"Seen one on that TV show—*Planet of the Animals*?" The handle of a golf club poked out of the overgrown yews behind me. The hedge blocked the house from view and nearly blocked the concrete steps up to the yard. An ancient man, his skin as dusty as his voice, stood on the top step, waving the club.

"Animal Planet," I said. "Yeah, I heard they ran an episode on Airedales not long ago."

"That's it. The King of Terriers. That dog hunt?"

Only once that I knew of, this past spring. He'd got his man but good. "He's more a lover than a killer. Say hello, Arf." Arf jumped out of the convertible and trotted over, his tail curved up. The old man extended a shaky hand, and Arf leaned his fuzzy golden brown head into it. Mr. Ambassador.

One of the dance students gave a demonstration whirl in the street, and the other kids clapped. "I don't know how those kids do those pairo—what are they?"

"Pirouettes?" I said, and he nodded. His gaze moved to the ambulance, then back to me, questioning. "One of the tenants was attacked. She—didn't make it."

"My word." He grabbed the iron railing, and I took a step forward, praying he wouldn't tumble down. His face turned ashen.

"I told those people, you put those fancy dresses in the windows, the gangbangers that been hanging around, they gonna think everybody around here's made of money. I told them, there'll be trouble. Mark my words."

Somehow, I doubted the gangs he had in mind would be interested in yards of organza or bags of tiny glass beads. And a knife or a gun would have been a more likely choice for a career criminal than a clay platter. But he'd been right about one thing: trouble.

"Who was it?" he said.

"Bonnie Clay. The potter. She hadn't lived there long. Apartment upstairs, studio below."

"Oh, Lordy. Older gal, skinny, looked tough. I'd have thought she could fight off almost anybody." He pressed his lips together, his hands tight on the head of his golf club cane. "Now if it had been the one in there before her, I'd have said no surprise, the way the two of them went at each other."

Arf ambled back to my side. I rubbed his ears, the pressure of his warm body against my leg reassuring.

"Hannah was her name," he went on. "Little gal, big paintings. What do you call 'em? There's one, over there."

I craned my neck for a better view. A giant mural of psychedelic flowers covered the side of the building. I'd been too rushed to notice it on my tumble down.

"So, who went after each other? Hannah and—"

"That boyfriend of hers. She's a jumping bean of a redhead, 'bout thirty. I'd hear 'em yelling, stomping out onto the street. Next day, they'd be all lovey-dovey. Some couples go for that, running all hot and cold, but I never could understand it."

Me, neither. The old man had a way with descriptions. He'd nailed Bonnie, and I expected to recognize Hannah in a flash.

"You hear anyone threatening Bonnie?"

"Nope. Never. We got acquainted when she was moving in—musta been April. Then I went in the hospital. She brought me flowers from my own garden, so I wouldn't miss out."

He started telling me about his angina and his kidney stones and how his doctor had wanted to do one kind of procedure but his daughter thought they ought to do another type instead.

I was still thinking about Bonnie. And the gangs he'd suggested. According to Josh, the outer door had been locked, but the studio door had been open. There were no signs of forced entry, or of a smash-and-grab. From what I'd seen, the place had looked neat and clean, except for a fine layer of pottery dust everywhere.

And the blood.

I shivered in the warm sunlight.

"The pain was awful. I couldn't keep anything down." The medical saga continued.

Across the street, Spencer stepped off the curb and headed our way. I would let her and Tracy puzzle out the access issue. Not my problem.

"Arf and I have kept you long enough," I said. "Thanks for the visit, and I hope you and your doctor get that problem straightened out."

"Well, Pepper, learn anything I ought to know?" Spencer held out a hand in a "stay right there" gesture, then extended her badge to my elderly friend and introduced herself. "Mr.—?"

"Adams. Louis Adams, Senior."

Mr. Adams had mentioned a daughter, not a son.

"You see anything out of the ordinary in the last day or so? Say, since about nine o'clock last night?"

"Just a fancy car tearing away. Driver went up on the curb, hit that post. That's when I looked out."

Spencer and I glanced across the street. Sure enough, a metal pole for a parking sign tilted at an angle the city street crew hadn't planned.

Spencer teased out more answers. The car had been new-ish and white. Boxy. "Friday night. One of those—what d'you call 'em? S—SUVs. What kinda sense it makes to drive a car that big in the city, I can never figure." The driver had been alone. Hair, age, gender, race? Mr. Adams couldn't say.

Ben drove a big SUV, newish, white, and boxy. So did Carl. I'd seen half a dozen of them last night on Kristen's block alone.

Spencer made notes, walking Mr. Adams through his sketchy memory. "And you're not sure what time?"

"No, ma'am. Late, like I said. I don't sleep too good these days. My daughter got me one of them DVRs for Christmas so I can watch my shows anytime. My granddaughter programmed it for me. Real smart, that girl."

"An unintended consequence of the DVR and streaming—we can't use the TV schedule to figure out when events occurred." She handed him her card. "If you think of anything else, call me."

Arf hopped back in the car, and I followed Spencer across the street, a little dazed. The caffeine and sugar had worn off.

"Pepper." Spencer spoke sharply, breaking my reverie. "Why don't I get a uniform to give you a ride home?"

"Are you kidding? I know it's not a bad neighborhood, despite Mr. Adams's gang theory, but if anything happened to that car, my father would kill me."

"I can call Officer Buhner and ask him to drive it home for you."

"Oh, good garlic, no. If—*when* Tag hears about this, he will become a serious pest." We stood on the sidewalk outside the bakery. "I'm fine. I just need to get back to work."

She dropped her chin and peered at me. "If you insist. Now, what's Mr. Adams's gang theory?"

I explained. To my surprise, Spencer didn't immediately dismiss the idea. "I'll check with the burglary unit and gang squad. But any burglar worth his salt knows high-dollar retail goods don't necessarily mean large amounts of cash on hand."

"And bridal gowns aren't cash purchases. Very little in the wedding industry is," I said. "Unless somebody imagined a potter would have a chunk of change on hand after a busy day in the Market. Did you see any signs of a break-in?"

"Detective, you want a last look before we move the body?" the medical examiner called out.

"Be right there," she replied, then to me, "You sure you're okay?"

I could drive safely, but that wasn't what she meant. I nodded.

Before leaving, I climbed partway down the hillside, more careful of my footing than I'd been an hour ago, and studied the wall. Outdoor murals had sprouted all over the city in recent years, a marriage of graffiti and public art. One day last summer, I'd stood outside the production facility in SoDo where we pack our tea and spice blends, watching an artist use ladders and a lift and crates full of spray cans to create a school of fantastical fish. Daunting scale, but then, artists make careers of what daunts the rest of us.

Like the best murals, this one appeared to burst from the wall, the layers of paint and shadow giving it such depth that you almost wanted to reach out and pluck a flower. The colors weren't quite realistic—a hint of fluorescence, a touch of shimmer—but that made them all the more intriguing.

On the lower right corner, at a hard-to-read angle, was the signature. I whipped out my phone, zoomed in, held it above my head, and clicked. Peered at the tiny screen. HART. As in Hannah Hart? Or H Art, Hannah's Art?

I snapped a few more shots, then tucked the phone away and headed for car and dog. Plenty of time later to Google the name—I know not to phone and drive.

Not that it was my problem, anyway. The police had this well in hand. They'd see that Bonnie got justice.

And I had an urge to be back among the living and breathing, the hustling and bustling. Back in the Market, selling sugar and spice and everything nice.

That may not be what little girls are truly made of, but it's a comforting thought, now and then.

Six

*No man is an island, entire of itself; every man is a piece
of the continent, a part of the main. If a clod be washed
away by the sea, then Europe is the less.*

—John Donne, *Meditation XVII*

ARF AND I TROTTED UP WESTERN TO THE MARKET
Hillclimb, trudged up the stairs, and made our way to the
pizza window. I fed him a chunk of sausage, then browsed
the newsstand, checking out the headlines and photos on
the foodie magazines. (Eyes only until my hands were
clean.) Arf trained his attention on a recently trimmed black
poodle whose owner was flipping through the postcard rack.

"Mind your manners, dog." I had to admit, she was rather
fetching. For a poodle.

First thing, call Kristen, I reminded myself as we hustled
down Pike Place. The Market was at its midday busiest, a
mélange of browsers and serious shoppers.

My shop was a madhouse. I sent Arf to his bed behind
the counter, tossed my bag in after him, and helped Reed
with a customer restocking the kitchen of her summer home
on Bainbridge Island. Matt had his hands full, assisting a
customer planning an Italian feast for twelve, and Cayenne

was on the phone, the customer grilling her, from the sounds of it, on everything from Jamaican allspice to Israeli za'atar. I scooped out four ounces of sweet marjoram—the last item on the customer's list—and asked Reed, under my breath, "Where's Sandra?"

"Back room. Meltdown. The new columnist for *Northwest Cuisine* is waiting in the nook. I gave her tea and cookies. You didn't answer your phone."

"What? She's here? On a Saturday?" I set the marjoram jar on the restocking cart, marched over to the nook, and held out a slightly grubby hand—no apron to wipe it on. "Pepper Reece. So nice of you to stop in."

A full-figured woman of about fifty, wearing a lime green twin set and a beaded necklace of black jet, gave me a once-over. A spiral-top notebook lay open on the butcher-block work surface next to her untouched tea, and she'd jotted half a page of notes in compact script.

"Nancy Adolfo. Apparently your staff forgot to mention our appointment. But I'm enjoying watching the place hum."

If she'd wanted to catch us at our crazy-busiest, she'd timed it right. "I promise, in two minutes, you'll have my full attention."

Adolfo smiled, revealing tiny, shiny, sharp white teeth. I headed for the back room and the squeaky door that kept it more secure than any alarm.

"Sandra? What's up?"

My assistant manager swiveled the desk chair back and forth, arms crossed, chin lowered. I could almost see steam coming out of her ears.

"She lies. Whatever she told you through those perfect veneered teeth is a lie."

I unfolded the wooden chair we keep behind the door and sat, knee to knee. Reached out and stopped the chair. "Sit still and tell me what happened."

"A woman called earlier this week and demanded to

know what days you work. Refused to let me help her or say what she wanted, but she made me hinky." Sandra huffed. "Now she shows up pretending she had an appointment and that I screwed up. She wants to catch you off guard and see how you respond."

Adolfo had joined the regional food scene a few months ago, reporting on Portland, Seattle, Vancouver, B.C., and the Northwest wine and orchard country. She'd quickly developed a reputation as a wolf in sheep's clothing. Her beat was specialty food retailers—wine tasting rooms, butchers, ethnic grocers. Spice merchants. I understood not making an appointment—if you want to evaluate customer service, product freshness, and retail readiness, best not give your marks time to clean up their act.

And she treated the producers and retailers like marks, taking aim and firing away. Her reviews ran the gamut from gnarly to nasty. There'd been talk of a boycott of sorts, modeled on one in another city where restaurants refused to give a harsh critic a dinner bill, forcing him to accept a freebie, an ethical no-no, or publicly demand a check, airing dirty linen in front of diners. How to make a similar standoff work in businesses that sell products and offer free samples, no one could figure out, so the effort had fizzled. I'd never worried about her showing up here—our spice tea may not be everyone's cuppa, but our reputation is solid. Reviews matter, but word of mouth matters more.

But a woman who would lie to me about my own employees bore watching.

The phone on the desk lit up, and the ringer made the tiny office feel like the inside of a bell. Despite the chaos out front, I left it for the staff.

I took a deep breath and placed my hands on Sandra's knees. "I know you're feeling off-center, and I don't blame you for wanting to smash in her teeth. But I need you at your best. Stick to the customers, and leave her to me."

She forced out another irritated breath, her dark eyes flashing. We'd talk later about what was really bothering her.

"All right then," I said. "Let's get spicy." She attempted to smile, mostly failing. I grabbed an apron, put on my pleasant HR expression, and charged out to brave the invader.

"Need a refill? Black assam and spices, our custom blend." I poured myself a refreshing cup. Funny how caffeine can hype you up or soothe you down, in the right dose.

The critic raised her head, her poofy red hair encased in hair spray, but said nothing. She had positioned herself in the booth so she had a full view of the shop—usually my spot. I slid in across from her.

"Charming shop," she said. I'd heard that sniffiness before. If you prefer your charm superficial and supersanitized, then don't come to an urban outdoor market that's been in continuous operation for well over a century. I ignored the patronizing tone.

"A detail or two from you, if you don't mind, then I'll let you get back to business." She oozed smarmy sweetness, and I reminded myself to keep my cool. "Just spell my name right" might have worked for P. T. Barnum, but us lesser mortals prefer our publicity to include a few kind words.

For the next ten minutes, she quizzed me about the shop's history and how I acquired it. "And you had no experience in retail or the culinary arts? None at all?"

Her incredulity gave me a chance to practice patience. "You can learn a lot by hard work and observation. Plus a top-notch staff. My customers and employees have taught me the business, and I keep up by reading, cooking, and eating."

Sandra walked by, carefully ignoring us. From behind the front counter, Cayenne shot me a wide-eyed look, biting her lower lip.

Finally, Adolfo closed her notebook and slipped her pen

into her purse. One of those sleek Waterman pens I'd learned to recognize from a particularly status-conscious lawyer at the old firm, and a Dooney and Bourke leather handbag. Wide-legged white palazzo pants, back in style. I'd seen a similar pair in the window at Nordstrom. If this spice gig didn't work out, maybe I could take up reviewing.

"May I offer you a bag of our spice tea? On the house," I said as she slid awkwardly out of the booth.

"What I would take"—she paused to get her footing—"is a sampling of your summer blends."

For summer, we featured a fiery grilling rub, a classic Italian blend, and our Herbes de Provence, a perennial favorite. I'd found a new source of culinary lavender to give the mixture the faintest hint of romance. I tucked the three tins in a small bag and handed it to her. "So glad you came by."

Her gaze traveled slowly from my wiry, weird hair to my black T-shirt, pants, and apron, and my black shoes muddied by the morning's adventure. "I'll admit, you've redeemed yourself nicely."

With that, she swished out, leaving other customers staring at her ample backside. Leaving me not knowing whether we'd garner a favorable review or a skewering worthy of our barbecue blend.

"What country does she think she's queen of?" Sandra said.

Cayenne bustled over. "Kristen called twice. She said it's urgent."

Oh, cardamom. The news had gotten to her before I had.

Matt was chatting with a customer keen on Middle Eastern food. I beckoned to the others, who gathered around me. "Sad news. Bonnie Clay was killed last night, in her studio on Beacon Hill."

"Oh, good Lord." Sandra clapped her hand to her chest.

The natural deep blush on Cayenne's high cheekbones faded, and she brought her hands together in front of her mouth. Reed slipped an arm around her. "I grew up on Beacon Hill."

"Spencer and Tracy are on the case. Don't be surprised if they come in later."

"What do we tell them?" Cayenne's voice quivered, but a flicker in her eyes betrayed a touch of excitement at being on the periphery of an investigation. She'd heard stories of past murders that had touched the Spice Shop; that had touched me and sucked me in.

"Everything you know," I said. "As honestly as you can."

"What are you going to do?" Reed said.

"Nothing. I barely knew the woman." Or did I? "It's hard to focus on herbs and customers after a shock, but—"

"But she's dead!" Cayenne said, and a customer snapped her head to look at us.

"Honor her by keeping the world turning." That's what my law firm bosses told us when the planes crashed into the towers on 9/11. If you let evil stop you, they said, then evil wins. They were right.

I could not let my mother hear the news of Bonnie-Peggy's death—*call it murder, Pepper, 'cause you know that's what it is*—from the radio or TV. Of course, they wouldn't release the name yet anyway, until the family could be notified.

How had Kristen heard? I'd told Spencer and Tracy about the party, but I was surprised they'd gotten hold of her so soon.

Back in my office, I tried my mother again. Still no answer. I strived for a message that balanced urgency with detachment and achieved neither. After fits and starts, I blurted out, "Mom, call me. The moment you can."

Next, Kristen, on a family outing. No answer. I sent a text. *I can't believe it, either. What's going on???*

Ben. His name popped into my head as if from outer space. I'd told Spencer we'd taken Bonnie to the party and dropped her off afterward. And then I hadn't given him another thought.

Which meant either I'm a terrible girlfriend, or . . .

No other viable excuses came to mind. If you don't think to tell the guy you've been dating that the woman you introduced him to last night—a woman who'd sat in his car—was dead, well, that would probably top *Cosmo*'s list of Ten Ways to Know He's Not For You.

Right above not needing his comfort.

I sighed. This was not the time to analyze my emotions, or lack of them.

But then, he might already know about the body. He worked the food and fun beat on the local weekly, but all the reporters savored a good, juicy crime story, and he followed the Seattle Police Department on Twitter for breaking news. He also took his turn in the rotation, calling law enforcement PR types for updates and attending official briefings.

Texting was made for moments like these. *Bonnie Clay found dead*, my thumbs spelled out. *Expect to hear from Spencer and Tracy.*

Too callous. I pushed the "clear" button and retyped. *Sorry to tell you, Bonnie Clay's been found dead. Call me.* I pressed "send."

I reached for the computer to check out Hannah Hart, then stopped myself. It was only curiosity, anyway. What couldn't—*shouldn't*—wait was telling Bonnie's friends and neighbors in the daystalls.

I took a deep breath, closed the office door, and told Sandra I was taking a stroll. I was a little embarrassed that I hadn't thought of calling Ben sooner. There was nothing wrong with him. But—and this was the crux of the matter—there was nothing *right* about *us*. And stringing along Mr. Good Enough For Now wasn't fair.

Pike Place never fails to amaze and amuse me. The

sidewalks were nearly impassible around the take-out joints—the piroshky maker, the Greek guy, the cheesecake bakers. The line for the original Starbucks—started in the Market in 1971—stretched all the way up the block. The coffee wasn't any better there than in any other location, or in any other espresso shop, but we humans relish our landmarks, and it's a big one.

Ten minutes later, I'd spoken to half a dozen vendors at the long craft tables, and word had begun to spread. Their cheeks were pale, and more than one hand trembled after hearing the news, as it held out a silver pendant for closer inspection or returned a credit card after a purchase. The Market artists are fiercely independent, yet deeply connected. We all feel a camaraderie with those who share our commitments, who make similar choices. Especially the choices that other people in our lives don't understand.

Like making art and selling it, practically on the street, practically outside, in a city where rain is more common than shine. Even with the occasional help of a sales assistant, it's a tad bit crazy.

Like buying a spice shop with zero experience. With nothing but guts and a small-business loan.

The kind of craziness that keeps a woman up late at night and gets her going early in the morning. The kind of craziness I hope everyone finds, at least once in their lives.

"I dreamed of owls last night." The fused glass artist folded her arms over her heart and bowed her head. "Told myself it didn't mean anything, but I knew better."

The soap maker squeezed into her neighbor's space and folded her into an embrace.

"Bonnie hadn't been here long," the Rasta-haired photographer in the next booth said, "but she did good work. She'd have done well."

"She mention any problems, any worries?" I'd vowed to not investigate. But in a brief moment between surges of the crowd, when I had the vendors' attention, I couldn't help myself.

"Not to me." The soap maker slipped back to her own stall where a customer fingered heart-shaped goat's milk soaps.

"Oh, remember? She and some woman were yelling— what day was that?" The glass artist held her hand below eye level. "Short, gray-brown hair, great tan. But I don't know who she was. Or who started it."

Wednesday, I didn't say, and, *That was my mother*.

The jewelry maker beckoned me over. I'd given her the five-gallon bucket full of rusty hardware my builder and I filled during the loft build-out. The necklace she made of tiny locks and keys is one of my favorites. "She was worried that she might have to move. She had a sublet, and the woman was making noises about wanting the place back."

Hannah? Bonnie hadn't mentioned that to me. But then, she hadn't said much last night. "What did she say?"

The jeweler's expression grew distant, one small hand fingering her chin. "She said she felt like she'd been on the move for thirty years. I said, you need a place of your own. We're not like people who work regular jobs. We can't just pick up all this"—she swept a hand over her display of ear-rings, bracelets, pendants, key fobs, and more—"and our materials and equipment and move on a whim."

I pictured the shelves of greenware, the boxes of clay, the wheel, the kiln.

"You have to protect your art and your space, I told her," the jeweler went on. "But she said—how did she put it? She said that was a trap. You put down roots and you get stuck, and before you know it, your creative spirit dies."

Ah, humans. We don't always make the best choices, de-spite thinking we know what we need. On the other hand, the Universe doesn't always offer us the best options. In recent years, Seattle rents had rocketed higher than the Space Needle.

"Those are cut from the passenger door of a 1957 Hudson." She spoke to a woman holding a pair of robin's egg blue earrings in a teardrop shape. Or maybe it was a raindrop. "Original paint."

The jeweler turned back to me, her voice low. "You are going to investigate, aren't you?" The customer held an earring to her face and consulted a mirror hanging on the pillar between stalls. I glanced at her reflection and saw her watching me, as if wondering what kind of fascinating mess she'd wandered into.

"Nothing to investigate. Whatever happened, it has nothing to do with the Market." A premature conclusion, but I didn't want the customer to leave with her tongue wagging.

"I'll take them." She handed over the earrings and opened her purse. "They're too fun. The perfect souvenir."

Now that's what we like to hear.

Seven

There's no more exotic plant out there. It's a member of the orchid family. It's a hard plant to grow; from start to finish, it takes eight years to get a finished product.

—Spice expert and merchant Patty Erd, on why vanilla is anything but "plain"

"TELL US AGAIN WHY YOU THINK BONNIE CLAY'S REAL name is Peggy Manning," Detective Spencer said. We were standing on the sidewalk alongside the shop. On my way back from the artists' stalls, I'd detoured to pick up Turkish delight for the staff and seen the familiar unmarked car.

"My mother told me. They knew each other decades ago."

Spencer and Tracy wore matching skeptical looks on their polar-opposite faces. Though we were practically standing on the spot where I'd found a man dead last September, seeing Bonnie-Peggy dead had been a shock. Heaven help me if I ever get comfortable being in close proximity to murder.

"Did you figure out how she died? Or who or why?" I said.

Tracy's eyes strayed to the white paper bag in my hand. "Let's go in and sit down."

The shop's spicy-sweet aroma—notes of cinnamon and

chile punctuated with crystalized ginger and a hint of that spilled Italian blend—enveloped me. *Home.*

Spencer poured tea. I set the treats on a tray and slid into the nook across from them for the familiar process of giving a formal statement.

Familiar, but still full of squirm potential.

"We're not quite clear," Spencer said, "how you knew her. Or why you went down there."

My vision fixed on a spot on the butcher-block work top, I massaged my forehead. "You never saw her eyes. They had an intensity I can't explain."

"And what does that have to do with the price of tea in China?" Sarcasm was among Tracy's more obvious talents.

"I met her on Wednesday. As an adult, anyway. I knew her eyes right away, but not her face, or her name." I explained my mother's arrival and our visit to Bonnie's table in the North Arcade, when my mother identified her old friend. I did not mention the phone call I'd overheard outside the Pink Door or my mother's obvious discomfort. Or about hearing her and Bonnie shouting. They would interview her before long; she could explain herself better than I could.

"But you remembered her eyes," Spencer prompted. "From her visits to your childhood home."

"I always notice eyes," I said. "We took a course once, when I worked in HR, on making a good first impression. The trainer suggested noticing a person's eye color as a way to be sure you make eye contact." Though apparently my interest in eyes—windows to the soul and all that—had started much earlier.

"And so you left your shop on a busy summer day and drove all the way down to Beacon Hill to check on this woman you barely knew. Why?" Tracy wasn't quite playing bad cop; call it dubious cop. He reached for a piece of candy, then stopped himself.

"Summer weekends in the Market are huge for the artists,

and she was psyched about it. So when she didn't show up, I called. And when Josh said there was trouble, I ran down."

"Of course," Tracy said. "Who wouldn't?"

I didn't know how to explain that it had been more than instinct, more than a hunch, that convinced me something had gone terribly wrong.

It was those eyes.

"Pepper? I hate to disturb you, but it's Kristen. Again. She says it's urgent, and I figured, well . . ." Cayenne held the phone against her chest, glancing from me to the detectives and back.

Ugh. Bad timing. I thanked her and took the phone. "I've been trying to reach you. I'm so sorry you had to hear—"

There is no getting a word in edgewise on Kristen Hoffman Gardiner.

I listened. Frowned. "What do you mean, it's gone? Are you sure that's where you left it?" She was sure. "Our detective friends are here right now. Make the report, and they'll pass it on to whoever."

I handed Tracy the phone. He listened intently and started scribbling. I filled Spencer in. "Kristen lives on Capitol Hill in a house her great-greats built in 1895. The house we grew up in. They just did an attic-to-cellar remodel, and she found a fabulous diamond and sapphire bracelet. She wore it for a few hours last night, but it was heavy and got in her way, so she took it off and left it on her dresser. Now it's vanished."

One eyebrow rose slightly, a sign of the wheels turning in Detective Spencer's brain.

We both looked at Tracy, still on the phone. "And you think this is linked to Bonnie Clay's murder?"

Tracy and I have our moments. He and Tag have their moments. Those moments had become less unpleasant since revelations a few months ago cast new light on an old conflict. And though I have done my share of griping and grumbling about Detective Michael Tracy, I have never thought him cruel, callous, or incompetent.

But he had stepped in it big-time. And his gaffe had been my fault.

"She didn't know?" Spencer whispered to me. Fingers over my lips, I shook my head. I should have made her slow down, stop, and listen long enough to tell her the news Tracy was repeating now.

"I don't know whether there's a connection," he said. "After Detective Spencer and I finish down here, we'll come interview you and your family. Meanwhile, I'm going to call this in and send up the burglary squad and the CSU. Any photos?"

I grubbed in my apron for my cell phone and started scrolling.

"While you're waiting, please make a list of all party guests, their addresses, and their phone numbers." He listened. "Mrs. Gardiner, I'm not accusing your guests of theft. The sooner we can rule them out, the sooner we can find the real culprit."

He handed me back the shop phone and nodded toward the cell phone Spencer and I were studying. "Party pictures? Send them to us."

"I don't see any showing the bracelet," I said.

"Send them anyway. So we can confirm who was present when, and match names to faces."

"You think there's a connection." They didn't actually shrug. They didn't have to. Two major crimes touching the same group of people in less than eighteen hours?

Doesn't take a degree in criminal justice to make that link.

"Baby Beluga, in the deep blue sea. Swim so wild and swim so free!" The lyrics, punctuated by giggles, spilled from a trio of unlikely sources whom I recognized before they tumbled into sight: my mother and her grandchildren.

"Hey, Aunt Pepper. We went to the Aquarium." She'd

stopped singing, but my twelve-year-old niece swayed to the music in her head as she leaned in to kiss me. Her ten-year-old brother reached over the back of the booth to wrap his slim brown arms around my neck.

"Glad you aren't too old for that."

"Never!" Two young voices rang out. My niece added, "Grandma loved it as much as we did."

My mother glanced from me to the detectives and back. Though she had never met them, they carried a somber air that had wiped the carefree joy off her face.

"If you promise not to tell your mother," I said, "I'll spring for ice cream."

My niece held out her hand while I pulled cash out of my apron pocket. "I don't know why you're bribing us," she said, "but I'm happy to help."

"Let's get doughnuts! Baby Beluga doughnuts," her brother said as they headed for the door. "And go Down Under to the Magic Shop."

"You're the baby," my niece said. "Can we take Arf?"

"Yes, but no treats for him," I said. She hooked up his leash, and the chime rattled against the glass as the front door shut behind them.

I wasn't sure how my sister-in-law would feel about me letting them wander the Market alone. With any luck, she'd never know.

"What's going on, Pepper? Do these people have something to do with the messages you left?"

The messages you didn't answer. But she'd been busy with the kids. I gestured for her to sit and made the introductions. "The detectives are here because this morning—I'm sorry, Mom. No easy way to say this. Bonnie is dead."

She stared at me, her face shockingly still. Finally, she said, "You'd better tell me the whole story."

I did. She listened without visible reaction. I finished with the jewelry maker's comment that Bonnie was worried about moving again, and my mother lowered her gaze.

After a long moment, she turned to Spencer and Tracy. "Peggy—I can't get used to thinking of her as Bonnie—and I met in college. We even shared an apartment for a while, with Ellen—Kristen's mother. The year the girls were born, we formed a household, a peace and justice community. Peggy was part of the group—on the fringes. But we made different choices, and until this week, I hadn't seen her in thirty years."

"She went to the party at the Gardiner home," Spencer said.

"Kristen invited her, and I'm glad. That house was home base for some important friendships. Movements were hatched there that changed this city, in small but significant ways." She reached out to touch my arm. "Children were raised there who are still changing this city, in small but significant ways. It was a house with open doors and open arms."

"And yet, your daughter claims not to remember anything about her. Except her eyes," Tracy said.

"Detective, do you remember all your parents' friends from when you were twelve?"

"Point taken," Tracy replied. "On another note, a valuable bracelet seems to have gone missing from the Gardiners' house. Did you see Kristen wearing it last night?"

"What? It's missing? Did someone break in?" She whipped around to face me. "Kristen and Eric? The girls?"

"Everyone's fine," I said.

She let out a breath. "No, Detective. I heard her mention it, but I didn't see it. A family piece, I presume. You may have gathered, Kristen comes from an old Seattle family. Moneyed, at one point. Not that money prevented tragedy. Ellen died of breast cancer, five years ago."

"Thank you, Mrs. Reece," Spencer said. "We can all hope the bracelet turns up in the house. If not, we'll find it.

Now, if you don't mind, we have a few questions for you about Ms. Clay. Or Ms. Manning."

A voice ripped through the shop. "She called to order the thirty-six jar set with all the spices and the spinning wire display rack, and you told her I wasn't registered. I was your first bride. Your owner signed me up herself at the Bridal Fair at the Convention Center."

The high-pitched complaints came from a tall blonde in a black silk tank, tight white capris, and platform sandals. One wooden heel made a loud clap on our plank floor as she stomped her foot.

"Excuse me." I slid out of the booth and sped to the registry. "I'm Pepper Reece. Nice to see you again." Bridezilla ignored my outstretched hand. "I'm afraid we don't carry any racks like that. Let's see what you registered for."

I peered at the computer screen. Reed had brought up her page, featuring an airbrushed engagement photo of the happy couple with their names and wedding date. *Two more weeks.* I gave Reed a quick nod to let him know I had this. Visibly relieved, he fled.

"Are you calling my maid of honor a liar?" Her heel thumped the floor again.

"Have a seat," I told Bridezilla, then scrolled through the items she'd selected. "The closest we have to what you're describing is a twenty-four jar starter set with a wall-mounted rack—"

"I chose the free-standing chrome rack. And no starter sets." She spat out the phrase as if she'd found an earwig in her coffee. She reminded me of those first-time home buyers on TV who insist on commercial-grade appliances and granite countertops, and who can't believe the audacity of their agent in showing them a home without a master suite and a jetted tub.

My jaw began to throb. I clicked to another screen. "A revolving rack like this? We can order a thirty-two or a forty, if you have the counter space." Hard to imagine her knowing what to do with forty spices, but I was letting my irritation influence my judgment. Maybe her fiancé was a serious cook. Heaven knows, he was going to need a good hobby, married to her. And he might want to keep the sharp knives well hidden.

"Our kitchen is spacious. Custom natural marble countertops. Order the forty-jar rack. My maid of honor will call you." She snatched the printout from my hand, and stomped out.

Difficult customers are the cost of doing business. While I was occupied, the detectives had finished questioning my mother and left. I updated Bridezilla's entry and placed the order, then plucked a rosewater-flavored square off the tray. The fruit and sugar melted in my mouth.

Time to attend to the business of selling spice. My mother emerged from the back room, face drawn, eyes wary. At one point, she and Sandra huddled in the nook, deep in conversation. My mother reached across the table and laid her hand over Sandra's. Then she spoke, and Sandra slid her hand out and covered my mother's.

I swallowed hard. It's never easy to watch grief, especially a grief whose edges and contours you don't understand.

And then the door flew open, and my mother and I rushed to wipe all sugary traces off the kids' faces and clothing to protect ourselves from their mother's wrath.

Ah, life. In all its messy glory.

Eight

"The time has come," the Walrus said,
"To talk of many things:
Of shoes—and ships—and sealing-wax—
Of cabbages—and kings—
And why the sea is boiling hot—
And whether pigs have wings."

—Lewis Carroll, "The Walrus and the Carpenter"

"THESE VEGAN HOT DOGS AREN'T ACTUALLY ALL that bad."

My mother saved me the trouble of giving Ben a deadly look. I have no problem with a vegan diet. Or with vegetarians, pescetarians, flexitarians, or I'll-eat-anything-atarians.

I have a problem with trying to disguise one food as another. A carrot–soy–oat flour stick will never be a kosher dog, no matter how good the mustard, pickles, and sauerkraut on top.

"We all have so much more energy since we started eating right." My sister-in-law began stacking plates, and the kids and Carl exchanged not-so-guilty smirks. They are a close family, and Carl adores Andrea, who is not as wicked as I make her out to be. Just a touch self-righteous.

But a mini doughnut or two never hurt anybody.

"Grandma, I'm sorry your friend died." My nephew wrapped his arms around my mother. She squeezed him back, then he sank to the ground next to me and draped an arm over Arf. Carl's house, on Queen Anne Hill, is a variation of the classic Seattle Box, smaller and newer than Kristen's. They're on the remodel-as-you-go plan, meaning projects get done when they have the money and Carl has the time. At the moment, new bathroom fixtures crowded the second-floor hall, waiting for the plumber to give them the go-ahead on ripping out the kids-and-guest bath.

Carl pushed his chair back from the patio table—not easy to do on slate pavers—and stretched his long legs. My mother says he's named for Carl Bernstein, while my father insists he's named for Carl Yastrzemski, the famed Red Sox left-fielder. In truth, the firstborn male Reece has been given some version of Charles for generations, a tradition even my sister-in-law could not change.

"I don't remember her," he said. "Did she live in Grace House? What was I, eight or nine when we moved?"

My niece stuck her head out the back door and called to her brother to come help get dessert ready. Boy and dog groaned as the boy stood, then shuffled inside.

My mother plucked a tiny leaf out of her wineglass. "You were nine and Pepper twelve. Peggy never lived at the house. That crowd thought owning houses too establishment. They hopped around, living in places other people owned."

"Did we camp at a farm with some of them once?" A wisp of memory teased me.

"On Orcas Island, yes. They were caretaking for an older couple one summer. Peggy, Roger, Terry—I don't remember who else. They stayed in the guest room a few times, after Debate Night."

Debate Night had been adults-only conversations about

politics and economics and who knows what else. We kids had been sent to the basement for Video Night, so rare in our TV-free household that it seemed like a treat, not banishment. Kristen liked to sneak up the stairs and sit on the top step, behind the door, to listen, but I was usually more interested in the movie. Some things hadn't changed.

"Roger." I squinted, trying to remember.

"So why'd she leave?" Ben asked.

Mom waved a hand vaguely. "Who knows? Seattle's always drawn people searching for the pot of gold, and when it isn't here, they drift away."

"What drew you to the Emerald City?" Carl asked Ben.

"I came for the job." The fabric and metal chair squeaked as Ben leaned back. "It was time to leave Austin."

"You mentioned jobs in Phoenix and Sacramento," my mother said. "And you were born in Chicago, though you need to find out the time of day so I can run your chart."

His full lips curved. "Itchy feet."

We were opposites that way. Was that the reason I'd been holding back on our relationship?

"Seattle's a great city. Love the culture. But it isn't necessarily the easiest place to make friends." He winked at me. "Some exceptions apply."

Carl fetched two beers from the cooler that serves as the fridge in what Andrea calls their outdoor kitchen, a lovely stone structure with empty spaces where the appliances should be, and handed one to Ben. "Ah, the Seattle Freeze. We're all so nice and polite. Newcomers feel like they've finally come home, until they try to break through that friendly veneer and get to know us. Bam! Frozen out. Local legend, anyway. I hope you haven't actually experienced that, because we need our newcomers. We need your passion and ideas and energy."

Not for nothing was Carl on the city payroll.

But his comments did make me wonder: Was I freezing Ben out?

"Your father always said he came here because of Bobby Sherman," my mother said. "After he got back from Vietnam, he saw *Here Come the Brides* on TV and thought, wow, the skies really are blue and the grass really is green. And the girls are pretty cute, too."

They all laughed, but I wasn't going to let my mother change the subject so easily. "Mom, don't you want to reach out to Peggy's family? To Roger—he was her boyfriend, right? You're the one who always makes the calls, sends the condolence notes."

"Let the police take care of it, Pepper." My mother reached for the wine bottle. "Everyone I knew is long gone."

There was something odd about her reply, or maybe it was the way her hand shook as she refilled her glass.

"Mom, Peggy was your friend. Years ago, yes, but now she's dead. Murdered. It's not like you to ignore that." To let a death go unobserved, a life go uncelebrated, even when the threads of connection had worn thin, as some inevitably do.

"We are having a perfectly lovely evening, Pepper. Why do you insist on ruining it by dredging up the past?"

Because you knew her. Because you were shocked to see her, then went back and got into a shouting match. Because you warned someone about her, and you won't tell me what's going on.

I opened my mouth, then closed it as the harmonies played in my mind's ear. Yoga, meditation, astrology, Feldenkrais, communal child rearing, Montessori schools— you name a trend from the 1970s, it swirled through our lives, first at Grace House and later in our own home. But all through that vortex of experimentation and exploration, there had been one constant: my mother's love of medieval songs and chants. When she was in the kitchen, or cleaning, or driving our old VW van, she'd pop in a tape and crank up the volume.

To this day, whenever I am stressed by choices, whenever I sense that people I love aren't being quite honest, whenever I feel tugged in a direction I do not want to go, those haunting sounds fill my senses.

There had been a second theme in our lives, best stated by a bumper sticker on that old van: PRAY FOR PEACE, AND WORK FOR JUSTICE.

The back door opened, and my nephew walked slowly down the steps, bearing a heavy plate. All I could see were three candles, unlit. Cake? Gluten-free, sugar-free, and taste-free, unless the kids had used "Grandma's here so let's celebrate Aunt Pepper's birthday two weeks late" to badger Andrea into relenting.

I shut my mouth and closed my eyes, letting my hand drop to my dog's soft head. Why was I acting so snarky, petty, and grumbly?

Because I was about to do the thing I had sworn all day that I wouldn't do.

I was going to find a way to work for justice, for Bonnie Pretty Pots.

WHAT *would Brother Cadfael do?* I wondered, as Arf and I hopped out of the Mustang Sunday morning outside Chinook's, at Fishermen's Terminal. As last night's family gathering wound down, Ben had seen the fire catch hold in my eyes, and he'd wanted to talk, to figure out how we were going to investigate.

Not wanting to give him the cold shoulder, but not feeling warm and cuddly, either, I'd pleaded exhaustion after a too-full day. Mostly, I needed to let my own thoughts heat up and simmer a bit.

So I'd gone home alone and buried myself in my book. I'd been devouring medieval mysteries ever since finding a box of Brother Cadfael books and videos my mother had left in my storage locker.

Now it was time to pack up my troubles and be social. Laurel had snared a dockside table overlooking Salmon Bay, part of the waterway system that links saltwater Puget Sound to the city's inland freshwater lakes, Washington and Union.

After a good hug, I smoothed my skirt—made by a Market vendor from upcycled T-shirts—and sat, feet happy in my pink shoes. Arf accepted the ritual petting, then laid next to my chair, muzzle facing out. Who knew when a sucker—make that a pet lover—might stroll by? Or another comely poodle?

"Glad I beat Mom here. The oddest thing, last night—" I paused, leaning back to let the server pour coffee.

Hurriedly, I filled Laurel in on last night's revelations. "They were friends way back when. Kitchen-table activists, saving the world one hungry kid at a time." Another household motto. "Now, Bonnie-Peggy shows up, after decades away, who knows where, and my mother goes all crazy-furtive. Then Bonnie turns up dead." My voice broke, and I reached for my water glass.

"You don't think—"

"I don't know what to think." But I knew what Laurel was thinking: that at best, my mother knew things she wasn't telling me, and at worst—well, I wasn't going to go there. I wasn't going to imagine my mother a murder suspect.

But Spencer and Tracy wouldn't be so hesitant. What had she told them, while I was off soothing the savage breast of Bridezilla?

"There you girls are!"

Did I imagine her hug a little more ferocious than usual, her eyes warning me to stay away from certain sore subjects?

"What a spectacular day! Laurel, so good to see you."

The server appeared at my mother's elbow. My mother reached out a hand. "Tell me, where do you source your coffee?" What followed was a Q&A on the beans, their origin, and the roasting technique that lasted a full three minutes—I timed it—before my mother flashed the woman a smile and allowed her to pour.

"Ahhh." She inhaled deeply. "The coffee. The food. My family. How I have missed this city."

She dithered between the oysters fried with bacon and served with spinach and eggs, or the salmon Benedict, served not on any old English muffin but on a potato pancake. Call it Northwest weird. Call it yummy.

Our orders in, my mother adjusted the ruffled neckline of her pale green tank and began the quiz session. Either she was nervous, or this was not her first cup of coffee. Or both.

"Laurel, tell me all about the restaurant and your boat. And Gabe's college plans."

"He's beyond excited. The local Notre Dame club is hosting a welcome picnic this afternoon. I confess, it's hard to watch how eager he is to leave Seattle."

"That's a good sign," I said. "He's ready to explore the world. Then if he comes back, you'll know it's his choice."

"Heck, I didn't leave Seattle until I turned sixty," my mother said. "Never considered leaving for college. If I had, I wouldn't have met your father."

"Seattle must have been so exciting back then," Laurel said. "What, 1970? The antiwar protests. Feminism. The environmental movement."

"We accomplished a lot," my mother said. "For a bunch of hippies."

I wanted to ask about Peggy. I wanted to ask where all the energy and ideas came from, and what causes mattered now, what we could do to improve the city we'd inherited. But what I wanted most was breakfast. Vegan hot dogs wear off, even when they're followed by double-decker chocolate cake and decidedly non-vegan vanilla bean ice cream.

"Perfect timing," I told the server as she slid before me a photogenic salmon cake alongside eggs with hollandaise and adorable baby red potatoes. Mom had chosen the salmon Benedict and Laurel the oysters.

"I was just a kid," Laurel said, breaking the silence that accompanied our first happy bites, "but I remember hearing about the march from the U-Dub to downtown that shut down I-5. Were you part of that?"

"May 6, 1970," my mother said. "It started as part of the student strikes sweeping the country. Tensions had been building, but when Nixon sent the troops into Cambodia, that blew the lid off. Five thousand people—mostly students, but also faculty and residents—marched down the Ave to the freeway." The Ave, aka University Way, the heart of the U District. "The rest of that week was chaos. Finally, the mayor closed the express lanes, and fifteen thousand people marched downtown. He welcomed us at City Hall."

"That's when you met Dad, right?"

"Some protesters didn't want the vets to participate. Called them Baby Killers and worse." A shadow crossed her face.

What could be worse than that?

"The freeway was backed up for miles. Drivers honking and screaming, protestors yelling back." Her brown eyes grew distant, remembering. "This big farm truck kept inching forward, until finally the driver decided to teach us a lesson. He barreled ahead, right into the crowd. Out of nowhere, this tall guy in army fatigues grabbed me and pulled me out of the way."

I stared. I had never heard the story in this much detail.

"Two months later, I married him." My mother picked up her fork. "Don't let this beautiful food get cold."

"So how did you decide to establish your group?" Laurel asked. "What was it called?"

My mother's sharp-eyed glance ricocheted between us. "Something smells fishy here, and it isn't in the water or on our plates. Did my daughter put you up to poking into my past?"

"Lena, she wants to help you."

"I am not in any trouble."

"Mom." I leaned forward. "You argued in public with a woman you thought was dead. And three days later, she was found dead. That is the definition of trouble."

"It was nothing. Old tensions we needed to get out of our system."

"The homicide detectives won't see it that way," I said. Her expression told me I was right, that witnesses had reported their argument, and her explanation had not satisfied the police.

"And how do you know so much about what homicide detectives think?" she snapped.

"Thirteen years as a cop's wife." I speared a potato and held it up. "And two murders solved on my own. Not to mention a few miscellaneous crimes."

Her small, lovely face twisted, but she kept herself from crying. "I don't want you to get involved."

I hadn't planned on it. I'd planned the opposite. Until last night, when it became so clear that my mother did not want to talk about Bonnie-Peggy, alive or dead. Not that I thought for one eenie weenie moment that she had anything to do with the murder.

But what about the person on the other end of the phone?

I wanted to push her. But it didn't feel fair. And I didn't feel ready. So I followed my mother's example.

I changed the subject.

"Gad, Laurel, I almost forgot to tell you. Nancy Adolfo

came into the shop yesterday. Unannounced. Told me she'd made an appointment and my staff forgot to tell me. Sandra was livid."

Laurel followed my lead. "That's her MO." She explained about the new critic while my mother and I ate.

"Sounds like she doesn't realize that people in the food business actually talk to each other," my mother said. "Eventually, she'll destroy her own credibility. Oh, what bliss, sitting here with you two on this gorgeous day. I love Costa Rica. Your father is so happy there. But"—she gestured toward the water, the sailboats lined up along the docks, the commercial fishing vessels moored beyond. "I miss all this."

Was she thinking of coming back to Seattle? First hint I'd had. What did Dad think of that? You never know your parents the way you think you do, but I was absolutely sure they were solid. When I'd left Tag, I'd asked my mother to tell me honestly if she'd ever considered divorce. "Divorce, no," she'd replied. "Murder, yes, but divorce, no."

The old joke didn't seem so funny right now.

"What about your volunteer work? With the kids?" I asked. Her Hungarian immigrant father had been so furious at her elopement—and no, I wasn't on the way—that he'd refused any more help with college tuition, saying she was her husband's responsibility now. She'd followed her dream anyway, opening a Montessori school and finishing her degree years later. With help, if I'd picked up on the clues right, not from her father, but from her mother, who'd wanted her daughters to have the opportunities she hadn't had.

"Oh, it's so much fun." Her face lit up. "The little ones are such a delight."

"Good thing you boned up on your Spanish before the move."

"And the parents all want to practice their English!" She cackled. "But children are children, in any language."

"Mom, yesterday, when you were in the shop—"

"Pepper, can't we please stop talking about it?"

"No, not about Bonnie. Sandra and I keep meaning to talk, but we haven't had time." The fib was the easiest way to get my mother to reveal a confidence. "Did she tell you what's going on? Is she ill?" My stomach started to roil.

"No. It's Paul. From the pain, they think it could be prostate cancer. They're running tests."

Holy moly. I sat back, mouth over my hand. "Ohmygosh. I had no idea."

Sandra is the rock the Seattle Spice Shop stands on. And Paul—the husband she calls Mr. Right, to distinguish him from her first, Mr. Oh-So-Wrong—is her rock.

If either shifted, we'd all be shaken. As if the tectonic plates that underlie the Pacific Northwest did the shimmy, the fox-trot, and the Charleston all at once.

But what hit me in the gut was that Sandra hadn't told me herself.

"Lena, are you coming to Flick Chicks on Tuesday?" Laurel asked later as we headed for the parking lot. "It's Kristen's week."

"We'll see." They air-kissed good-bye, and my mother unlocked Carl's white SUV. I couldn't help remembering Mr. Adams's description of the vehicle he'd seen race away Friday night.

"I thought you might bring Ben along this morning," she said, hand on the door.

"Sunday morning is girl time," I replied.

"He's a good man, but even without seeing a chart . . . Well, don't let him push you into investigating because he wants a big story."

As I'd feared when we met, during another unfortunate incident. "That worries me, too. Is his job kismet, making us a good match, or coincidence?"

She climbed into the SUV, a tiny woman in a big rig. "There are no coincidences, Pepper. Everything happens for a spiritual purpose. Your soul knows what experiences it needs for growth. To raise your vibration and cultivate a deeper meaning."

"Mom, where do you get this stuff? It's like you're talking Greek."

She switched on the ignition. "Oh, honey. This language is much older than Greek. Chalking things up to coincidence means you don't trust the Universe."

Arf's leash in hand, I waved as she drove away. I trust the Universe. It's people I wonder about.

Nine

Under the wide and starry sky
Dig the grave and let me lie.
Glad did I live and gladly die. . . .
"Here he lies where he longed to be,
Home is the sailor, home from the sea . . ."

—Robert Louis Stevenson, "Requiem"

I THINK BEST ON MY FEET, AND MY DOG NEVER SAYS NO to a walk, so we wandered back to the waterfront. Despite its trendy restaurants, Fishermen's Terminal is a working marina, owned by the Port of Seattle, and home to the North Pacific fishing fleet. A medley of human, bird, and mechanical sounds played around us: laughter and shouted greetings, the squawks of pigeons and seagulls, the cranks, creaks, and squeals of ocean-going gear. An engine stuttered, then caught hold, punching a stinky blue-gray cloud of smoke into the air.

Two men rolled a cart of silvery fish to the seafood market, doing a brisk business late on this sparkling morning.

A shiny new sailboat motored past, its engine barely purring, headed for the Sound in search of wind.

So much for my view of myself as caring and honest—big-hearted, in Detective Spencer's words. So caring, I didn't have a clue what was going on with my assistant manager until I lied to my mother to find out.

At least I'd never hidden behind any pretense of minding my own business. In HR, we learned to never pry, but to spot potential problems and figure out the best ways to address them. My mother, alas, was resisting my efforts to help her solve those problems, and I feared she was about to run headlong into a bigger problem: our friendly homicide detectives' need for a suspect.

Some people say you can't help those who don't help themselves, but I've never believed it. My childhood had taught me otherwise.

I stepped around a young couple, arms around each other's waists as they exchanged murmurs and kisses.

Why had Bonnie-Peggy come back to Seattle? I wasn't sure what to call her, the two names hopelessly intertwined in my mind. My mother had not seen her in eons. Bonnie had told the photographer in the Market that she'd been on the move for thirty years.

Had she meant that figure literally? People often round up to the next decade when they recount time.

Was it a coincidence that our family had moved out of Grace House thirty years ago?

My mother didn't believe in coincidence.

I paused to watch a fortyish man crouched on the deck of a blue-and-white gill netter, distinguished by its cabin-forward profile and the giant reel mounted on the deck. He appeared to be working on a badly tangled net.

Near the entrance to the Terminal stands a statue I've always loved, the Ancient Mariner in a wide-brimmed yellow hat and a slicker, cut like a nineteenth-century frock coat, his long beard and broad mustache iron gray. This was a modern fisherman, clean-shaven, in brown canvas work pants and a white T-shirt that showed his biceps and pecs quite nicely.

He straightened and raised a hand. I returned the greeting and walked on.

I walked past the port offices and the headquarters of the big seafood companies, closed for the weekend. Past the terminals, their big metal doors shut, where men and a few women repaired engines, rebuilt hydraulics, and sold parts. Past smaller buildings, dark for the day, that reeked of fish and grease, saltwater and sweat. It was not an unpleasant smell. It smelled like good, hard, honest work.

I walked past all kinds of boats equipped with all kinds of nets for catching all kinds of fish. Bonnie had feared being trapped. Caught. Did she mean by the mysterious Hannah and the troublesome sublease, or something else?

Or someone else.

I had no reason to think Bonnie's predicament related to the past, except for my mother's odd behavior. She claimed not to know anything about Bonnie's present life, and yet, she had been worried enough to call someone with a warning.

Someone from back then. Who knew them both and knew their secret.

I stopped abruptly.

If Bonnie had been killed because of a secret from the past, was my mother in danger, too?

Arf fixated on a child preparing to toss a french fry to a mallard. I reminded him who was leader of the pack. "Sit, Arf. Stay."

The child tossed, the duck swam, the child clapped. Her father picked her up and carried her past us. "Doggie!" Arf stayed put. I never have figured out where my dog learned his excellent manners, or his unusual response to certain commands. Ever since he'd taken down a bad guy at the Seattle Center fountain in April, I'd been watching my words around him, wondering if another unexpected combination would set him in motion.

Was it coincidence that Bonnie and my mother had reappeared in Seattle at the same time? Bonnie had been back here a few months. I squinted, remembering. She'd expressed surprise, last Wednesday in the Market, at my mother's presence. So how had she known my mother had moved to Central America?

A dozen or more Friday night partygoers had known them both. But I'd picked up no clues that Bonnie had been in touch with any of them.

"Coincidence means you don't trust the Universe," my mother had said.

Clearly, my mother was not telling me everything. *She's a grown-up. She has the right to decide for herself what you need to know and what you don't.*

But I'm a grown-up, too, and I have the right to ask questions.

"Humans, Arf. What are we going to do about them?" My companion retained his gentlemanly silence.

I stepped around a cluster of young boys eyeing a super-duper modern vessel, no doubt boasting all the latest techno-hoorah. Hey, if that's what it takes to get the next generation out on the high seas . . .

So who had my mother called? Not my dad or Kristen's father, out of reach in the Queen Charlotte Islands.

I thought back to the party. Faces I hadn't seen in years, names I barely remembered. A couple who'd been instrumental, along with our parents, in setting up Jimmy's Pantry, the free meals program. The first yoga teacher on Capitol Hill, who'd held classes in our third-floor ballroom. The women who'd been my mother's compatriots at the Montessori school and day care. Terry Stinson, who'd had a finger in every pie, a hand in every project.

Wasn't it odd to go back to a city you'd lived in once and not reach out to your old friends?

Maybe not, if you'd been gone a very long time, as Bonnie had been.

Or if those friendships had ended badly.

The fisherman stood when we neared his boat the second time, and I had the sense he'd been waiting for us.

"Pretty lady on a pretty day."

I like to think I'm not easily flattered, but I stopped anyway. Next to the net, a tangled heap of rope and seaweed, lay a crumpled crab pot. "You're a netter, right, not a crabber?"

"This pot came up in my morning catch. It's a ghost trap. Thousands of nets and pots get lost in storms every year. Or they get cut loose when another boat runs across the line. But they're still fishing. This one snared an old float." He plucked a small green glass ball out of the mess and tossed it to me. He gestured toward a larger glass float caged in a rope and tied to the dock post, next to an old creel. "You never know what you'll find."

"Ghost traps? I've never heard of them."

"They can be a big problem. Care to come aboard?" He made a sweeping gesture, and I noticed the boat's name. *Thalassa.* The goddess of the sea.

It was tempting. "Uh, thanks. I need to get going."

He picked up a corner of the tangled net, his green-eyed gaze on me. "Another time, then. I'm here most Sundays."

If Kristen were here right now, she'd say, "Go fish."

"I'll keep that in mind." Because as much as I love boats and crab and handsome men with hard-earned muscles, my dog and I had places to go and snooping to do.

KRISTEN'S front door was locked. I rang the bell, and Mariah let me in.

"Mom's kinda freaked out." She stooped to bury her face in Arf's neck.

I raised my eyebrows. The woman who'd gone toe-to-toe with a neighbor who threatened to call the cops last year when she let Mariah, then eleven, and her ten-year-old cousin walk to the grocery store alone? Who'd orchestrated dozens of contractors and their crews and faced hordes of city inspectors without losing her temper once?

The woman who, daily, kept me in line?

"Oh, Pepper, it's you." Kristen piled her hair on top of her head and fastened it with a binder clip. A hank immediately fell loose, but she didn't take notice. I followed her to the kitchen, where she poured two glasses of lavender limeade. She set a bowl of water on the floor for Arf and took the seat next to mine at the island.

"I'd add a jigger of tequila if I didn't have to take Mariah to a birthday party in an hour." She did a half swivel on her stool, and I glanced down, surprised to see a chip in the polish on one big toe. The Ice Queen was melting.

"So do they think they know who broke in?" I took a sip. Tart, sweet, and—I say this with all honesty, even though I created the recipe myself—surprising.

"That's just it. There's no evidence of a break-in."

I pictured myself peering in the windows of Bonnie's studio. I'd left fingerprints on the window frame and sill, and footprints in the dew-damp ground below. But a gloved burglar, someone with a plan, could have left no trace.

Kristen plucked one of Laurel's lemon thyme cookies off a tray. "Detective Tracy thinks I mislaid it, or that one of the girls took it and doesn't want to 'fess up. What Spencer thinks, I don't know. That woman keeps a stone face better than a marble statue."

"But how could its disappearance possibly be related to Bonnie's murder?"

She sighed. "I can't believe she's dead."

"Me, neither." I took a cookie. "Let's go over it all. When did you take it off, when did you last see it, when did you notice it missing?"

"I took it off during the party, but what time, I don't know. Me and my big mouth. I had to make sure everybody knew what we'd found."

"Natural reaction. We were celebrating the house, after all. And the house gave you the bracelet." I scrunched my face, thinking. "Did you take it off before or after you gave the tour?"

She cocked her head a moment. "During. I slipped into the bedroom and laid it on our dresser."

Had someone seen her and sneaked back to help themselves?

"Nothing else is missing, right? So it has to be someone who knew about it, and who knew you'd taken it off. A burglar wouldn't come in, go upstairs, and take nothing else."

"That's what Eric thinks. 'What's the point of installing a security system,' he said, but—"

"But if that's what happened, no security system would have made a difference. Who went on the tour?"

"Lena, Cayenne, Bonnie." She ticked them off on her fingers, then named half a dozen others. Some I knew and some I didn't.

"And Sharon, right? What about her kids?" A soft snore caught my attention, and I glanced down at Arf, stretched out on the floor, feet twitching as if he were running in his sleep. "I think I saw her go in with you."

"Yeah, but I'm not sure she toured the whole house. She never saw the place in its before condition, and I don't think she cares much about design. She's one of those moms who's all kids, all the time. That reminds me, Detective Tracy wanted to know the name, address, and parents of every kid here, like being a kid made them automatically larcenous. Like they would care about diamonds and sapphires."

"They would know the bracelet was valuable. Cops have to cast a wide net. This early, they don't know what's going to be important."

Her shoulders sank in an "I hate to admit you're right" gesture. "He made me feel kinda stupid. I didn't think I had to keep tabs on who went inside, and I didn't mind if someone went upstairs alone. I didn't expect my friends to steal from me."

As recent conversations with my mother proved, even our nearest and dearest can hide a secret or two.

"Okay, so let's think about this from the other direction. That bracelet is unique. The thief can't just pawn it. Did he—or she—know you had it and plan to take it? Or did they snatch it up on impulse? Who knew about it before the party?"

"No one, except Eric and the girls. My sisters." She refilled our glasses. "I asked my dad where it came from when we found it, but he didn't have a clue."

I cooled my hands on my frosty glass. "You have a lot of old family photos. Does the bracelet show up in any of those?"

"Scary, how much you think like Detective Tracy." Kristen pointed to the albums open on her breakfast table. "Nothing yet. There's no other family to ask. We did take pictures after we found it and cleaned it up—Eric insisted, for insurance—so maybe the most we can hope for is that it shows up in some secondhand shop. I mean, I don't know its history, but I want it back."

I flipped idly through an album, stopping at a shot of Kristen and me sitting on the front porch. "What do you remember about Bonnie Clay? Or Peggy Manning. And Terry—were they friends?"

"They were all friends. A community."

"Until they weren't."

"Meaning what?" Kristen's voice took on an unfamiliar edge.

"Meaning Bonnie shows up and my mother clams up.

That makes me think something happened that she doesn't want me to know about."

"No law says she has to tell you everything."

"No, but if it relates to Bonnie's murder—"

"Hey, I gotta change and go." Kristen gestured toward her bare feet, her cutoff sweatpants, and her Disneyland T-shirt. Any other mother would have no trouble wearing that outfit to drop off a kid, but not her.

Two shakes later, my dog and I stood on Kristen's front porch. The dead bolt snapped shut behind us.

"Tossed out on our ears, Arf." I tightened his leash, and we started down the steps. "Musta been something I said."

Ten

*Now home to a fish market, a creamery, produce stalls,
and apartments, the Sanitary Market, built in 1910, got
its name from being the only building where horse-
drawn carts were not allowed.*

—Market history, City of Seattle website

"BOY, AM I GLAD TO SEE YOU."

The day the deal closed, the Spice Shop felt like home.
It still does. I am more myself here than almost anywhere,
except in the loft or at the rail of a Puget Sound ferry in a
stiff breeze.

But while I appreciated Cayenne's enthusiastic welcome,
I suspected it was chased by a problem.

"That customer," she said. "He's—weird, but I can't put
my finger on it."

Late thirties, wearing cargo pants and a loose shirt. His
pockets appeared to lay flat, not hiding any merchandise. His
left elbow jiggled in a hyperactive way.

Oh, the things you learn in retail.

"Go to bed, Arf." The dog obeyed, and I crossed the room
quickly. There wasn't much to shoplift—spice grinders,
boxes of tea, tins of our custom blends—but any theft hits the
bottom line. "Hi. What can I help you find?"

The customer practically jumped out of his worn brown deck shoes and let out a squeal that made me want to grab the WD-40. "Oh, I—umm." He glanced from me to the jar-lined shelves, then back. "Umm, you sell spice, right?"

I nodded.

"What about—" His gaze darted around the shop, landing briefly on Cayenne, who watched him as though she had her finger ready to call the police, then on the couple browsing cookbooks. His voice dropped, so low I had to lean in. "What about marijuana? I mean, it's legal in this state, right? Not that you would sell it, but who does?"

There's a first time for every question. "Both medicinal and recreational marijuana are legal in Washington," I said, "but they can't be sold within a thousand feet of any place intended for children, meaning schools, libraries, parks, and playgrounds."

He tilted his head in a question, dark hair flopping over one eye. He needed to visit the Market barbershop, Down Under.

"There's a preschool and a park in the Market," I said. "But if you're after a taste of Seattle, our tea will give you a pleasant glow. It's a blend of spicy and mellow. Not exactly a high, but quite nice." I held out a box.

He took it in both hands, studying the label and our salt-shaker logo.

To my surprise, he bought three boxes. "For my mother and sisters," he told Cayenne before wandering out. The moment the door shut behind him, we started giggling.

"Remember the Walmart lesson," I told her. "The best way to prevent shoplifting is to greet every customer."

Reed came in, bearing two iced coffees. Other than the pot-seeker, my staff had the shop well in hand. They didn't need me. I suppressed a pout and headed for my office to do a little research.

Okay, call it snooping.

Like any good HR manager in the modern world, I'd

developed a few skills for checking out potential employees online—all perfectly legal. Call it self-defense after a handful of self-inflicted hiring failures.

Time to apply those methods to this case.

Searching two names doubled the work and the frustration. Neither Bonnie nor Peggy had a Facebook account, Twitter handle, or website. That was a puzzle. Most artists I know set up a public portal, for curious browsers who find them by serendipity. Or tourists who get home to news of a grandbaby on the way and wouldn't those adorable stuffed critters they saw in the Market be just the thing?

I checked all the usual suspects: Etsy, Pinterest, Instagram.

Big fat zeros, all around.

Either Bonnie wasn't market-savvy or she hadn't gotten around to it.

Or, she didn't want to be found.

For fun, I searched myself, under both my names. Nothing under the legal one, thank heavens. Good news only for Pepper Reece, including the terrific profile Ben had written of me when he first came to town.

I sat back, arms crossed. What else? With no idea where she'd lived all those years away from Seattle, or under what name, I had no clue where to start the hunt.

But I knew who to call. Though I didn't know what my mother saw in Ben's stars, and I understood her warning not to let myself be used for a story, he was a good guy. And he had research skills.

"Hey, you busy? I need a little help from my favorite investigative reporter."

"Ha. That's a glorified label for a news grunt, but I'll take it. What's up?"

I explained.

"Meet you at the loft in, say, thirty minutes?" he said, and I agreed.

On my way out, I asked my staff their Sunday evening plans.

"Family dinner," Reed said. "The one day a week my mom cooks Chinese."

"Going to my grandpa's house," Cayenne said. "We tend his garden and cook up a storm. The leftovers last him all week. There's been trouble in his neighborhood, and my mom's worried. But he's too stubborn to move."

"He's lucky to have you close by."

Arf and I strolled down Pike Place to my favorite produce stand for greens and tomatoes. We ducked into the Sanitary Market—happily, no longer strictly an animal-free zone—and grabbed peppery Genoa salami and mild, slightly sweet *provolone dolce*, and a chunk of Parmesan. Backtracked for another box of Turkish delight. Those things are addictive.

Across Pike Place in the artists' stalls, I caught my friend the jewelry maker in a good mood after a big sale.

"You said Bonnie was worried about her sublease and having to move again. Were the problems with a woman named Hannah Hart?"

"Honestly, Pepper, if she mentioned the name, it escapes me now." She pinned a pair of earrings onto a gap in her display board. "Got my eye out for a piece of a car like you drive."

"Nightmist Blue."

And then I had—well, not a brainstorm. A slight ripple in the weather. Arf and I trotted over the Desimone Bridge, pausing to toss a couple of dollars in the violin case of an all-women trio. How the bass player coaxed music from an upside-down plastic bucket, I could not fathom. In a quiet spot overlooking the construction site for the new Market Front, I fished in my bag for my phone. Tory Finch wasn't one to gossip, but I'd crossed a few lines for my former employee last fall, and she knew it. Besides, if I asked too much, she'd say so.

"Painter. Muralist," Tory answered without hesitation. "Let me see what I can find out."

"Thanks. How's Zak? And the gallery? I miss you guys."

"We miss you. And the Spice Shop. We're having a big opening end of the month, including pieces inspired by my grandmother's work. Zak's band's playing. Say you'll come."

"I'll come. Anytime—you know that."

A few minutes later, I hoisted my overloaded tote higher on my shoulder, switched Arf's leash to my left hand, and unlocked the door to my building. We climbed the wide staircase, greeted by the odor of stale popcorn mixed with eau d'ancient sawdust, a smell that would probably never go away completely, and a touch of bacon.

Ever since my neighbor Glenn's husband had gone back east to care for his ailing, elderly mother, Glenn had been indulging in comfort food. Not that I blamed him. In the month that I'd camped at Kristen's house after leaving Tag, I created roughly two dozen varieties of mac and cheese, my routine broken by the occasional baked potato extravaganza and regular doses of homemade chocolate chip cookies. Only nervous energy had kept me from gaining fifteen pounds.

Inside the apartment, I gave Arf fresh water, then started on an appetizer.

"So," I asked my dog over the ka-thunking of the food processor. "Why would you sublet your studio and your apartment, then demand them back early?"

Plans change, heaven knows. I stepped through the window and snipped a handful of chives from the happy green jungle on my narrow deck.

How had Hannah's plans changed? More trouble with the boyfriend? A new job that didn't pan out?

The whir of the food processor matched the whir in my mind as I added herbs, seasoning, and oil.

Other reasons were possible, but romance and career cover most of life's disappointments and dilemmas.

But Hannah's change in direction had created problems for Bonnie. Deadly problems, or merely inconvenient ones?

The intercom sounded, and I buzzed Ben in. Put the bowl of cheese spread on a pressed tin tray, and laid out crackers and smoked salmon.

I kissed him and carried our appetizers to the round cedar picnic table, a gift from my former mother-in-law. She'd salvaged the table and one bench from a neighbor's trash after a windstorm, and I'd added mismatched chairs.

Ben set a bottle of rosé on the kitchen counter. "Crawling around in the past is dirty, messy business. Wine will make it easier."

Just when I thought this guy wasn't right for me, he said something that made me relax and laugh. And that's always a good thing.

He sat on the cedar bench and fired up his trusty laptop while I opened the wine. "We'll start local. Seattle had two dailies back then, right?"

I handed him a glass and perched on the pink iron chair that looked like a refugee from an ice cream shop, disguised by a fluffy tropical print pillow. "Yes, but I don't know what we're hoping to find."

"Neither do I. That's the fun part."

I held out my hand, surprised to see my fingers tremble. "Ben, I'm not sure I want this to be a story for your paper. I mean, any murder is news. But this one involves my family. And Kristen's." An invisible ice pick stabbed me in the jaw. I hadn't shared my fear that if Bonnie had been killed to protect a secret from the past, my mother might be in danger, too.

"No worries." Eyes on the screen, he scrolled and clicked. "We investigate all kinds of stories that don't pan out."

"What I'm saying is, we might uncover things I'm not willing to see in print."

He took his hands off the keyboard and faced me. "Pepper, you called me because I'm a reporter. I'd like to think you also called because we're friends. Maybe not as close as I'd hoped—I kinda sense that you're holding back—but I would never do anything that would hurt you or your family."

He sensed . . . My chin rose and my jaw clenched. "Even for a story?"

"Even for a story. I will not publish a word without your one hundred percent approval. And if my editor asks me, I'll tell her I didn't find anything that works for us. We're not general news—it's gotta speak to our audience in some way. If someone else finds the story I didn't, I'll take my lumps."

Oh my. Was he honestly this generous? And this interested in my well-being?

I studied his open face. He didn't know all the details about Tag, or the hard-luck love stories that had dogged me (*sorry, Arf*) since my divorce. In my opinion, a new love doesn't need to know all the down-and-dirty of the past. It just gets in the way.

Maybe this push-and-pull, this uncertainty, this questioning was not a warning, but a natural phase in developing a stable relationship.

Truth was, I hadn't dated enough in recent years to know. Truth is, you never know—until you know.

I slid off the chair and onto the bench, and wrapped my arms around him. Kissed him lightly, then again, more deeply. Because you never know, until you risk the answer you aren't ready for.

Eleven

Be careful what you wish for.

—Every grandmother's advice

"SHE WAS TIGHT WITH YOUR MOM WAY BACK, RIGHT? Any chance their projects made the newspapers?"

"What would we learn from a photo op on the opening of a preschool or a yoga studio?"

"Reporter's credo: Follow every trail." Ben spread cheesy goop on a cracker. "This stuff is fabulous."

"You only love me for my cooking. Let's start dinner. I'm starving." I swung my leg over the bench, feeling antsy.

The sun had begun to slide behind the Olympics, flinging fractured rays of colored light into the loft. Why the original builders had installed twelve-foot-tall windows on the fifth floor of a trackside warehouse, I had no idea, but on evenings like this, I was grateful.

"The light is the same color as the wine." Ben twirled his glass and sat at the butcher-block counter dividing the kitchen and main living area. The only walls in the place surround the bed and bath, and the plank floors, high ceilings, and exposed beams and pipes give it classic loft style.

I'd played that up, adding mismatched furniture and bright and funky finds for a look I hope is both welcoming and intriguing.

"Vinny would spin some theory about how the French discovered that leaving the skin on the grapes until the wine reaches the same shade as the sunset over the Rhone Valley on the first day of summer creates the perfect blend of sweetness and acidity." I tossed chopped romaine in a big wooden bowl and reached for the salami.

"Vinny believes in ghosts."

"Don't you?" He knew my theories about what had happened in April, about the mysterious little lady who'd pointed me in the direction of a very bad man. "I feel like we're chasing ghosts. Make yourself useful and scrub this cucumber."

Ben scrubbed while I mixed the dressing for my version of the Pink Door's Italian chopped salad, adding a generous pinch of Celtic sea salt from Bonnie's pig, a piece that had become even more special in the past hours.

My chest felt heavy, and I forced myself to take a deep breath.

We carried our dinner out to the veranda and the round bistro table.

"I always feel like I'm stepping through the looking glass," Ben said. "Sliding down the rabbit hole. Choosing the red pill."

"It's not that different out here from elsewhere in the city."

"To continue mangling the movie metaphors, the Emerald City is on a completely different planet from where I grew up. Your family, the commune, the causes and projects—might as well be Mars."

"It wasn't a commune." I twisted a strip of salami around my fork. "Although we did have chickens, but the neighbors complained, so we ate them."

He gestured with an open hand. "See? That's what I mean. You were hippies. We were—conventional."

Conventional or not, it was lovely to relax on the veranda amid the herbs and flowers, in the rosé light, conversation weaving in and out of the various corners of our lives.

But I couldn't forget that a woman was dead, and I wanted answers.

Ben reached out a hand. "Pepper, can we talk? Seriously, about us."

"Nineteen eighty-five. The year we moved." The startled look on his face barely registered as I shoved my chair back and gathered plates. "Bonnie didn't live her life the way the rest of us do. The clues are not online."

"So where are they?"

"With any luck, downstairs."

Ten minutes later, we hauled a dusty wicker trunk out of the service elevator and into my loft. I began unloading the scrapbooks and photo albums my mother had boxed up before the move south. Andrea, bless her, had other plans for their basement than housing family archives, so they'd landed in my storage locker. I set aside two shoe boxes wrapped in newspaper comics. The books covered the picnic table.

Ben let out a low whistle. "I'd never have figured your mother for the sentimental type."

"All mothers are sentimental. They just show it in different ways." As a preschool teacher, my mother had been a big believer in projects involving round-tipped scissors and glue sticks. She'd loved those albums with self-adhesive pages covered in flimsy plastic. The stickum had loosened over time, and a Wonder Woman Valentine's card fluttered to the floor. I picked it up—the pencil scribble on the back had faded, but I made out the name of a boy in my second grade class—and started searching for the page it had come from.

A damp nose poked my leg. "Go back to bed, Arf." *Flip, flip, flip.*

"I'll take him out," Ben said.

"Oh, I'm sorry, boy," I told the dog, embarrassed. "Thanks," I told the man.

I refilled my wineglass and carried it and a thick black album, the binding embossed in gold, to the couch. When I moved out of the Greenwood bungalow Tag and I had bought from his elderly aunt, I'd taken my books and clothes, some kitchen collectibles, and a few treasured pieces of furniture. He'd been deeply hurt that I left our wedding album behind, but it, like so much else in the house, belonged to the past. To a time gone by—a time that had perhaps never really existed.

The things we save illustrate the choices we make. What matters to us.

My mother's collection included baby books, school record books, and the scrapbooks Carl and I had made, our childish handwriting as dated as the cards and photos. But this album had been hers.

I sipped and flipped. My parents' wedding photo, he in a dark suit, she in a yellow mini-dress, a matching ribbon in her long, straight hair. *So young.*

A shot of my mother and Kristen's parents standing on the front porch of Grace House, each woman cradling a baby. Kristen's and my first joint appearance. My father must have been behind the camera, as usual.

Several pages later, I found a solo shot of him, blurry enough to make me think I'd taken it. He'd been a fun dad, but he always looked serious in photographs.

I turned the pages. More photos of the two families as they grew. Carl and me with our Hungarian grandparents, looking old and stodgy, though by the date printed on the photo, they hadn't been much more than fifty. My first day of school, and three years later, Carl's. The two of us with Grandpa Reece at a Cardinals game, Carl clutching his glove. Over the years, he'd collected enough foul balls to fill a shelf in his office.

A newspaper clipping of opening day at Jimmy's Pantry. In one photo, a row of eager adults posed at the kitchen window, ready to serve the first meals. Another showed a long line of men, women, and children outside the Cathedral's side door, as Terry Stinson studied his watch and waited for the five o'clock dinner bell.

Terry, tall and thin, a grin on his homely face. Next to him stood a small woman, her hair long, straight, and blond.

The caption confirmed what her eyes told mine: Peggy Manning.

Other pages told of the free clinics the Grace House community had worked to establish in the Central District, with partner groups, including the local chapter of the Black Panthers; a grant to expand the Montessori school; and later, a national award for work with the HIV/AIDS foundation. An editorial about the Archbishop of Seattle's decision to withhold half his income tax to protest the country's nuclear deterrence policy, symbolized by weapons stockpiled in Puget Sound. For his pastoral leadership, the bishop had his wages garnished by the IRS and suffered through a years-long Vatican investigation.

I browsed pages of clippings and photos, rallies for this cause, that protest, this candidate.

But no more mention of Peggy.

Then, as the headlights whizzed by on the soon-to-be-demolished Viaduct, I came across a page I couldn't explain.

Holy coriander.

In 1985, a man named Roger Russell was killed in a shoot-out in a wealthy neighborhood north of the university. Apparently the homeowner—Walter Strasburg, a computer whiz consulting with the government on code for its nuclear subs—had come home unexpectedly to find Russell destroying his computers. Strasburg had dug a gun out of the bedroom closet. Russell had pulled one, too. An explosion created a cloud of debris and confusion, and the two men shot each other to death.

According, at least, to the sole eyewitness, Strasburg's ten-year-old son.

My hand flew to my mouth.

The door opened. "Honey, we're home!" Ben called, his tone light and teasing. Dog claws tapped across the floor, and Arf gave me the "time for treats" look.

I pointed to the laptop, unsure if I could speak. "I need you to find an obituary. Walter Strasburg. June 1985." I spelled the name, then grabbed Arf's treat jar off the counter. The lid finally popped off, and a pawful of liver chews fell on the floor. I didn't bother to pick up the extras, instead stumbling past man and dog into the bathroom. I threw cold water on my face. Buried my damp face in my damp hands, pressed the heels into my eyes. Raised my face to the mirror, spread my fingers, and stared at my horrified self.

My mother had mentioned Roger last night, and he'd obviously been close to Peggy. Had he killed the man in some kind of protest? Why had she kept the clipping all these years?

After a few moments, my heartbeat slowed and I returned to the living room, a towel around my neck. Ben had settled on the couch, and I sat next to him, one leg tucked under me. Wordlessly, he handed me the laptop, then picked up the album lying on my packing crate coffee table, open to the clipping that had stunned me.

The obituary shed no light on Walter Strasburg's death. It described his childhood in Seattle and his passion for electronics, extolling his achievements as a computer genius of the type Seattle is famous for—bits and bytes of code that changed the world. He'd been a Little League coach, a budding philanthropist, a son, a husband, a father.

Survived, it read, *by his wife, Elizabeth, and two sons, Brian and David.*

My mother's clipping had not named the young eyewitness.

But I knew Brian Strasburg. As the HR manager responsible for staff, I'd been the one to console legal assistants left in tears after his tirades. The one who'd counseled him on adopting milder manners, often ending up close to tears myself.

Ben studied me, questions on his face.

"Brian Strasburg was a lawyer at my old firm. Hard-nosed, difficult. Some of the staff loved him, others hated him."

"Was he part of the downfall?" Ben scratched Arf behind the ears.

"Surprisingly, no. Two senior partners deliberately withheld information in a med mal case, and the court levied huge sanctions on the firm—half a million dollars. Then it came out that the IT director had embezzled two and a half million. Almost overnight, the firm dissolved, and the lawyers started teaming up. Strasburg offered me a job, but I'd already decided to buy the Spice Shop."

"No regrets?"

"Not one." I sipped my water. "He'd been married to another partner. They had a kid. She divorced him and left the firm, long before it blew up. I always thought she was too nice for him. Now I'm wondering whether it doesn't all trace back to Grace House. To 1985."

"Pepper, you can't say—"

"Yes, I can. I don't remember Roger Russell, but my mother referred to Peggy and Roger, and she kept this clipping. It's gotta be the same guy. Maybe Roger went off the rails. Maybe no one knew what he had planned. But if they didn't know, then they failed him *and* themselves. Not to mention the Strasburgs. By not living up to their own code of making the world a better, safer place through nonviolence and *community*."

"I think you're being too hard on them. And on yourself."

I sank onto the bench in front of the middle window, made of reclaimed wood found in the building. Below the seats, bookcases held my treasured volumes: *Anne of Green Gables*. The Little House books. Remnants of an innocent time.

"So what does this have to do with Peggy?" I mused.

"Why do you think it has anything to do with her? The article doesn't mention anyone but Russell." Ben clicked off the laptop and slid it into its case. "I hate to leave you alone with all this running through your head, but it's getting late, and I've got to be in Olympia at eight o'clock. Fact-finding hearing on highway infrastructure." He rolled his eyes.

"You? You're the food and fun guy."

"Except when the government reporter goes on vacation and the editor drafts me. If I get a chance, I'll dig a little deeper into all this, but Pepper . . ."

I cupped his cheek and jaw in my hand. He'd wanted to talk about our relationship, and instead I'd stumbled deeper into a family crisis. "Thank you. All this work and you might not even get a story out of it."

"I got a great dinner and an evening with a woman I'm very fond of. How about a kiss for dessert?"

Dessert. I'd left the Turkish delight in the kitchen. I kissed him. Seattle delight.

The door closed. Back on the couch, I tossed the damp towel on the floor and pulled the heavy album onto my lap. My mother had not saved any other articles about the incident—maybe it didn't mean that much after all.

No. I know how my mother thinks. She saved this one for a reason. The date—in her handwriting—said June 15, 1985. The day before Kristen's birthday, almost two weeks after mine. Birthday memories run together, unless something special or out of the ordinary occurs. My sixth stands out because Grandpa Reece visited, and my sixteenth, because he died that morning. My twenty-first was a blur, my thirtieth a lovely day with Tag on Whidbey Island. My fortieth a vision of hell, as I'd ranted and raved against him, unable to imagine his betrayal—or that I would ever get over it.

My twelfth, and Kristen's, came up blank.

How on earth could Roger—or anyone—have imagined doing such a hateful thing, in the name of justice?

A tiny spot in the center of my heart burned.

If Peggy and Roger had been a couple, how had all that affected her? If she meant what she'd told her neighbor in the daystalls—that she'd been on the move for thirty years—had she left because of grief?

I laid the flat of my hand against my chest, the cool touch oddly calming. "The question is whether the past has any connection to her death."

Arf opened one eye, then let it drift shut. He's used to me talking to myself.

But there were more questions. Brian Strasburg was a man of sharp edges, who had the skills to trace a person. Did he hold a grudge? Had he found Peggy Manning, aka Bonnie Clay, and taken vengeance?

And what was I going to tell my mother?

Twelve

Unlike sights or sounds, researchers say, odors are processed through the brain's limbic system, also the center of emotions—which might explain why scents often trigger memories with emotional overtones.

NOTHING LIKE THE FREE-WHEELING, FAST-MOVING, get-going-or-get-out-of-the-way pace of Monday morning in the Market to get the juices flowing.

Not to mention a triple shot latte and a cherry turnover.

I locked myself into the shop and breathed in the sweet scent of refuge.

Now that Matt and Cayenne were mostly trained, we'd resumed a semi-normal schedule. Sandra took both Sunday and Monday off. I worked six days a week, but that's the nature of retail, especially in high season. By fall, I hoped to score a day midweek for myself.

But not yet. Arf and I surveyed the place, and I plugged in the LED sign mounted in the front window—our salt-shaker logo, sprinkling salt on the waves. Then it was time for the Monday morning paperwork. No shortage of paper-work in HR, but little of it had involved money and none of it actual cash handling. Most days, Sandra or I tally up after closing, but with neither of us working Sundays, that had become a Monday task. So I dirtied my fingers thumbing bills and sorting coins, ran the sales figures and credit cards, and counted myself lucky that the totals were only off by fourteen cents.

Then it was time to open the doors for my staff, brew tea, and welcome the hordes.

Not *hordes*, on a Monday, but a girl can hope. And even Monday traffic picks up in June.

"Boss." Using Sandra's nickname for me, Cayenne cast a long-lashed look toward the front door. Tag, in full bike cop uniform, the tight shorts showing off his long, lean legs, an older woman at his elbow. He pointed uphill, then down Pike Place, giving directions.

I took a deep breath and stepped outside.

"Good morning, Officer Buhner. What brings you by?" His stops had become less frequent the last month or two.

"Hey." His tone was light, but he kept his sunglasses on and offered none of the usual flirty platitudes that both flatter and annoy me. "Just checking on you. Market vendor gets murdered, you'll get involved. Though why you would divorce a police officer then turn amateur cop beats me."

My spine stiffened. For a man who does not fish, Tag does a bang-up job of baiting me. *Keep calm and carry on.*

"She was a friend of the family. You don't honestly expect me to walk away from that."

Three years ago, I had walked away from him. We had worked our way back to being friends, and for a short time, I thought we might give it another go. He'd made his interest more than clear, and then, the flame died, leaving me confused.

That happens more often with men than I care to admit.

"That was uncalled for. I'm sorry." I touched his arm in apology. "Tag, I know how to find old files in civil cases, but what about records of criminal investigations?"

"Depends. Were charges filed, was there a conviction?" He described the process of submitting a public disclosure request, online or in person. "What do you want to find?"

I grimaced. "Not exactly sure. What if the case is old? Thirty years."

He took off his glasses and fixed me with a steady glare. The new SPD uniform shirts are a deep navy, unlike the medium blue street officers wore for years, and his shirt no longer matched his eyes. The eyes burning into me right now.

"Be careful, Pepper. Don't let that new boyfriend of yours drag you into investigating so he can get a story." He threw a leg over his bike and sped off, weaving through the obstacles, somehow staying upright despite all the hazards.

I stared after him. He'd turned off the automatic flirtation switch. Still protective, but not the way he'd been in the past. Still interfering.

He'd echoed my mother's comment about investigating with Ben. But I wasn't worried. Ben had assured me he wouldn't go to print without my agreement, and now he was off chasing another story.

Was Tag involved with someone else? Did I care?

I let out a long, ragged breath. Life gets tricky sometimes.

THE circles under Kristen's eyes were the color of her stolen sapphires.

To my eyes, she lacked her usual sparkle, but no one else seemed to notice as she went about her routine, tending to the books and the tea accessories.

"The extra bamboo strainers should fit in the lower half of the apothecary," I told her. "Behind the baskets of Spice Shop kitchen towels."

"I know where they go." She swished past me, her scrunchie sliding off her blond ponytail. I grabbed it before it hit the floor and held it out. She snatched it without a word.

Oh-kay. There's nothing like your first time as a crime victim.

"Boss, what about these?" Cayenne stood in front of the display of Bonnie's salt pigs and cellars.

"Oh, good garlic. I have no idea what to do." Decisions, decisions. "I'll take them to the Market office. Let them decide what to do with her stuff."

"Those new replica English tea canisters will fit in the space."

"Good thinking." I wrapped up the pottery and clicked Arf's leash onto his collar, and we made our way to the Market office, on Lower Post Alley in the Economy Building. Spitting distance from the grossly infamous Gum Wall, ranked as one of the germiest tourist attractions in the world, right after the Blarney Stone.

Alas, the Market Master was making his rounds, and decisions on Bonnie's belongings were up to him. Where we might find him was anyone's guess.

"To the park, then?" I asked my four-footed companion. With typical agreeableness—or it may have been the magic word "park"—he turned in the right direction, and off we went.

We kept to the streets—easier than weaving through the crowds on the sidewalk. I kept an eye out for the Market Master, a tall, gangly man with a too-long face.

There he stood, next to the fresh pasta stall, head cocked, listening.

I tugged on the leash, and we changed course, stepping into the narrow passage between two long rows of stalls. The pasta seller pointed up the Arcade, then down the ramp. Curious as the mythical cat but wanting to observe some degree of tact, I paused to inspect the flavored oils.

"Call me if you think of anything else," another man told the vendor. "Well, if it isn't the official market snoop."

I met the taunting-yet-teasing gaze of Detective Michael Tracy.

"Hello, Detective. I need a word with the Market Master, if you don't mind." I held up the bag of pigs and pots. "Bonnie Clay left a few display pieces in the shop, and I'm wondering what to do with them."

The Market Master's thick lips twisted like an unbaked pretzel. "Bit of a problem for us. The emergency contact on her application turned out to be her landlord, who doesn't have any more info on her than we do. I was hoping Detective Tracy would have better luck, but he tells me they haven't located any next of kin yet."

"Can I leave them in her storage locker?" I asked. Most craftspeople keep one. "Until you find someone to take her stuff. You probably want it cleaned out fairly soon."

"That's a fact. We're going down to open it up right now. Come along if you want."

I wanted. "Sure. Did the pasta maker have any useful information?"

Tracy snorted. "Saw her cart stuff back and forth every day and didn't even know her name. Your 'Market family' isn't so close after all. Other than a handful of the artists, I doubt anyone exchanged more than a few sentences with her."

"She was new," the Market Master said quickly. "She hadn't had time to become well acquainted yet. Our people work too hard for chitchat."

"How long—had—she been—here?" Tracy's words came in spurts as we scurried to keep up with our long-legged guide.

"Two, three months. I'd have to check the file to be sure."

That caught me off guard. I hadn't seen her until last Wednesday, though I try to walk through the Arcade at least once a week, to visit and see what's new. The vendors and the merchants have an important relationship. If a customer asks an artist where a spice shop is, I want the answer to be: "Well, there's a couple, but I shop at Seattle Spice, right across the street." And nearly every day, we field questions about where to find the best meat, the freshest flowers, fun jewelry, and great baby gifts.

Plus, I like the artists. Their energy is infectious.

So either I'd walked the aisles on Bonnie's days away, or she'd kept a low profile.

The Market Master used his key to call for the elevator. The ancient cogs and pulleys creaked into action, and we began the descent. No point asking Tracy if he had any leads—any suspects, a working theory. No point seeing him roll his eyes at my audacity.

Besides, Tracy appeared to be lost in his own thoughts.

The elevator stopped, then gave a sudden jerk, and my guts rose and dropped. Arf was unfazed.

I'd never been to the lockers, deep in the Market's belly. The Market Master halted at a space four feet wide and six feet deep, a two-by-four frame covered with chicken wire. He opened the lock, stepped inside, and rustled around, then strode off, tool in hand, his jingling keys beckoning us forward.

I felt a bit like Gretel plunging deep into the dark forest, but with no Hansel to hold my hand, and no bread crumbs to lead me back out.

He stopped in front of another stall. Bonnie's business card was stapled to the wood frame. "This is it. Never had any security issues, but we tell folks not to leave anything valuable down here."

Tracy took a few photographs, then gestured to go ahead. I saw now why bolt cutters have long handles. Even a man as strong as the Market Master had to lean into them.

The metal snapped and the lock fell apart. Gloved, Tracy slid it out of the hasp and opened the wood-frame door. I watched closely as he opened box after box of pottery—bowls, cups, plates, crocks, all in the style, colors, and glazes I'd seen in her booth.

I exhaled slowly, my hand on my heart. There would be no more of her work.

"Business supplies." Tracy riffled one gloved hand through a plastic container full of brown paper bags and boxes of business cards, and another filled with tissue paper and bubble wrap. He popped a third lid.

"What's this?" He held up a copy of a tabloid-sized newspaper, folded to show, in living color, a photo of my shop. And me.

Thirteen

*It seems to me that our three basic needs, for food and
security and love, are so mixed and mingled and
entwined that we cannot straightly think of one without
the others.*

—M. F. K. Fisher, American food writer and essayist, in
The Gastronomical Me

"YOU SAID YOU HADN'T BEEN IN TOUCH WITH HER
before last week. You want to correct that statement?"

I stared at the newspaper in Tracy's hand. Nothing Bonnie had said, in the Market or at the party, suggested she'd
known she was working across the street from the daughter
of an old friend before we swung by her table last week.

And yet, she'd held on to a two-month-old newspaper . . .

It's creepy-weird to realize someone's been watching you
from the shadows.

"Nothing to correct," I said.

"Hrmmph." Tracy could say more in a few consonants
than most people with an entire dictionary.

He was saying he didn't trust me or my mother. At the
moment, I didn't blame him. I held out my hand. "May I?
To refresh my memory?"

Tracy pulled a second set of thin gloves out of his pocket. I slipped them on, then took the paper and sidestepped to the nearest light—a dim bulb that looked as old as Edison himself. I'd read the article when it came out, and allowed Kristen to hang a framed copy above the tea cart for customers to see. But the details had grown vague.

I searched for the detail that had been bugging me. My mother's surprise at seeing Bonnie-Peggy had been genuine—she'd thought Peggy was dead, though why remained a mystery. Obviously they had not been in touch. So how had Bonnie known that my parents had left the country?

Yes. Because Ben had reported that I was a Seattle native, raised on Capitol Hill by parents deeply involved in the community, who now lived in Central America.

Bonnie had gotten the country wrong, but if I'd read her response right, she'd been more than happy to believe my mother safely away in another hemisphere.

Why?

The forces that had drawn her back to Seattle had overcome the impulses that drove her away.

"Care to tell me what's going through that mind of yours?" Tracy slipped the newspaper into an evidence bag.

"We about done here? I've got a schedule to keep." The Market Master had reappeared, another lock in his hand. "I'll put one of our locks on this cage for now. Detective, the sooner you get these things outta here, the better. Space is tight."

I held up my bag. "What about these?"

"Better you keep them," Tracy said. "Until we make a more thorough search and inventory. Wouldn't want to find your fingerprints on a bowl in her stash and not be sure why."

They returned the boxes to the locker, Tracy promising to do his best without actually promising to take charge of

Bonnie's personal items. I wondered what would happen to that lovely pottery. To her life's work—at least, in recent years.

And to her memory.

SO that's how a miner feels, emerging from underground. Arf and I blinked against the sunlight.

"Okay, buddy," I told him. "I haven't forgotten." We trotted up Pike Place to the park and did our thing, including a stop at the railing for the human to take in the view, and let the motes of sunshine mingle with the salt air on her face.

Part of my skin care routine.

If the dog minds, he never says a word. I appreciate a male who doesn't feel obliged to take charge.

Back at the shop, I took Cayenne aside. "How did you meet Bonnie?"

"In the Arcade. Her pottery was gorgeous. I thought it would be perfect for us."

"Did she know the shop, or me?"

"Everybody knows you, Pepper." Her head tilted slightly, and her voice wavered, as if she worried about displeasing me. "I wanted to connect with the merchants and vendors, like you do."

I touched her forearm. "You are a great ambassador for the shop, Cayenne. Thank you."

Of course Bonnie had known who I was. She'd already seen the newspaper story. Had she come to the Market on purpose, to keep an eye on me? Or had she'd joined the arts and crafts crew first, then discovered my presence? How had she felt about our proximity?

Had it worried her, like it worried my mother?

Reassured, Cayenne flashed me the smile that won over customers, and turned to offer tea to a fleet of incoming tourists.

I sensed eyes on me. Kristen, across the shop. I longed to tell her what Ben and I had uncovered last night, and that a woman we barely knew had a newspaper article on me tucked away, and ask what she thought.

But for reasons I couldn't articulate, not even to myself, I wasn't quite ready.

In the modern world, there are a million ways to reach out and touch someone. Sometimes a phone call is best; other times, a text or an e-mail.

Certain moments call for face-to-face.

"Hey, I'm late making the bank run," I told my staff. "Keep an eye on the pooch, would you, please?"

I left the Market and made the deposit. We were doing well, slightly ahead of my projections, even after the expense of the gift registry. Although if I had to send too many more apology gifts to brides we hadn't actually wronged, our profit margin would get mighty slim.

Then I followed my nose.

At Third and Cherry, I passed the white terra-cotta Arctic Club building, long one of my favorites, now repurposed as a hotel. Who wouldn't love a building adorned with walrus heads? (They're terra-cotta, too; no actual walrii were harmed in its construction.)

My target lay in the next block. Inside, I checked the directory on the lobby wall, then took the elevator—as old, or older, than the one in the Market, but more elegant and less spooky. Got out on the third floor. Took a deep breath. Found the right oak door, the name stenciled on the frosted glass. Turned the brass knob, the hinges creaking as I walked in.

The worn brown carpet and scuffed white walls marked this a low-budget operation. No one sat at the reception desk, but the stainless steel water bottle and vase full of zinnias said its occupant was away temporarily. Early lunch, maybe. My tummy rumbled with envy.

A man called from a back room. "Be right there!"

And before I could do more than pick up a brochure about the assistance available for vets struggling to obtain their full benefits, Uncle Sam himself strolled in.

"Pepper!" Terry Stinson called in his dry baritone. The red-and-white striped pants made him seem taller and thinner than he was. His white shirt lay open at the collar—no red bow tie today—and the rolled-up sleeves revealed lean, muscular white arms. "Come in, come in. What brings you here?"

"Sad news. You heard about Bonnie. Peggy, I mean. You were old friends—I wanted to check on you."

His skin paled, matching the gray-white hair and goatee. He sank against the desk, his shoulders and spine curving forward, fist to his forehead as his eyes closed briefly.

"Your mother called me Saturday. Sharon and I are devastated."

I perched on the love seat, a faded blue floral number that was never in good taste, even ages ago when it was new. Something sharp poked me. I shifted my weight, looked down, and pried a small medal out from between the cushions. I fastened the pin and set it on the dusty coffee table.

"You knew her way back when."

He nodded, eyes lowered, unfocused. "Met her and your mom about the same time. Both smart, dedicated. Hot chicks." He raised his head, and the left side of his mouth curved. "We were so serious back then. Change the world, get us out of Vietnam, blah blah blah."

"The world is a better place because of what you did."

The tendons in his thin neck pulsed. "I suppose so, but it never seems like enough."

A natural reaction, in his line of work. "When did you last see her?"

He lifted his eyebrows in a playful gesture. "Why so many questions, little Pepper? Are you investigating? I read about you, you know."

"Actually, that's one of the odd things. The Market Master took me to Peggy's storage locker to help him figure out what to do with her stuff, and she had a copy of the newspaper story about me and the shop. Seems strange. She'd been away thirty years, right? Why keep the article about me?"

"That's easy. A kid she knew, making good."

And yet, she had not reached out to me. She had not swung by to say, "Hey, remember me? Old friends. How's your mother?"

"I suppose. But I have to wonder, why come back after all this time? And why did she leave in the first place?"

He pushed himself off the desk and stood upright. "Don't know. It was all a long time ago."

"Terry, was Roger Russell Bonnie's boyfriend? Peggy's, I mean?"

The good-hearted, old-friend facade slipped. He opened his mouth, as if trying to decide what to say. The door opened. He bounded forward and threw one arm around his wife, who held a paper bag that smelled of lunch.

"Hey, honey! You remember Pepper, don't you?" He continued, more somber. "She stopped by to offer her condolences. About Peggy. Bonnie."

Sharon pressed her lips together, her gaze shifting from her husband to me. The diamond studs in her ears glinted. "Terrible, isn't it. After all she'd been through, to be killed in her own home. And with her own handiwork. I hope they catch the thug."

Her expression seemed less than sincere. But then, she'd barely known the woman, a face from her husband's distant past.

"I'm sure they will. The old man across the street saw the car."

A cough wracked Terry's thin shoulders. Sharon reached past him and grabbed the silver water bottle from the desk. He held up a hand, warding her off, but she remained vigilant, her upper body tense as if ready to battle whatever ailed her husband.

"You're working here now, Sharon? Keeping him in line?"

Her chuckle bounced around the room's blank walls, no carefully chosen art or objects warming it up. Kristen had said Sharon didn't seem to care much about the house, though she'd gone along on the tour—no doubt out of curiosity, as the house and community had been part of her husband's life long ago. She didn't seem to care much about the office, either, the vase and flowers on the desk the only personal touch.

"As if anyone could. His assistant left to have a baby, so I'm filling in." She wagged a finger at him. "And you've got clients scheduled all afternoon, so you've got just enough time to eat your lunch and look over their files."

In other words, time for me to leave. I pushed myself up and kissed Terry's cheek. Stretched a hand toward Sharon as I headed for the door, not quite touching.

The door creaked shut behind me, but I swear, I felt them watching me through the frosted glass.

SINCE I wasn't far from SPD HQ, and my dog and shop were in good hands, I swung in to ask about old case files. One old case file—the Strasburg incident in the fateful year of 1985.

"Normally, you need to submit a request and we get back to you. But I've got a moment," the records clerk said, "so I'll see what we have."

My heart beat more quickly than it should have as I watched her watch the screen, her brown coral-tipped fingers flying across the keyboard.

"That case was never closed." Her forehead creased in concentration. My muscles tensed, and I feared what she might say next. A few more clicks, then her hand moved to open a drawer I couldn't see. "The original detectives are both retired. That file is with our cold case detective now. We're lucky to have one—with budget cuts, many departments don't."

Detective John Washington, the card she handed me read. In my years with Tag, I'd met a lot of cops, but some stood out. I pictured a tall man, at least fifteen years older than we were, with close-cropped black hair. He calls Laurel every few months to assure her that the murder of her husband, Patrick, is still on his mind, but his calls no longer give her much hope.

I thanked the clerk and walked down the hall. Nothing in *The Complete Idiot's Guide to Private Investigating* told me how to ask Detective Washington to fill me in on the Strasburg case. *Because I used to work with the victim's son, and my parents might have known the man who killed him, and I might have just met the killer's ex-girlfriend, and everything changed after that, and I want to figure out why.* That didn't seem like it would fly.

Worse, my trumped-up explanation might make Detective Washington take a closer look at my family and our friends.

No, it couldn't be possible—no one I knew could have had anything to do with the tragedy in 1985.

So why did it keep coming up, everywhere I turned? Roger Russell had been loosely connected to the Grace House community, as had Bonnie Clay. Or Peggy Manning. From the way my mother talked about them, I suspected that Roger and Peggy had been a couple.

But the way Terry Stinson had looked at her, and his reaction to Roger's name, made me think it might have been more complicated than that.

My clerk informant had said Detective Washington had a rare private office where he spent his days poring over thick files and consoling distressed relatives. That's part of any detective's job, but for a cold case detective, the days often become years.

Not for the first time today, I felt like Sam Spade or Lew Archer—make that Samantha or Louise—my all-black retail outfit adding a touch of noir. All I lacked was the 1940s fedora.

"Oh pooh, Pepper. Go home."

"What an excellent idea." Detective Tracy appeared at my elbow, and I jumped, unaware that I'd spoken out loud.

I glanced at the number on the nearest office door, then at the card in my hand. He must have just left Washington's office.

He put his hand on my elbow, an odd, old-fashioned gesture that might have been chivalrous if we were Humphrey Bogart and Lauren Bacall. I wrenched away and shot him a spiky glare.

But it's not a good idea to antagonize a detective—or to call attention to yourself in police HQ. *Down, Pepper.* I was careful not to speak out loud this time.

The occurrence of another murder had dissolved our temporary truce.

Or maybe I was a teensy bit worried about what I might uncover. Nothing in the *Idiot's Guide* advised on how to dig up the past without tearing up your own roots.

But maybe I should have paid more attention to the section on how to make friends and influence police detectives.

He punched the elevator button. "After your marriage to an officer and your—shall we say, unfortunate experiences, you should understand murder isn't a game. Don't play detective, Pepper."

The elevator door opened, and I stepped in. *No. That's your job.*

Fourteen

Salt is born of the purest of parents: the sun and the sea.

—Pythagoras

NOTHING GETS ME GOING LIKE TELLING ME NOT TO DO something.

I stomped down Fourth Avenue, swearing at Detective Tracy in my mind. How dare he send me running off like a dog with her tail between her legs.

Why he was so determined to keep me from talking with Detective Washington, I didn't know, but it didn't matter. More than one way to skin a cat.

I shuddered. Tortured animal metaphors may be commonplace, but that they were creeping into my own thoughts was a serious sign of stress overload.

My stomach rumbled as I neared Ripe, at the base of the black tower dubbed "the box the Space Needle came in," a nod to its origins as a bank. Brian Strasburg's firm had taken over part of our old offices on the fortieth floor.

But no way was I going to confront a lawyer on an empty stomach.

A few minutes later, Laurel set a toasted tomato, basil,

and goat cheese sandwich on a two-top in the corner and sat across from me. Between bites, I filled her in.

"So Bonnie knew who you were all along." She took a swig of her lemon Pellegrino.

"And I didn't have a clue," I said through a mouthful of fabulous flavor. So much for being a natural investigator.

That had been Laurel's phrase last fall, when she urged me to probe the death of a stranger at my shop's front door. And experience in HR gives some insight into human behavior, and hones both perception and problem-solving skills.

But personnel problems don't involve unearthing old crimes and sifting through clues that might tie them to the present.

I swallowed and reached for my own fizzy, fruity water. "I'm baffled—why keep her eye on me? And what is—*was*—the tension between her and my mother? I'm almost certain it goes back to those days in Grace House, if not before."

"So focus on that."

I leaned back in my chair, arms folded. "Kristen's mom is dead. My mother won't talk. Our dads are off battling wind and wave, not that mine would tell me what she won't. Terry Stinson's moved on. The others from that era—oh, Kristen's working on a list of who came to the party."

"Call them. See what they make of their old friend all these years later."

"Bonnie seemed eager to come, but then she didn't circulate much."

"She looked scared to me. She sat on the stone wall by herself most of the evening."

"Speaking of scared, I wanted to talk to Detective Washington about the Strasburg case, but Tracy literally steered me away."

Laurel's eyes took on a sheen of grief. She spoke, her tone uncharacteristically flat. "Detective Washington has brought justice and comfort to a lot of families."

But not hers.

I finished my fizzy water and laid my napkin on the table. "Now that my stomach's happier, I'm thinking more clearly. Better to talk to Callie first, find out about Brian Strasburg's family before I confront him." A law librarian and researcher in Strasburg's firm, Callie Carter had given me invaluable help, both when we worked together and more recently.

"Good plan," Laurel said, her thoughts obviously elsewhere.

Even quicker of wit and tongue than your average lawyer, Strasburg's life and personality had been shaped, I was beginning to understand, by loss and anger.

We'd had a marginally decent relationship—improved by the passage of time—but if I was going to dig up his past, I didn't want to get buried in the rubble.

Because, as I could see on Laurel's face, cases might grow cold, but the pain never cools.

THIS elevator was swift and quiet. I rode up alone, texting Ben. *Dig up any dirt on Roger Russell?*

The door opened on the fortieth floor, and I stepped out, staring at the little screen. He texted back almost instantly. *Stuck in Olympia. Don't know when I'll be free.*

Rats. I dropped my phone in my bag and reached for the law office's door. Before I could grab the handle, the door opened and out strode Brian Strasburg, a sleek black leather briefcase in one hand.

"Pepper! Haven't seen you since spring." He grabbed my hand and moved in for an air hug. "What brings you to the old haunt?"

"Oh, uh—I had an errand down the street, so I popped in to see Callie. You know how she loves to bake. We got a new cookbook I thought she'd like."

"Oh, too bad. We just wrapped up a big trial over in

Spokane. I got back Saturday. Her kid's been at her mother's in Chelan, so she's spending a few days there. If you want to leave it . . ." He gestured with his thumb, back to the office.

"Thanks. I'll wait till she's back—more fun to give it to her myself."

Ten seconds later, we were in the elevator, speeding down.

You can know someone for ages, then learn something new and see them in a whole different light. But he was still the man I'd known.

And there was no easy way to say, "Hey, after all this time, I finally found out what happened to your family. Is that why you've got the personality of a yo-yo on steroids?"

Saved when we stopped on the seventh floor. We stepped back automatically as the doors opened and a young woman entered.

"How'd the trial go?" I asked Strasburg.

"Got everything we asked for. Commercial property dispute. Callie was invaluable—I can't tell you how many thousands of hours we spent researching. Hey, you ever want a real job again, you call me. We'd make room for you."

The door opened. "Thanks. I'm exactly where I need to be."

"That's good. Not everyone can say that."

He strode off, leaving me standing on the broad steps of the black box.

I flashed on an image of another famous box, snakes and secrets spilling out. The gods had told Pandora to keep it shut. Had Bonnie opened it, or was the guilty party my mother? Or me?

The gods always get their revenge.

DEEP in my bag, my phone buzzed. Still on the move, I fished it out and read Kristen's text. *MJ waiting 4U. Save us!*

The light changed, and I crossed Madison.

"Glad to see your ears didn't fall off," I whispered to Kristen a few minutes later in the shop. Behind the counter, Matt and Reed refilled tea canisters, trapped by Mary Jean.

"Does the woman never shut up?" She rolled her eyes.

"Not that I've noticed. You get a chance to make that guest list for the detectives?"

She drew a folded piece of paper out of her apron pocket. "I think I got everyone who came. You can double check."

"Thanks. Hey, has Sandra talked to you about—"

"Pepper! Have you been out investigating? My class was fabulous. The students were so attentive. I told the director, I said, if you ever need a substitute again, call me no matter how short the notice."

I tucked the list into my bag and gave Kristen an "I've got this" look. Mary Jean the Chatty Chocolatier had grown on me, though I did wonder how she managed to stay alive, given her talent for talking without taking a breath. Me, I need oxygen. And chocolate, so I put up with her.

"I've got your cocoa." She slid into the booth, opened three tins, and began to detail the origins, processing, pricing, and other merits of each variety. I sat across from her and reached for the tasting tray we use when creating blends—a canister of clean stainless steel tasting spoons and another for the used spoons, along with small bowls, notepads, and pens. While she gabbed, I tasted. (Mary Jean doesn't require responses to her commentary, making it possible to keep working without annoying her.)

"This one's a little darker, richer," I said. "The middle one has a slight bitterness that will pair well with paprika and a little cayenne, a dash of thyme." I'd been stockpiling ideas for a spicy cocoa rub. Maybe Ben and I could sample two or three tonight with steak, to make up for my SIL's vegan barbecue.

Mary Jean stacked six smaller tins on the tabletop. "I

brought extra samples, for Sandra and Cayenne. You've got hibiscus blossoms for me, right?"

Parsley poop. I'd plumb forgotten.

Think fast, Pepper. "Mary Jean, I am so sorry. We'll get them on the next order." When that would be, I didn't know. And then, a moment of retail genius struck. "Hey, you know Josh, who used to run the deli at the Italian grocery? He's got his own place now. He does a lot of catering, including weddings. And he just lost his chocolatier."

She pinched the skin below her collarbone. "Everybody loves chocolate, but you can't make a living one truffle at a time. I called dozens of wedding planners to offer party favors—gift bags for guests, in custom combinations or flavors, but they already had their suppliers. It's mid-June. Wedding season's half over."

"Did they try your chocolates? And September's getting to be almost as popular for weddings as June. I'll talk to Josh. Meanwhile, we'll test steak rubs, and I'll get those hibiscus blossoms." Egad. I'd turned almost as chatty as Mary Jean. A side effect of theobromine, or of my guilt in forgetting her order?

She rummaged in her bag, a cloth tote that dwarfed mine, and handed me a shiny brown box tied with her signature raspberry pink ribbon. "Samples. I made them as a gift for a new hotel concierge, but you take them for Josh."

I sent a silent prayer that the stars aligned.

Whew. I dashed to the office and called my dried flower source. I could have six ounces this week, at a shipping cost triple the not-inconsiderable price of the blossoms, or I could get two pounds, free shipping, for less than the combined total of the smaller order. I bit the bullet, then beckoned Cayenne. Despite lacking Sandra's experience, she'd proven herself an adept taste tester and recipe designer.

"Think beyond tea," I said after explaining how much

hibiscus I'd had to order. The wheels started turning as she hustled off to greet a customer.

Alas, no time to squeeze in any research. My to-do list for the shop was much too long, and that's the list that pays the bills.

Sandra and I were deep into a project that kept one of us in the office, on the phone, for at least an hour every day. Today was my turn, and if I blew it off, she'd blow her top. And I wasn't about to add to her stress level or mine by doing that. I sipped a tall glass of our iced tea and settled into the chair with our list of potential commercial customers. Today's targets had bought from us in the past. Customers leave for a variety of reasons. Spice follows the chef, and when a new man or woman takes over a kitchen, they often bring their own suppliers. But with a personal nudge, the door may open.

So far, we were batting .500. Half the folks we'd called had agreed to try a few samples. We had a good on-base percentage—quite a few had ordered a product or two. None had made us their main source, but I didn't honestly expect any restaurant or producer to ditch their suppliers and switch all their loyalty to us—grand slams are as rare in business as in baseball.

"Put me in, coach—I'm ready to play," as the old John Fogerty song says.

We were banking on the blends. I'd turned Sandra loose, and our offerings had become far more adventuresome. The Spice Shop founder, Jane Rasmussen, had been a visionary, one of the urban pioneers who revitalized the Market in the 1970s. But her idea of spice mixes ended with lemon pepper and an Italian blend.

The times, they do change.

For the next hour, I pitched our wares, our sources, our reliability, and our prices. Promised samples, and made appointments for private tastings.

My last call was to the owner of a specialty canning

company who'd reached out to us. His longtime salt supplier had changed hands, and the quality no longer measured up. Could I do better? *You bet.*

"I should be able to get those samples shipped off today, tomorrow at the latest."

"That's great," he said. "My rival got Adolfo'd, and I don't want to suffer the same fate."

"Adolfo'd?" New word, but I feared I knew its meaning.

"Yeah, Nancy Adolfo. New reviewer for *Northwest Cuisine*. She reviewed the pickle company down in Tumwater. They make good stuff. Been around for ages. She said their kosher dills were soft and the spicing lacked imagination."

If you're craving a pickle, you're probably not seeking imaginative spicing. You want crunch and familiar flavor. "They buy caraway and mustard seed from me."

"She even griped because she couldn't park in front of their shop—too many customers. We should all have such problems. Stay clear—she's vicious."

The image of Adolfo's sharp little teeth popped into my head. *All the better to eat you with, my dear.*

We hung up, and when I stood, I literally shook off the dread. Customers pick up on negativity.

I put on a friendly face and headed out to the shop floor to pack up the salt samples. I gathered my jars and stepped behind the front counter. Set them down and bent to scratch Arf's ears. When I straightened, Kristen was standing in front of the cash register, gazing into outer space.

"Earth to Kristen."

She jerked her head toward mine, one hand flying to the silver-flecked scarf around her neck. "Pepper, you startled me. I was thinking about the bracelet. I don't know what's worse—that someone may have broken into my house, or that someone I know is a thief."

I stared at her, thoughts sparking, a jar of North Sea flake salt in my hand. A customer approached. Kristen weighed out his basil, thyme, and red pepper flakes and suggested he try our "perfect for pasta" Italian blend, in the refillable jar. Few customers—especially the male variety—refuse her. She added the blend to his order, and he left, whistling.

I'd been wondering how the killer got into Bonnie's studio, and why a woman would leave her door unlocked. More likely, I realized now, the killer had left it open.

"Neighborhood thugs. That's who Mr. Adams blames for Bonnie's murder," I said. "He lives across the street."

"You said her place didn't look ransacked. Burglars and thugs would have made a mess, searching for cash and jewelry."

Our eyes locked. "No mess at your house."

And that meant the murder and the theft had something in common, besides the links between Kristen, Bonnie, and me. Both the killer and the thief had, in all likelihood, known us. No common criminal, despite Mr. Adams's theories, but someone who had walked into Kristen's house—her home, her warm, gracious, welcoming home—and walked out carrying thousands of dollars' worth of jewels. And who had then sauntered into Bonnie's studio—and taken her life.

Someone connected to the deaths of Roger Russell and Walter Strasburg? That, I wasn't sure about. But if that's the direction Detective Tracy thought the evidence pointed, then he would point Detective Washington at my mother.

And that was terrifying.

"So who had a key to her studio?" Kristen asked.

I weighed out salt and dumped it into a bag. "Hannah, who sublet her the place, but wanted it back. The landlord, maintenance people, property managers. Though why they would kill her, I can't imagine."

Kristen picked up the jars of salt, cradling them like twins. "Then find Hannah."

Fifteen

Greeks and Romans burned thyme bunches to purify their homes and temples and to build courage in those who inhaled its smoke.

—Michelle Schoffro Cook, "All About Thyme," *Mother Earth Living*

I HOPED JOSH GIBSON WAS A WORKAHOLIC, LIKE MOST entrepreneurs—though one who stayed in his shop more often than I'd been staying in mine.

The sight of cars idling in every parking spot told me a dance class was just letting out. As I glanced in my rearview mirror, a dozen girls and a couple of boys surged up the hillside on the south end of the building. By the time I'd circled around, a space had opened in front of the gift shop.

The Dr Pepper cooler in the window called to me. *Someday.* I opened the door, a bundle of cards advertising our wedding registry in hand. The owner was out, and the salesclerk hadn't known Bonnie or Hannah. I refilled my slot in the rack labeled "More gifts from the heart."

In the window of the dress shop next door, closed on Mondays, wigged mannequins showed off bridal cream puffs—yards of white lace and satin festooned with seed pearls or glass beads. In a corner of the display, a headless dress form held a one-shouldered emerald green silk, above the knee.

If I ever have another wedding . . . Unlikely. Especially the way my life was going. *Focus on the challenge at hand, Pepper.*

Inside the bakery, two women about my age sat at the front table, drinking espresso and chatting with girls flush from class. The familiar twinge of regret over not having children—at having waited for Tag, only to find out it was too late for both my body and our marriage—zinged through me.

"Josh around?" I asked the barista over the noise of her machine and the alt-rock blaring through the speakers. She flicked her eyes toward the kitchen. Through the open window, I saw the baker/chef/delivery man's bandanna-wrapped head bob in and out of view. "Thanks."

I stood at the pass-through and watched Josh work. He pulled two huge trays of roasted eggplant out of the oven and slid in two of summer squash. Poured olive oil into a giant bowl full of chopped onion and spread the glistening white chunks on a waiting tray. Threw handfuls of herbs on a cutting board. Turned to grab a knife and spotted me.

"You're still cooking this time of day?" I said.

"The fun never stops. Roasted veggie salad for tomorrow." He pointed the knife toward ingredients piled on the worktable behind him. "Prep cook makes the tossed salad fresh every morning, but I make our deli staples every afternoon."

"I hate to interrupt, but I was wondering—" I started, at the same moment he said, "Any news?"

"You took the words out of my mouth," I said. "So I guess the answer is no, for both of us."

"Cops keep finding excuses to pop in, me being an important witness and all, but I notice they keep their lips zipped tight." He stretched out of view and reappeared, a green water bottle in hand.

"You mean because you found her? Yeah, that does get their attention." As I knew too well.

He drank, then wiped the back of his hand across his mouth. "Apparently, I was the last person to see her alive. Except the killer."

"What?" With all the commotion Saturday, and Josh speeding off to the wedding, I'd missed that.

"About nine thirty Friday. We close at six thirty, but I was sitting up front, working on my dairy order. Surprised me to see her walk by—most nights, she worked even later than me. Lots of times, I took dinner to her—leftover quiche, a day-old brownie."

"No chance you saw anyone else, I suppose."

"Sorry. Right after that, I headed upstairs to my place. Baker's hours on top of owner's hours make for a long day."

And the circles under his eyes.

"The Market Master's pushing me to find a place for her stuff, because I knew her," I said.

"He called me, too. I suppose I'll have to clean out her studio and apartment, unless I hear from a relative pretty quick. And find a new tenant."

Before I could ask if that wasn't Hannah's responsibility, I remembered the other reason for my visit. "I nearly forgot." I slid my tote off my shoulder and dug around for Mary Jean's truffles. "I heard one of your counter people say you'd lost your chocolatier. A woman in the Market might fit the bill. You'll make a killing from the dance moms alone."

The word "killing" hung in the air between us. Josh set his water bottle on the pass-through counter, wiped his hands on the white apron tied over his black-and-white pants, and reached for the box.

"So your tenants have keys to the main door. Cleaning

people? Anyone else? Any idea who would have a key to her studio?"

"Street-level tenants and the dance school have their own doors—they don't have keys to the main entry. I clean the hall and stairway—not very well, I'm afraid. The studio . . ." Box in hand, he sagged against the counter.

Patience . . .

"They say don't mix business and pleasure, but for me, they've always run together. And I guess I didn't know where to draw the line." He exhaled heavily. "The tenant who sublet to Bonnie—"

"Hannah Hart. I've been wanting to talk to her, but no one seems to know where she is. Bonnie was a friend. I'm hoping Hannah remembers something helpful."

He studied the floor. "When I decided to start my own restaurant, my parents urged me to buy rental property. They put up half, and I borrowed the rest. The rents pay for the place, and that's giving me time to develop the business. Anyway, the building came fully occupied, including Hannah." He paused, face flushed. "She's quite—alluring, and I wasn't thinking. Not with my brain, anyway."

"What? You mean *you're* her boyfriend?"

"Ah. I see our reputation precedes us," he said wryly.

I set my tote on the floor. "Mr. Adams said she and her boyfriend fought a lot, but he didn't mention any names."

"I finally called it quits. Her lease was running out, and I told her I wouldn't renew it. She blew up and moved out early. Not that I minded, but then Bonnie moved in, and I had no idea what was going on. Turns out, Hannah rented the place to her without telling me."

"Whoa. Wait." My brain felt like it was caught in the high-speed mixer bolted to the worktable. "How could she sublease without your permission? And why? To help you out, or cause you trouble?"

"Oh, trouble, no question. Hang on." He sprang across

the kitchen, out of sight, and I heard him shuffling papers. A minute later, he was back, waving a newspaper.

"I kept the advertisement as evidence." He began flipping to the back. "In case I had to evict Bonnie, or whatever."

I reached through the window and stopped him, then drew his attention to the front page. The page showing me in my black apron, standing next to the old samovar. MISTRESS OF SPICE, the headline proclaimed.

The same article Bonnie had read and kept. What did this coincidence say about the Universe?

Poor Bonnie. She claimed she wanted a home and yet she chose a temporary arrangement. Did she sense that it wouldn't work out?

Was he saying—? "Josh. You don't mean Hannah would kill someone to make trouble for you?"

"No. I don't know." His fingers grazed his forehead, ran over the bandanna, and tugged at his hair. "No, she would never go that far. Ever since she left, I've been expecting a time bomb to go off. But murder? I can't imagine that."

I couldn't see the connection, either. "You said you might need to evict Bonnie. Why?"

He leaned against the wall and folded his arms, his biceps bulging below his white T-shirt sleeves. "She was a great tenant. But Hannah stuck herself in the middle, overcharging and interfering, telling Bonnie to contact her if she had a problem, not me, because I'm an ass—" His voice had risen, and a woman standing at the counter while her young son chose a cookie glared at him. "Sorry," he called, then to me, "Big-shot downtown lawyer I talked to said change the locks, wait till the lease expires, then write Bonnie a new lease. But I didn't trust Hannah not to have some trick up her sleeve."

I didn't tell him Hannah had been pestering Bonnie to give her back the space—that little trick he'd feared. "At least she doesn't have a key anymore."

The tips of his ears reddened. "We've been so busy, I never called the locksmith."

Holy cardamom.

So Hannah could have let herself in Friday night and confronted Bonnie. But it's a long way from using someone to get revenge on an ex-lover to murder.

For that matter, Josh had a key, too. But as much turmoil as Hannah's petty scheme was causing him, he had no beef with Bonnie—and getting rid of her would not have solved the Hannah problem.

Besides, Mr. Adams had seen someone speeding away. Josh lived upstairs.

"One more thing. Mr. Adams across the street said there have been questionable people hanging around. Thugs, he called them."

He stuffed his hand in a big oven mitt. "Lou worries too much. Any guy under thirty wearing baggy pants, he thinks they're a gang member. Last week, he saw a couple of guys he didn't like the looks of, and he hobbled over to warn me, in front of my customers. They were just doing odd jobs for the dance school."

"I suppose even gang members get a cookie craving now and then."

He grinned. "Truth. Hey, I don't know where Hannah is—mooching off somebody—but when you find her, wear your tap shoes." The oven timer rang, and he went back to work, tossing one more comment over his shoulder. "Because the truth and the redhead have a way of dancing around each other."

Sixteen

I love cooking with wine. Sometimes I even put it in the food.

—Cook's motto

"GOT A SPECIAL SHIPMENT OF A WALLA WALLA WHITE." Vinny disappeared behind a stack of boxes, but his voice trailed after him. "Crisp, light, with a hint of grapefruit. From all that Central Washington desert sunshine."

"Thanks, Vinny. It's steak night, so I need a red. I'm working on rubs using cocoa, espresso, and a bit of heat, so—"

He reappeared. "So you want something bold, but not overpowering. Lemme show you this primo Pinot from Benton-Lane in Oregon, in the Willamette Valley."

"Sounds too rich for me."

"Nah. Get a good Pinot Noir, the fruit and tannins pair with beef like . . ." He kissed the ends of his fingertips, eyelids fluttering as he raised his face heavenward. "And your employee discount makes it affordable."

I am not in Vinny's employ, thank goodness, but he likes me and always gives me a good price. Not a sign of unrequited romance; just a sweet touch.

I walked out carrying two bottles, the second from a

small winery near Paso Robles in central California, having promised to give Vinny a report on the steak rub tasting and a free jar of the final product. Not all Market merchants work together like we do, but it's high on my list of job perks.

Arf and I strolled through the park, then down Western to the loft. After my chat with Josh, I'd wanted to talk to Bonnie's neighbors in the building. But with Sandra off today, I'd had to rush back before closing. And I wanted to think over my approach carefully. If I found Hannah first, I might not need to ask Josh's tenants to dish on their landlord and his love life.

Ben had sent his regrets to my texted dinner invitation. Still on the trail of infrastructure funding, traipsing down to Portland to interview an expert on regional planning. After that, I'd called my mother—with some trepidation, as my efforts to question her had sent her hackles, whatever they are, into overdrive, and she was sure to spot this as an excuse to continue probing. But she'd gone to a summer solstice celebration.

My conversation with Josh still had me puzzled. Women scorned—and men, too, for that matter—will resort to all kinds of chicanery, but there had to be more he wasn't telling me. Unless she was a whack job.

He doesn't owe you the whole truth, Pepper. We're obligated, one human to another, not to kill or steal or lie.

There's a lot of room in between.

But when someone you both know dies, and you call a friend for help, doesn't that create a sort of bond?

Cool it, Pepper. Not everyone feels your weird sense of loyalty.

As Arf and I climbed the steps to the loft, I decided it was not a night to eat alone. And taste-testing is easier with a buddy. I knocked on my neighbor's door.

"Care to join me?" I raised my two bulging tote bags. Downtown living is great exercise. "Red meat, red wine."

"And I have red hair," Glenn said. "Beats reading the monthly statistical analysis from the police department. Or updates on the tunnel project." The glamorous life of a city councilman.

In the loft, Glenn chose a bottle and found a corkscrew, entertaining me with city nitty-gritty while I unpacked the groceries and considered flavors. When I bought the Spice Shop, I'd retrofitted one long shelf on the kitchen wall for spice jars. My collection had since grown to three shelves, as collections do.

"Continually amazes me," Glenn said, "how stupid some crooks are. You hear about the doofus who sat in his truck drinking beer and selling rock cocaine in front of City Hall Park?"

I pulled spices from shelves, measured, and mixed, jotting down proportions.

"Thing is," he went on, "catching the idiots takes resources that would be better put to use on other crimes. Dang, this is good. Try it."

He slid a glass toward me, a tasting pour. I sipped. "Vinny knows his Pinot."

"Not that every crime isn't serious, but you know what I mean." He topped off my glass.

I did. I climbed out the window to fire up the grill. Back in the kitchen, I julienned jicama and a red pepper and dumped them into a wide mahogany bowl, piled high with sturdy greens. Found a jar of my wasabi salad dressing in the fridge. Unwrapped two beautiful filets.

"Here's the plan. I've made four combos, ingredients known only to me. I'm cutting each steak in half, and we'll split them." I massaged a different blend lightly onto each piece, then speared them with numbered metal flags Sandra's Mr. Right had fashioned for this very purpose.

We carried our wine outside, and I put the steaks on the grill, telling him about the murder on Beacon Hill. He's a great listener—a precious quality in a politician—and he took off his glasses to massage the bridge of his nose.

"Thank you, Pepper. It's important to hear about the lives behind the statistics. I gripe and grouse, but you know I have complete confidence in our officers. The new chief—she's turned things around."

"Tag thinks so, too." I'd seen her in the Market and around town, a sharp-eyed woman with a pleasant Irish face who wore pearls and dress blues equally well.

"But how are *you*, Pepperoni? This can't be easy."

My eyes watered, and not from the smoking grill. I grit my teeth to quiet my quivering chin. It didn't work. Kindness has that effect.

Glenn slid an arm around my shoulder, careful of the hot spatula in my hand.

Minutes later, we sat at my inside table with salad, wine, a baguette, a plate full of numbered steaks, and notepads and pens. We inspected, sniffed, tasted, pondered, and talked. Used words like bite, bright, pungent, peppery, sweet, sharp, acrid, bitter, coffee-tinged, dark. Balance and nose. Punch and heat, edge and mmm . . .

"You know," Glenn said, leaning back in the pink wrought iron chair and raising his glass, "this is the first time I've enjoyed dinner since Nate's been gone."

This neighborly thing goes both ways.

After he left, I compiled our notes and snuck Arf the last bite of steak. Although it isn't sneaking if no one else is watching. I poured the unused rubs into clean, numbered jars so any willing soul on staff could try their hand. Grilling, pan frying, slow cooking, and using different cuts of meat all give different results. Spice making is a collaborative process. I hoped we could add a midsummer bonus to our lineup.

"Ooh," I told Arf. "What about a rotation, like brewers with their seasonal ales? Or managers with their pitchers?" I pumped my fist.

My dog ignored me.

Though Glenn had drunk his share, I'd gone easy on the wine, to keep my palate clear. After Arf and I took our evening stroll along the waterfront, I poured another glass and tuned in to the Mariners' road game. Like my father and grandfather, I'd rather listen to a game on the radio than watch it on TV. The radio announcers give you more details—more color, as it's called, to paint the pictures you can't see. Plus you don't have to stare at the screen to follow the game.

And that brought me back to murder. Killers and other crooks don't stop while you try to catch them. They zig and zag, responding to your moves, covering up their tracks and trails.

What was happening while I wasn't watching?

Like two teams on the field, two competing possibilities were at play: Was Bonnie's killer someone from the past, or the present?

So far, I'd focused on time gone by. Bonnie had not made many new friends, but no one in the Market seemed to harbor any ill will toward her.

That led me to her neighbors at home. Had Hannah seriously believed she could move back into the building? Why? Carrying a torch for Josh? Easier to worm your way into someone's graces if you're close by. Or maybe she was a little crazy. Not thinking things through. I didn't buy into the impulsive artist stereotype—my experience with Tory, Fabiola—our graphic designer, and many of the Market folk proved that artists can plan ahead. Creating a business isn't all that different from creating an art piece; it's just a different medium.

But plans are notorious for changing; it's their worst feature.

Where had Hannah gone? As the jeweler had said, it's not easy for an artist to find good working space. Maybe she'd been so desperate to get her studio back that she'd have risked the wrath of Josh. If she got rid of Bonnie . . .

But even she had to understand that when the lease expired, she'd be SOL. She'd have bought herself weeks or months, at best.

What if the argument wasn't over getting the place back? What if Hannah had stored things in the studio and needed access Bonnie hadn't wanted to give her?

A sharp crack of ball on bat caught my ear. Line drive to left field, no throw. One out, one in, runners at the corners. The Ms had tied the game, top of the seventh. I crouched by Arf's bed to rub his ears, then rooted in the kitchen for the Turkish delight I'd brought home over the weekend.

"Mmm. Pistachio. Peppers and pistachio are classic. What about adding a dash of cocoa?" I made a note. Sandra says no combination is ever too weird to give a second thought, although some don't warrant a third. The ones you think are brilliant may flop, but the ones you dismiss might make a million bucks.

A woman can dream.

I poured more wine, sat on the couch, and waited for the next pitch. Curve, strike one. I licked powdered sugar off my fingers. Low, ball one. The announcer's words created a picture of the two teams concentrating, players and coaches fidgeting in the dugout, fans rising, rubbing their arms.

Full count.

If Tory's contacts didn't pan out soon, I'd have to try another tack to find the slippery Ms. Hart.

"Swing and a miss. He strikes out." I groaned, and the crowd in a faraway stadium cheered. Time for the seventh-inning stretch and the singing of "God Bless America," to be followed by the crowd belting out "Take Me Out to the Ball Game."

Traditions are great, but sometimes they keep us from seeing other possibilities.

What was I not seeing?

My mother's scrapbook still lay on my packing crate

coffee table. I studied the single photo of Terry and Bonnie—Peggy, back then—and the line outside the cathedral door. The paper had yellowed, the black-and-white photo had faded, but the way he looked at her . . .

At his office this morning, it had been clear that her death touched him deeply. They'd been close. They'd all been close.

Bonnie had been involved with Roger, I was all but certain. Where had that left Terry?

And then Roger died . . .

Thirty years ago. Why did the memory hold such power to trigger present grief, to open old wounds of loss and betrayal?

"Why," I asked my dog, "does every question beget more questions?"

He ignored me, no doubt thinking, "Humans."

The Mariners' ace reliever sent the other team down one, two, three, and we moved to the top of the eighth.

My thoughts turned to Kristen's missing bracelet. The police wondered if someone had seen the party and snuck in, hoping to be overlooked amid the hubbub. On the other hand, a party meant more witnesses, more people to spot someone who shouldn't have been there.

As Glenn had said, most criminals are not too bright.

Kristen's list of partygoers was in my tote. I got up and dug it out.

No one missing. No brainstorms; no connections I hadn't seen. Her family and mine. Her neighbors. Spice Shop staff and folks from Eric's firm. Friends from the dozens of walks of life we all travel. From the Grace House past, Bonnie, Terry and his family, and a few other couples and solos—men and women I hadn't seen in years but who'd been delighted to see my mother. And vice versa—no obvious tensions.

The burglary detectives had probably contacted most of them by now, with Spencer and Tracy keeping a close eye on the investigation. I could not imagine anyone from that community a thief.

Two out, two on. The batter laid down a bunt, and the runner on third tagged and scored. "Dang it." The Mariners returned for the top of the ninth, and a buzzing snagged my ear. I fished my phone out of my tote—I never remember to tuck it carefully in a side pocket—and read Tory's text: *A mutual friend will reach out.*

Would Hannah talk to me, a friend—more like an acquaintance—of Bonnie's? Depended, I supposed, on whether the police had already found her and left her feeling under suspicion. Approaching her through the artists' web was good. Less threatening.

The radio relayed a low rumble from afar. Top of the ninth, a one-run game.

Ball one. Ball two. I sat up. Strike one. "Take your pitch," I told the batter. "You got this."

The batter took his time, stepping out of the box, stepping back in, working his way to a full count. My shoulders tensed. I quieted my breath, hands in loose fists, arms ready to cheer.

My brain kept firing possibilities at me. I had to find Hannah. Because only two people were known to have had recent tensions with Bonnie, and the other was my mother.

I was fishing. Sometimes, like the fisherman I'd met on Sunday, who talked of ghost nets and traps, you catch more than you expect.

And sometimes, as the roar from the radio made clear, you strike out.

Seventeen

Time waits for no one, and it won't wait for me.

—Mick Jagger and Keith Richards,
"Time Waits for No One"

"WHICH ONE DID GLENN PICK?" SANDRA ASKED THE NEXT
morning when I set out the jars of steak rubs.

"Not telling. You think he's got better taste than I do."

"Well, he's married to Nate, and you're not."

I rolled my eyes. Then, a hand on her arm, I plunged in.
"My mother told me about Paul. I'm so sorry." This wasn't
the time to say, *And I'm sorry you felt you could tell everyone but me* . . . "The test results?"

Her whole body breathed a sigh of relief. "Good. They
came back good. But they can't figure out what's causing
the pain, so he's going back in later this week. I need Thursday afternoon off."

When life hands you trouble, it never checks first to see
if this is a good time. "Sure. Take all the time you need."

"Just keep me busy, to take my mind off all the scary
possibilities."

"Then you're in luck. Besides the cocoa rubs, we're launching Project Hibiscus." I filled her in. "Cayenne's raring to go.

Anything's game—a rub for beef and pork, a drink mix, sorbet. Salad dressing. Focus on local produce and fresh herbs. We'll make recipe cards for customers and vendors."

"You got it, boss," she said, and I hoped the prospect of experimentation would keep her mind off her fears for Mr. Right.

Fat chance.

A few minutes before we opened, my jeweler friend rattled the front door, her photographer neighbor behind her. I let them in, their anxious faces giving my hands the shakes.

"Has something happened?"

"No." The jeweler's pale yellow '76 T-bird earrings swayed. "The detectives interviewed us again, but nobody's telling us anything. We were hoping you know what's going on."

"Wish I did," I said as Sandra handed them each a cup of tea. Hot or cold, it does soothe the nerves. "But I doubt they think Bonnie's murder has anything to do with the Market."

"How can you be sure?" the photographer said. "The pasta seller saw you take off with the Market Master and that detective. Tracy. I always want to call him Dick, but it's Mike, right?"

"Or Michael, though plenty of people do call him dick and not with a capital D." I shivered, remembering what we'd found in the locker. "This may sound weird, but did Bonnie ever say anything about me?"

The photographer's brow furrowed. "No."

"Now that you mention it," the jeweler said slowly, "you came through one time, the way you do. She was next to me that day, and I was going to introduce you, but she got all busy unpacking stuff and didn't hear me. You left, and I glanced over, and she was standing there, watching you, a big clay platter clutched to her chest."

Like the one that killed her.

"What were you worried about, Peggy?" I said, as if to her spirit. "Why were you afraid of me?"

"Peggy?" the jeweler asked.

"Bonnie's real name," I said. "Or at least, the name she used when my mother knew her, when I was a kid."

They made faces of surprise but quickly recovered to pepper me with questions. When they left a few minutes later, they seemed relieved.

Business buzzed along steadily all morning. When Cayenne's customer asked sourcing questions, I stepped in, to the customer's amusement.

"I can't believe you're named Pepper and Cayenne." She handed me her platinum American Express card.

Cayenne ran a bag of Aleppo pepper through the sealer. "Nobody ever thinks this is my real name that I was born with, but it is. My grandparents came from New Iberia, Louisiana, and my granddaddy worked in the Tabasco plant. They moved up here when he got a job at Boeing, when my mom was little, and they all missed the smell."

Everyone within earshot laughed. "The moment you introduced yourself," I said, "I knew you were destined to work here. Whether your parents named you, or you chose it." I handed the customer her shopping bags, each stuffed, and thanked her. Reed held the front door.

"Why do you suppose Peggy changed her name to Bonnie?" Cayenne said.

"I changed my last name when I married Mr. Wrong, and it bugged me to pieces," Sandra said. "I don't know how you could change your first name. Your name is your identity."

I reshelved the pepper and paprika, careful of alphabetical order. "This has been my name since I was three. It feels like my real name, like who I am."

"What's on your driver's license?" she demanded.

"That's for me to know and you to forget about."

"You were a little kid when you got your nickname. That's how you think of yourself. How everybody thinks of you." The last pot of thyme had gotten scraggly, and Kristen tucked it behind the counter, out of sight. "Even if your parents wouldn't let you change it legally."

So long ago, I'd nearly forgotten about that argument. The summer we turned twelve. *Nineteen eighty-five.*

"Well, what is it?" Sandra said, gaze darting between us.

"You tell her," Kristen warned, "and you'll never hear the end of it."

"A girl needs her secrets, don't you think?" I picked up a shaker-top jar that had strayed from its shelf, and closed the subject. But I knew we hadn't heard the last of Sandra's curiosity.

After lunch, I packed up my samples and my lecture notes, put on my lucky pink shoes, and headed for my weekly gig teaching the food service students about spicery. I was eager to talk marjoram, not murder, basil, not bracelets. To do my small part to help the students reach their dreams.

Flavor as public service.

I set my samples on the tasting table at the front of the classroom and, for the next hour, talked flavor, storage, blends, and extractions. I doled out bits of history: how ancient traders spun tales of mythical birds building nests of cinnamon on impossible-to-reach mountains, to keep their sources secret and prices high. The desire for spice stoked the Age of Exploration, sparking wars and colonial strife. In medieval times, herbal healers were highly valued—I invoked the sainted name of Brother Cadfael—only to have that knowledge decimated by centuries of European witch hunts. Students tasted, compared, opined. I passed out sticks of cinnamon and cassia, and we discussed the evocative power of spice and the relationship of scent to memory.

"It's just salt." A thirtyish man with a wispy blond goatee stared at my tasting table and the open jars of salt—crystal, flake, and granulated. Next to them sat bowls of peppers and bags of bay leaf, basil, and thyme. He waved a hand over the lot.

"You don't need to understand it all now," I said. "Just be aware of the main characteristics and flavors so you can follow your chef's orders."

"It's just SALT." He shifted his weight from one foot to the other. His arms began to swing, and his torso swayed. His face reddened as his movements picked up speed.

"Hey, man. Don't sweat it." The calm words came from a black man in his fifties, whose questions had shown genuine interest and a fair amount of kitchen savvy. "Step by step, buddy, remember? We're all in this together."

"It's JUST SALT." The wispy man tore off his white jacket—students all wear standard kitchen clothing, a sign of their new path—and flung it at me. I caught the crumpled bundle before it landed on the samples. He glowered and charged out of the classroom.

My fingers shook as I scrolled down my notes, wondering where I'd left off.

"You were saying how some flavors balance and some compete," the man who'd tried to calm the distraught student said. His gentle tone worked on me, too.

"That's right. Thank you. We talked about the five tastes: salty, sweet . . ." They joined in and repeated the rest: "bitter, sour, savory."

And off we went, discussing how herbs and spices could be used to balance the tastes of various foods and how to combine them. Their classmate's departure had sharpened their focus, as if his meltdown exposed their vulnerability. I struggled with my own balance: give them enough info to pique their curiosity, but not enough to spin their heads. They deserved my full attention. It wasn't their fault that one of their classmates couldn't handle the pressure.

It was mine. I'd worried about sending the innocent Mary Jean into the lion's den, and I was the one who got bearded.

"You've been a great class. Now for a treat, combining the

spice lecture and the talk on chocolate." I wound through the group, passing out salted dark chocolate–covered caramels. "Take a nibble. Taste how the sweet and bitter come together in the chocolate, how those flavors complement the caramel. Then, when you get that first hint of salt, notice what happens in your mouth."

They grew quiet, faces thoughtful as they identified the flavors and textures. Some were naturals; others were just discovering good food; and yet others chose the program for its job opportunities. All good reasons. The rattle in my chest left by the earlier disruption had eased. I watched with nervous anticipation as the chocolate worked its magic, bringing all we'd talked about to one delicious moment.

"At this point, they all get a little overwhelmed," my staff minder said after class ended, when he came in to help me pack my samples. "Happens in every group, though you can never predict which students will boil over."

But I was supposed to be the HR whiz. The woman who could spot a problem before it ripened into crisis, who could salve a temper before it erupted.

Who could keep an employee—or a student, or a friend— from spur-of-the-moment rash actions that had long-running consequences. But I couldn't shake the impression that I'd blown it. Kristen and my mother were keeping their distance. Sandra had chosen to confide in others. And I had no idea how I felt about Ben, let alone how to talk with him about it.

So much for my communication skills, and my lucky pink shoes.

I dragged myself out, stopping by the office to thank the director for giving Mary Jean a go. And to check on another project. "I know him as Hot Dog. Black, fortyish, wiry. A former boxer with sweet manners."

"I know the man you mean. He came to an information

meeting, but he didn't take an application. And he hasn't come back."

My dejection must have shown. The director came out from behind her desk and put her hand on my shoulder.

"Pepper, it's a reality of this business. You can't help everyone. You can't solve everyone's problems."

Cardamom. I couldn't even solve my own.

Eighteen

*Beyond lay Cadfael's herb garden, walled and silent,
all its small, square beds already falling asleep, naked
spears of mint left standing stiff as wire, cushions of
thyme flattened to the ground, crouching to protect
their remaining leaves, yet over all a faint surviving
fragrance of the summer's spices.*

—Ellis Peters, *The Raven in the Foregate*

"LOOKING FOR SOMETHING IN PARTICULAR?" I ASKED A
woman staring at the wall of spices.

"Oh no. Just killing time."

It's only an expression, but it's always irritated me. Time
is not meant to be killed. It's meant to be savored. Relished.
Celebrated. Because it's gone before you know it, like Bonnie Clay's time on this earth.

I struggled to keep my pleasant retail smile in place. I struggled to keep my inner turmoil from spilling out and flooding
the shop, washing away hard-won camaraderie and goodwill.

To keep from feeling like a total muck-up.

"Let us know what we can help you find," I said, before
I said something I might regret.

I'd half expected Kristen to cancel Movie Night after the

theft. And the murder. And the widening chasm between us. But no. "See you at six thirty," she said, and waved good-bye with the end of her scarf.

You don't have to go, I told myself. You don't have to go back to that house, to sit in the elegant home theater that had replaced the dark, dank "rec room" carved out of the basement, between the laundry and a spare bedroom that made me shiver with cold and damp.

After the near-disaster at Changing Courses, order maintained largely by the steady hand of a student—for whom I predicted a successful career—I longed to go home and curl up on my couch. Under a blankie, despite the heat. I was trying to do too much, and doing none of it well.

Keep calm and carry on, I told myself as the last employee waved good night.

And walk my dog. We wrapped up the closing routine, locked the door behind us, and took the long way home. Then I fetched the car. Drove up to Capitol Hill and squeezed into a parking spot a block from Kristen's house.

Because inviting as my couch might be, deep down there was nothing I would rather do on a Tuesday night than gather with my girlfriends to eat, chat, drink, and pretend to watch a movie.

Make that girlfriends plus one. Across the street, my mother climbed out of Carl's car.

"What's tonight's feature?" She slipped her arm through mine, and we picked our way down the sidewalk, the concrete heaved and cracked by tree roots. "Another of Kristen's romantic comedies?"

"I wouldn't be surprised if she makes us suffer through some artsy, broody film noir." Last time she'd been in a mood, she'd picked a Ben Kingsley movie, *House of Sand and Fog*. Girl doesn't open her mail; everybody dies. She thought it brilliant and provocative. I'd had to cleanse my palate with *The Princess Bride*.

My mother groaned. "It's genetic. Her mother adored Ingmar Bergman. How can the Scandinavians create such bright fabrics and such depressing movies?"

"And now they're writing depressing mysteries. Jen at the Mystery Bookshop tried to get me to read a couple, but I couldn't finish 'em. If I wanted pages full of angst, I'd reread my teenage diaries."

"Now you know why I love historicals. Life could be harsh, and people haven't changed a whole lot. But reality is easier to take when it's dressed in period clothing." She raved about her latest finds.

We started up Kristen's brick walkway. I dragged my feet. "Mom, the other night, I found—"

"Great timing," Laurel called.

Not exactly. The moment vanished in the flurry of hugs and introductions.

I had one foot on the bottom step when Seetha grabbed my hand. "I was hoping she'd come," she whispered. "I'm so excited to meet her."

"I was hoping she wouldn't," I whispered back. "So we could talk about her."

"Kristen's done a wonderful job," my mother said as the four of us headed inside. "A picture-perfect family haven. But the old place had its charms, didn't it, Pepper?"

"If it did, I've forgotten what they were." Gleaming woodwork, Persian rugs, and an artful mix of abstract paintings, family photos, and grade school artwork will do that.

She made an exasperated sound and headed for the kitchen, lured by Kristen's welcoming call. I trailed behind, wondering if the walls knew the secrets that would solve Bonnie's murder.

And told myself, *No.* Firmly, emphatically, *No.* I was keeping my nose in my own business tonight.

I followed the others downstairs.

"*Casablanca* again?" Laurel pretended exasperation. The choice was a clue to Kristen's stress, the kind of movie we were allowed to watch as kids. Classic film is her comfort food, like popcorn to my neighbor Glenn, and mac and cheese to me.

"It cheers me up," Kristen said. "After the theft, I need cheering up."

"Theft?" Seetha said. Laurel shot me a questioning look. In all the other turmoil, I'd forgotten to mention the bracelet. Kristen filled them in.

Seetha's naturally red lips made an O. "One of your friends stole your heirloom? On the tour?"

"I'm still trying to figure out if it is an heirloom. I don't remember it. Do you, Lena?" Kristen said. Her blond pony-tail swung, held by a silver butterfly clasp.

"The bracelet? No, I have no idea where it came from."

"Round up the usual suspects." An antique oak sideboard held a tray of champagne cocktails. I picked up a flute, a raspberry in the bottom, and ignored my mother's glare. One of the things I like about being a grown-up is playing the smart aleck whenever I want.

But even at forty-three, I can feel my mother's disapproval like a cold hand on my shoulder.

"Do the police have any suspects yet on the theft?" Seetha asked. "Or the murder?"

Kristen's eyes flicked toward me.

"You all keep telling me this is dangerous, leave it to the police, yada yada, then you want me to investigate, and pester me to tell you what I've found out." I picked up a plate and spooned up a too-large serving of Laurel's black bean and pasta salad, redolent with herbs. Felt my mother's eyes on me. Felt all their eyes on me. Felt a sharp stabbing behind my jaw, right below my ear. I picked up my glass and plopped into one of the red leather chairs facing the screen. "Isn't it movie time?"

The champagne kicked in, and for the next hour and a half, we sang the songs and recited the best lines in a movie packed with great lines. "Of all the gin joints in all the towns in all the world, she walks into mine," we chimed, and I heard it as a comment on coincidence and fate.

"Play it, Sam. Play 'As Time Goes By,'" we said along with Ilsa.

And I thought about what we owe the past.

When the camera panned the crowd at Rick's singing "La Marseillaise," the diamonds glinting in Rick's sometime-girlfriend Yvonne's ears reminded me of Kristen's missing bracelet.

Apparently they reminded her, too. She grabbed the remote and hit pause, and the movie screeched to a black-and-white halt.

She stood in front of me. "The bracelet is connected to Bonnie's murder. I'm sure of it."

A chill passed through me, and not from the basement or the champagne. "How you can be sure? You don't know where it came from."

"I'm sure it wasn't a family piece. I've pored over those albums, and I didn't spot it in a single photograph. If my grandmother had lost that bracelet, I'd have heard stories. And if my mother had inherited it, she wouldn't have lost it. She'd have sold it to pay our school tuition, or the orthodontist."

"Okay." I leaned forward and set my glass on the table. "But what makes you think the bracelet has anything to do with Bonnie?"

"I think Bonnie stole it and got killed for it." At Kristin's words, my mother gasped.

"Why would she take it?" Laurel tucked a strand of her long gray-brown curls behind her ear. "She came to the party in a T-shirt and an old peasant skirt, wearing Birkenstocks.

She looked like the last person who cared about fancy jewelry."

I got to my feet and started to circle the room. "You haven't seen her pottery. She loved beautiful things. Kristen may be right about a connection, but who would have known she took the bracelet? She was killed only a few hours later." And there had been no sign of a struggle. Had Hannah gone to the studio to confront her about the lease, seen the bracelet, and taken it, with deadly consequences?

Or had Bonnie come home and found Hannah waiting?

None of that made any sense.

"You think the thief was someone who knew the house in the old days. Who stayed here sometimes."

Kristen nodded.

"Someone who knew about that bracelet." I glanced from her to my mother and back. "Did Bonnie—Peggy, whoever she is, or was—leave boxes stored in the basement?"

"No idea. No one had been in the storage room for decades." Kristen described digging through box after box, most of them unmarked, all of them filthy. The clothing had gone to rag recycling, except for a few vintage pieces the girls had claimed, including a leather jacket that fit Mariah. Few other items had been salvageable.

My mother said nothing.

"The bracelet is the MacGuffin," Laurel announced.

I turned to her, slowly, deliberately, annoyed by the non sequitur. "And what, pray tell, is that, and why does it matter now?"

"It's a plot device. It drives the story, but it also distracts the characters and the audience from what the story's actually about. I wouldn't have thought of it if we weren't watching Bogart." She scooted forward in her seat, launching into lecture mode. "The classic example is *The Maltese Falcon*. I learned about it when Gabe wrote a paper comparing

Hammett's book and Huston's film. The story isn't about the search for the Falcon. Just like this isn't about the bracelet."

"Oh, right," Seetha said. "They kill for the bird, because they think it's valuable. They want the prestige of owning it, or to sell it for megabucks. The bird is a symbol of their greed."

And only Sam Spade could see it. Like maybe I was the only person who could weave all the threads together in a pattern that made sense. I waited for the telltale pain in my jaw, the pain that told me I was listening to others instead of myself.

It didn't come.

"What we don't know is what really drove Bonnie," I said.

"Or her killer," Laurel added.

Footsteps upstairs signaled the return of Eric and the girls. No one said a word about finishing the movie. We all knew how it ended, and the thrill was gone.

"It's still the same old story. A fight for love and glory . . ." I sang almost to myself, and I drained my champagne.

Outside on the sidewalk, my mother kissed my cheek, keys in hand. I reached out and touched her arm.

"Mom. I found the album. I saw the newspaper clipping from 1985, about the attack on Mr. Strasburg and Roger Russell's death. That's why we left this house, isn't it?"

She gave me a long look, her wide brown eyes studying the hazel ones I'd inherited from my father. She sagged against the giant maple in the parking strip, between the sidewalk and the street.

"Why didn't you tell us?"

"You were children." Her head snapped up, and she spoke sharply. "We had an obligation to protect you from things you weren't old enough to understand. Things we barely understood."

"We haven't been children for a long time."

"Pepper, please. It's late and I'm tired."

It was barely nine o'clock, and my mother is a night owl.

"Mom, I understand this is hard. Things you'd rather forget come roaring back, and you don't know why, and it hurts all over again. But tell me this much. What did Bonnie have to do with the Strasburg incident?"

Her lips tightened, and she stared into the past. "I wish I knew, Pepper. I wish I knew."

Nineteen

*In ancient Greece, it was believed that unless the
sowing of basil was accompanied by cursing or railing,
it would not flourish.*

—Nava Atlas, *Vegetariana*

I CALLED DETECTIVE SPENCER BEFORE THE STAFF
arrived for our Wednesday morning meeting. She listened
without interrupting, then said she'd get back to me.

My cell phone buzzed with her summons right as the
staff and I finished discussing the calendar of upcoming
events. We'd be sprinting till October. I didn't have time for
distractions.

Take a lesson from Brother Cadfael. No herb went
unharvested, no tincture unbrewed, no patient untreated,
but he always found the killer.

That old motto: "Pray for peace, and work for justice."

As soon as the till was up and running and the door open,
I left my dog and my shop in practiced hands and headed
downtown.

Detective Spencer met me in the hallway. "Detective
Washington is expecting us."

John Washington was the man I remembered from SPD

picnics and parades, his hair now more gray than black, his chest thicker than I'd recalled. He welcomed us into his private office with a kind but curious expression and a warm handshake.

"You guys always say, when a witness to a crime reports another crime, you look for the connection," I said. The matching client chairs needed new upholstery, likely salvaged from the old HQ a good dozen years ago. "This is an extension of that theory. It may be a coincidence that a woman intimately involved with a man killed while committing a crime thirty years ago is killed now. Or not."

And another woman, who knew them both, had just returned to the country. *Oh, Mom.*

"Violent crime is like a rock thrown into a pond." Washington held his two large fists together, then opened his fingers and spread his hands. "The ripples extend far and wide. That's why investigation is a public responsibility. I take all concerns seriously. And, I gather you see another connection."

He studied me as I told my story, leaning back in a brown leather chair not quite big enough for him, steepled fingers resting on his chin, lips pursed. Every so often, he shifted slightly in the chair, as if his low back hurt. Or as if my story made him uncomfortable.

"The storeroom wasn't locked, but Kristen says it hadn't been touched in decades. The house was informal headquarters for a much bigger community. Over the years, kids—young adults volunteering with some program or another—used that basement as temporary storage. Most of the stuff was probably theirs—mainly old clothes and household items, books, things that were easier to leave behind than retrieve. The bracelet was the only thing of value she found, in a black velvet case inside a shoe box tucked behind the other boxes."

"Sounds like whoever put it there didn't want it to be found," Spencer said.

"Right," I said.

Washington reached for a thick black binder, its pressed vinyl seams splitting from age and use. He flipped to a section of clear plastic photo sleeves, snapped the binder open, and laid a sleeve in front of me. It held two photos: a faded Polaroid, blurry at the edges, of a woman's wrist, and a color print dated 1981, with an insurance agent's name and address stamped below it. Next to it he placed a photo of Kristen's bracelet, taken when they'd added it to their homeowner's coverage.

Each showed the same bracelet.

"Tell me," I said, my voice as dusty as the now-demolished basement storeroom.

"The bracelet disappeared in the course of a shooting and subsequent explosion. A man and his family came home unexpectedly and discovered an intruder. The homeowner went for a hidden gun. The intruder pulled his own weapon, and the two men shot each other."

I wrapped my arms around my cramping stomach.

"We called in experts from the fire department. Working theory was that the intruder brought an explosive device with him. Simple, but powerful. When it all cleared, two men were dead. And this"—the detective tapped the plastic sleeve with a thick finger—"was gone."

"Roger Russell and Walter Strasburg," I said. "June 1985."

He nodded.

"That's why this is a cold case," I said. "An open file, even though you reported that Russell and Strasburg shot each other. The stolen bracelet meant someone else was involved. You kept that detail out of the papers."

"I must have visited every pawn shop and secondhand store in the city at least twice."

"You? This was your case?"

"I was a young patrol officer. The detective squad was shorthanded, and I was eager and available. Lucky break for me. I got to work closely with a veteran detective and eventually became his partner. He taught me a lot." The look on Detective Washington's face said one lesson had been the pain of leaving unsolved a murder that destroyed a young family. The Strasburg case was personal to him. "It had been a family piece, left on display in the master bedroom. The only thing missing, and it never showed up."

Until another homeowner unearthed it in a long-neglected corner of a house where countless people had come and gone. Until she shined it up and showed it off at a sparkling Seattle garden party.

Someone had not forgotten.

"And now it's missing again," I said. "Is Bonnie Clay—Peggy Manning—the missing link? Was she—was she *there*?"

"We never knew. Now, of course, we have new questions."

"Why she came back," I said, "and why she's dead."

Washington glanced at his watch and drew the photographs toward him. My cue to leave. I leaned forward, hands on the arms of my chair. "The bracelet is the MacGuffin."

"The what?" he said, and I explained the theory.

If we found the bracelet—the Falcon—would we find the killer, and discover what this was all about?

OUT on the sidewalk, I exhaled. Even magnified by the concrete and asphalt, glass and steel, the sun's warmth barely touched me.

My belief that there are few coincidences when it comes to crime had convinced me that Bonnie's death and the stolen bracelet were linked. My discovery of the 1985 tragedy complicated the picture.

We were trying to fit a key piece of the puzzle into a hole that kept changing shape.

If Bonnie had been at the Strasburg house, that would explain why she'd fled afterward. But it didn't explain why she'd returned.

Or why she'd been killed, or where the bracelet was now.

It was beginning to seem that Kristen's house—*our* house, back then—had been ground zero for a terrible crime.

What had my mother known—and when?

And what about Brian Strasburg? Had he gone from being victim to suspect, now that Bonnie-Peggy had surfaced and been murdered, now that a family heirloom had reappeared and disappeared again?

The whirl of questions made me dizzy.

I didn't have to ask what Brother Cadfael would do. He would ask those questions; he would listen to the answers; he would note what was said and what wasn't. He would not walk away.

Neither would I.

And so, I hiked downhill to Seattle Mystery Bookshop. For the wisdom of the pages, and of those who sell them.

"Super-good choices. No TSTL damsels in distress. The heroine solves the case on her own." We reached the historical section, and Jen noticed my blank look. "Too Stupid To Live."

Oh. That would be me, more often than I cared to admit. "Mom reads 'em on her iPad, but I like book-books. They don't break when I fall asleep and drop them on the floor."

"Some readers insist on starting a series with book one, but the flip side is, authors get better as they go along. Not a worry with your mom's authors—both real pros. But it can be fun to watch the characters develop, especially the romantic relationships." She handed me a copy of *Murder in Morningside Heights* by Victoria Thompson.

"Maybe I can pick up a few pointers." I flipped it over to read the back cover, then chose the first two books in the series. "Might as well start at the beginning."

Jen added two Rhys Bowen paperbacks—*Murphy's Law*

and *Death of Riley*—to my stack. "These ought to keep you out of trouble for a while."

Ha. If it were only so easy.

I followed her to the front counter. "Jen, you seen Callie lately?"

"Not much. She's been a working fiend, in trial with Strasburg, keeping track of all the exhibits, running the computer projector. Last-minute research. All the stuff I don't miss."

"She happy with her job?" Callie hadn't called me to complain or get a reference, both good signs.

"Oh, yeah. They totally need her, and they know it."

"Strasburg can be pretty high-test."

"I hear he's a new man. No temper tantrums, no last-minute freak-outs—no keeping the legal assistants so late they miss the last bus. He took the whole staff to lunch at Ivar's on Secretaries Day. Inside—not the take-out window."

He claimed he'd gotten home Saturday, but what if he'd flown back sooner? If he'd gotten long-nursed revenge by killing Bonnie last Friday night? "That's quite a change in his MO. Wonder what happened."

She set my books on the counter and handed back my credit card. "I should ask why you're asking, but I think I won't."

"Just curious. You know I watch out for my employees, even when they move on. I got the idea she found the job pretty stressful."

"She said it was like a switch flipped. His son's teachers said his anger issues and mood swings were harming the boy. His wife had complained about that for ages—that was part of why she left him. But it finally sunk in, and he started seeing a therapist. The transformation was amazing. Kinder and gentler practically overnight. And it's stayed that way for months now."

"Good advertisement for therapy. Thanks for the intel." I tucked my books in my tote and headed out.

Strasburg's personality change made him an unlikely suspect, but not an impossible one. You can make peace with the past, but it doesn't always stay made.

Problem was, none of the usual suspects—family, friends, coworkers—seemed any more likely. I needed to know more about what happened in 1985—not just the terrible tragedy that killed Walter Strasburg, but what had led to it.

If Bonnie-Peggy had been involved, why had she come back to Seattle?

I got the chills. It had to do with the house, with my family and our friends. The main focus had been programs for children, the hungry, and those in need of medical care. Necessary, occasionally controversial, but not truly radical.

The Strasburg attack, though . . .

I'd let my mother avoid a confrontation long enough.

The prospect called for planning and fortification. Happily, the bookshop is next to one of my favorite coffee shops—the one with the amazing mural of the Goddess Coffea on the back wall, bringing us the gift of the coffee bean. I carried my double shot to a tiny table on the lower level, near the old bank vault that houses the owner's office.

Most people think radical activism belonged to the 1960s and early 1970s. That by the 1980s, the country had been lulled to sleep by capitalism, by the soft sounds of peace and prosperity, by Ronald Reagan's soothing baritone. But I knew better. I remembered protests against nuclear buildup, pleas for disarmament, fears of nuclear holocaust. Bumper stickers had continued the fight, everything from VISUALIZE WORLD PEACE to BOOKS, NOT BOMBS.

I remembered taking a ferry with Carl and my parents to Bremerton for a rally against the nuclear submarines.

I remembered boycotts of GE lightbulbs to protest the giant corporation's role in building nuclear warheads. I remembered prayer vigils for immigration reform and anger over the Iran–Contra fiasco.

But I did not remember Bonnie-Peggy. And I was one hundred percent certain that my parents would not have tolerated any discussion of violence in the name of peace. They had never allowed guns in the house, not even cap guns at the Fourth of July, and they'd made Carl give away the G.I. Joe a relative sent for his birthday.

But my mother was so guarded about that time that getting her to talk seemed about as likely as the city's tunnel project finishing on time and under budget.

Who else could I ask? I pictured faces from the party and settled on one. A woman who'd been on the fringes of the group but might recall some pertinent details. We'd always gotten along. I didn't have her number, but I knew who would. Alas, I doubted he would answer his own phone.

And some questions are better posed in person, when you can see the emotion they trigger and spot where to aim the follow-up. I drained my espresso, gathered up my things, and took to the streets.

Once again, the gatekeeper's desk sat empty. The flowers had begun to droop. Three orange petals lay on the open appointment book.

My focus wasn't the fading zinnias. I didn't need to check the vase to know its origins, but I lifted it up and peered at the bottom anyway. The same mark I'd seen on the salt pig that now graced my kitchen counter.

On the rare Movie Nights when my father inflicted a western on us, I'd usually fallen asleep. But I'd seen enough John Wayne movies to read a brand. And this was a double diamond.

"She always worked with her hands, so it shouldn't have surprised any of us that she took up pottery for a living."

Terry leaned against the doorway, arms folded, wearing khakis and a blue button-down. Without the boost of spirit the Uncle Sam outfit gave, he looked older. Tired.

"You knew she was back, didn't you? My mother called you last week from outside the Pink Door, anxious to warn you. But you weren't worried."

"Peggy—*Bonnie*—was no threat to me. Nor I to her. I think she finally understood that."

"Why would you be threats to each other? Tell me, Terry. It may be why she died."

He lowered his gaze, shaking his head—in a gesture of refusal, or lack of understanding? "The loss gives me great pain. She had so much to give."

Was an answer hidden in his reply? He'd always seemed like a straightforward guy. But nothing about any of this was straightforward. "Why did she come back to Seattle, after all these years?"

"I think she was tired of running." His voice was flat, matter-of-fact. As if pointing out the obvious. But I didn't quite see.

"From what?"

The door opened a few inches, and I half turned, expecting to see Sharon. Expecting her to glower and demand to know why I was keeping her husband from his work. It began to swing shut, and a thirtyish man in a wheelchair rolled partway in, left arm extended. He pushed the door a second time, his skin too dark for me to make out the tattoo rippling over his bare forearm. Behind him, on foot, came another man, dark blond, a military tattoo of some kind on his arm, wearing an olive green T-shirt and the same style of loose camo pants as the man in the wheelchair.

"Good to see you, gentlemen," Terry said.

"Your wife in?" the second man said. "We were hoping—"

"She left to run an errand, then pick up the girls from dance class. Go on in," he told the first man.

The client rolled past us, toward Terry's office. The other man's hooded gaze shot between us, and I wasn't sure whether he was going to throw a punch or sit on the faded floral love seat.

Terry shifted his piercing blue eyes to me, answering the question I'd almost forgotten I'd asked. "From herself."

Twenty

It is impossible to determine both position and momentum at the same time.

—Heisenberg's uncertainty principle

"THREE PINK ELEPHANTS, THREE BROWN OWLS, THREE teddy bears, and three Scottie dogs." The closest shape to an Airedale in the cookie case. "And one ferry boat—I'll eat that now."

In my determination to reach Detective Spencer first thing this morning, I'd skipped the sacred ritual of treats for the weekly staff meeting. My bad. But a midday snack would heal the wound.

While the woman behind the counter bagged my cookies, I checked my messages. A text from the shop, telling me a potential customer in south Seattle had called. Ben replying to a text I'd sent this morning, saying the trip to Portland had gone well, but he had more research to do in Olympia and wasn't sure when he'd be back. He missed me and was sorry he hadn't had time to follow up on Roger Russell.

And one from Tory saying Hannah Hart would meet her at the gallery at eleven this morning and could I come.

Ten minutes ago. *Dang.*

On my way, I texted back. With a bite and a promise, I tucked my cookie in the bag and trotted the few blocks to Pioneer Square.

When I rounded the corner onto Occidental, I slowed to a walk. *Remember your goals*. The point was to find out how Bonnie fit into the whole Hannah-Josh drama, without scaring Hannah off. *Probe gently*.

Outside the gallery stood a treelike sculpture made of found metal objects, a relative of *The Guardian*, which Tory and her stepmother had bought for my shop. Odd bits of metal danced and sang in the soft breeze.

The door stood open. I walked in, expecting to recognize Hannah from Mr. Adams's description.

But there was no one to recognize. The redbrick walls showed their paintings and fiber art to no one. Clay masks stared vacantly. Blown glass chandeliers hung from the high tin ceiling, shining light in empty corners.

"He-LOH-oh-h! Tory?" I peered around the cases displaying jewelry and other small objets d'art—glass boxes, carved stone totems, beads, porcelain netsuke.

No sign of her. No sign of anyone.

What was stranger, no sound. The gallery usually rang with chatter and musical inspiration. Tory and her pals were among the coolest, weirdest, most creative, most *alive* people I knew. And seldom quiet.

But where were they?

Where was Hannah Hart?

The cookie taste in my mouth turned sour, and I swallowed as I picked my way through the space, craning my neck to peer behind the pillars. I crept by the stage—filled with the electronic gear and drum kit of the Zak Davis Band, all eerily silent—and entered the narrow hall that ran to the open back door. A gust blew in, and dried leaves swirled around my feet, dust stinging my nostrils. A red straw, the kind that come in carryout lattes, skittered to a stop at my feet.

I held my breath, willing my heart to beat more quietly. Took another step, my back foot poised, head angled, listening. Listening.

"Tory?"

The silence was killing me. Had my calls, my questions put her in danger?

Then, outside, a door slammed, followed by a clapping sound, an "all finished" swipe of one palm against the other. My heart jumped. Voices neared, female, still indistinct. Footfalls echoed.

On the long wall were three paneled doors with dented brass doorknobs. I grabbed the first. No go. Grabbed the next, twisted, yanked. The door opened, and I fell inside.

But the door would not close.

By the thin light creeping in, I saw that I'd stuffed myself into a closet crammed full of cleaning supplies. I held my breath. Turned the knob again—slowly this time—and pulled the door toward me.

No luck. It wasn't quiet, and it wouldn't close. I flattened myself against the wall as best I could while straddling a shop vac.

In the hall, the voices grew louder. "This door keeps popping open."

My chest wanted to explode.

"Yeah. I keep meaning to ask Zak to look at it—I can't tell if the problem is the lock or the hinges. And when your rent's a dollar a month, you hate to call the landlord."

The voice. The tension flooded out of me, and I collapsed against a mop—judging by the shape poking my back and the stringy things brushing my neck.

"What was that?" In the hallway, Tory spoke sharply, on alert.

"It's me." I lifted one leg over the vacuum and shoved my way out. Blinked against the sunlight streaming in the back door. "Where were you?"

Tory glanced at the closet, then burst into laughter. The woman beside her was not Hannah.

"Sorry," Tory said, wiping her cheek with a knuckle. "I was out back, helping Jade load up for a show."

"What if Hannah came and went while you were messing around outside? What if—?" My temperature rose as anger and irritation flared through me. Just as quickly, it plummeted. My knees buckled, and I collapsed against the wall.

"Pepper, chill. I was outside three minutes max. If she isn't here by now, she's blowing us off."

"This is serious, Tory."

"Hey, I get it. Remember? I've been through this. I get what you're doing and why it matters. Oh." She jerked her head backward in surprise. "You thought—you were afraid—Pepper, I'm fine. We're all fine."

That pissed-off, post-adrenaline jittery mash of nervous energy pulsed through me. "I know you do. I know you are. I'm sorry." I ran both hands through my hair, wondering where I had left my tote. Tory hugged me, then introduced Jade, who made the clay masks and Japanese stoneware.

"We used to show in the same gallery," Jade said, "so when Tory asked me about Hannah, I tracked her down. I guess she can't go back to her studio yet—because of the murder. 'Course, she's not sure she wants to—"

Tory shivered visibly, and I remembered how we had all felt last fall, knowing what had happened outside the Spice Shop.

So the artist network didn't know that Hannah had moved out. Been kicked out. But if she'd killed Bonnie to get the space back—and get back at Josh—would she care that a woman had died there?

Only a psychopath wouldn't be bothered by reminders of violence, even by their own hand.

"Tory suggested we offer her work space in the basement. She said she'd come look, but then . . ." Jade extended her hands, palms up, in a "who knows?" gesture.

"I texted her," Tory said. "Don't worry, Pepper—I'm sure she's fine. You know artists. We get caught up in our work, and all of a sudden we've lost half a day and don't have a clue."

I was embarrassed to admit I hadn't worried about Hannah's safety. Who would be after her?

Bonnie's killer, that's who. If Hannah knew something . . .

"I heard she's unpredictable," I said. "That she's—"

"Off her rocker?" Jade laughed. "You talked to Josh. They're both great, but too intense. They blow up, get back together, then blow up again. They'd be better off if they could just walk away, but—well, you can't ever tell what's going on in other people's relationships, can you?"

And sometimes, not even your own.

What was I doing here? I should be in my shop selling spice, not gallivanting around the city, asking questions. And certainly not shutting myself in closets at the slightest unexpected sound.

But for reasons I hadn't yet fully grasped, Bonnie Clay's murder affected my family and other people I love. And that mattered way more than marjoram.

"Sounds like this time, he really meant it, but she wasn't convinced," I said. "Tory, tell me you have lunch stashed somewhere and I'll forgive you for scaring the parsley out of me."

"I can do that, but let me talk to this customer," Tory replied, nodding toward a woman who'd just walked in.

Before Jade left, I asked if she'd known Bonnie Clay.

"Sorry, no. There's so many potters in Seattle. And I've never sold in the Market. That's a lot of work."

"Bonnie seemed like she'd rather hang out alone than make small talk with customers all day."

"A lot of artists feel that way. Me, I spend so much time with the clay that it's nice to get out among real humans now and then."

At the law firm, we'd brought in a consultant who ran Myers-Briggs tests on the lawyers and staff. Easy to tell the introverts from the extroverts, the thinkers from the feelers. There ought to be a category for ambiverts—people like Jade who draw energy from both solo activities and social interaction, at different times and in different ways. It's too easy to put people in narrow categories that don't fit.

Jade jangled her car keys. "Great to meet you. If I hear from Hannah, I'll call you."

I wished her well, then headed up front. Bonnie had been part of a group years ago, then walked away and made herself into a loner. I was convinced the Strasburg incident had been the trigger.

But it wasn't the whole story. And that showed how much I know about people.

Then I remembered the newspaper article in her locker. Had she chosen to sell her work in the Market because it was the best place to make a living?

Or to keep an eye on me?

I watched the gallery while Tory dashed into the tiny communal kitchen—the third of the doors I'd seen in the back hall—to rustle up lunch. And music.

"Zappa Plays Zappa," Tory said. "I turned it off so I could hear customers when I went outside. Don't know how I missed you. Sorry we scared you."

We settled onto two bar stools behind the sales counter and tucked into turkey-and-provolone on croissants. "Thish ish prrfct," I said through a mouthful. "Investigating makes me hypoglycemic."

A few minutes later, after Tory had sold a woman a blue picture agate necklace and lunch had me feeling like myself again, I told her about the sublease. "Why would Hannah want the space back? To mess with Josh?"

Tory held up a hand, signaling me to wait while she

swallowed. "Might be as simple as not finding another place. Not everyone wants to rent to artists. We spill paint, use turpentine, keep crazy hours."

Maybe that was why Bonnie had jumped at Hannah's rental offer. I didn't know where she'd been all these years, but according to my friends in the Market, she'd been on the move.

Tory continued. "We're going to have to move soon, too—our building sold, and they're going to replace it with some micro apartment garbage."

"What? I love your place. So much character—all those old tiles and moldings." Tory and Zak rented the lower unit of a four-plex on Capitol Hill, a century old and suffering from age, neglect, and the rise in property values. A deadly triad. Tory painted in the attic, and their metal sculptor neighbor worked her welded magic in the decrepit garage out back. "What about Keyra?"

"This co-op thing's worked out so well that we're all hoping to find a place together. I've got some insurance money from my dad. Owning a building will give Zak and me some security." Her golden brown eyes turned serious. "Artists always fear being one step away from failure. Can you support yourself without a day job? If you get a day job, can you make time to make art? Are you giving in, giving up—wasting time you should be painting?

"And then, if people like your work"—she gestured toward her own paintings, a bloom of color against the faded redbrick—"are you a success, or have you sold out?"

I tilted my head, squinting.

"My gallery mates are all great." She sipped her iced tea, the Spice Shop blend. "But the art-for-art's-sake crowd thinks if you consistently create work that regular people buy, you must be sacrificing an essential element of your artistic soul for popularity."

"Sounds like jealousy to me. Or a head game."

She let out a wry laugh. "Artists. Head cases, all of us."

"Nah. Just human."

"Anyway, I get why Hannah might have freaked out. Short on money, short on options. Maybe Bonnie freaked out back. Maybe they argued and fought."

I drained my tea. "That would explain the lack of forced entry. But there was no sign of a struggle. And why confront her late on a Friday night?"

A trio of women came in, reminding me that this was a working gallery and that I had a business of my own to tend. Tory promised to call if Hannah showed up, but I wasn't betting on her appearance.

A block away, Yesler Way, the original Skid Road, separates the first platted claims in Seattle from the streets to the north, which other pioneers laid out to follow the shoreline. I stepped into the street.

Shouts pierced the air, and a hand jerked me back. Tires squealed. I landed on the curb, on my butt and elbow.

"What were you doing?" a man asked. I scrambled to my feet, my right knee already complaining. "You stepped right in front of that car."

My head swung right, then left, as I tried to orient myself. "What car? I never saw—"

He pointed as a white SUV rounded the corner and disappeared from view.

"It wasn't your fault," a woman said. "The driver came flying down Yesler and changed lanes at the last minute. Almost like she wanted to hit you. It was crazy."

Images zipped around in my brain, forming no discernible pattern. I couldn't think in complete sentences, let alone speak them. My pants were torn, and my elbow hurt to high heaven.

"The plate started AL, and I think it ended with a 2." She scribbled on the back of a parking lot stub.

"Thanks." I took a deep breath and took the ticket. The

street, the buildings, my rescuer, the witness—everything seemed normal.

Except the sidewalk, where my frosted cookies lay shattered, bits of pink, blue, and yellow covering the dark gray concrete like a mosaic. A pigeon landed with a squawk, zeroing in on a broken teddy bear.

Another white SUV? They were everywhere.

Had the driver truly wanted to hit me?

Talk about crazy.

Twenty-one

BY THE TIME I GOT BACK TO THE SHOP—CARRYING A BAG of biscotti from the Italian market, in place of the broken animal cookies—my fear had sharpened into anger. I could not believe anyone had tried to hit me on purpose, but it didn't matter. The incident fueled my determination to get to the bottom of things.

The first step is knowing where to start. I had two options. I picked the easy one.

My mother could wait.

"C'mon, dog." Arf obeyed.

"You've got the samples they asked for?" Sandra asked. It had taken her about two seconds to suss out that I'd been rattled, not once but twice, and that I would not be deterred. "Be safe, boss."

Business before investigation. But as I drove down First Avenue South to meet a prospective customer—a butcher ready to spice up his sausage business—I considered my theories. And the holes in them.

Hannah Hart might have flailed out in anger at Bonnie. She was the only person I knew who wanted Bonnie gone and had access to the building and studio. Josh had keys, but I'd seen his shock at the discovery of the body. But Hannah might have been wound up enough to confront her tenant, even late at night.

Her former neighbors might know if she burned the night oil. Whether she was likely to rage at anyone other than Josh. What she drove and where she might be now.

She was reportedly a small woman. Hard to imagine her attacking Bonnie viciously enough to kill.

And she had no link to Kristen or the stolen bracelet. But I had to agree with the police: Odds were that the two crimes were connected. We needed to figure out how.

I signaled and switched lanes. By that logic, I couldn't rule Hannah out until probing a little deeper.

Brian Strasburg, on the other hand, had an obvious tie to the bracelet—a family heirloom that went missing the night his father was killed.

But while Kristen and I believed Bonnie had been involved in the Strasburg incident, how would Brian have made that connection?

If he had, then all bets were off. Despite his reported personality transformation, I could imagine him harboring a deadly grudge. It's one thing to control your moods around your kid, another to let a potential accessory to murder slip away. Again.

Lawyers know how to track down facts and people.

I steered the Mustang into the butcher's small parking lot and sat, pondering. How would Strasburg have known the bracelet had surfaced, let alone its link to Bonnie-Peggy?

Unless some piece of evidence—known to Detective Washington and the victim's family, but never publically revealed, like the missing bracelet—put her in the loop.

Something they knew, and she knew, that was the reason she left Seattle.

And the reason she came back.

Maybe she thought she could hide in plain sight. That the passage of time would protect her. In a city, we run in circles that barely touch. Now that I live blocks from my work, my experience has changed, but when I worked downtown and lived in Greenwood, work and home were worlds apart. I never ran into a coworker in the grocery store. If Tag and I went out for Sunday breakfast, we didn't run into the bank teller I chatted with every other Friday.

A secret big enough to send a woman on the run for thirty years didn't just lose its power.

Had she come back to make amends?

The absence of signs of a break-in or a search for valuables in the studio ruled out my final option, random criminal violence.

Arf stuck his head over the seat and poked my neck with his nose. I reached up to stroke his bearded chin. "Okay, you're right. No more woolgathering. And I'll bring you a treat, promise."

Inside the butcher's shop, a glass-front cooler dominated the retail space up front. Swinging double doors led to the workroom and giant coolers and freezers in back. The butcher had given me a tour, and I rubbed my bare arms to warm up.

"So here are the samples we talked about. And some of our smoked black peppercorns," I said.

Once upon a time, butchers were big men with broad chests, full bellies pushing out their spattered white aprons, beefy arms bulging out of white T-shirt sleeves. No longer. The modern food entrepreneur can be anyone. Inspired by a love of backyard grilling, this one had left computer programming for meat cutter's classes, then bought this shop from an old-school butcher ready to retire.

"For the first year, I bought my spices from the same people he did. But then you called, and I thought, yeah, check it out. I'm ready to move beyond the basics, offer customers a little more."

He had a good palate and a good nose. We talked spices for sausage—red and black peppers, sages, fennel, oregano, garlic. We talked salami, the popular cured meats, and wild game variations. We talked salt.

He placed a respectable opening order, and I gave him a gift bag of our grilling rubs to try. "Your customers will love these. They'll think you're a brilliant butcher—"

"Which I am," he said, a dimple forming in his left cheek.

"Which you are," I agreed. "Because you give your customers what they need to make their friends and family think they're brilliant cooks. We're working on a cocoa and pepper blend, and one with hibiscus flowers that will knock your socks off."

He raised a finger and disappeared through the swinging doors, emerging with a small white insulated box. "Two pork loins and a small roast, and our sweet Italian sausage and maple breakfast sausage. Love to hear what you think about the flavors. And I put in a treat for your dog."

"You just made a friend for life. I like you, too."

Business accomplished, my copilot and I headed for Beacon Hill and Wedding Row. My intention was to chat up the tenants and find out more about Hannah and Bonnie, their habits, and the tensions. I had a hunch that in a building full of artists and retailers, little escaped observation.

The parking spaces out front were roped off to make room for a fleet of art cars. Need a distinctive way to arrive at your wedding or reception? Search no further! While it's hard to ignore the Yellow Cab repurposed as a shark or the Chinese dragon stretch limo, my personal fave is the Barbie Dream Hearse—billed as "Seattle's only hearse for the living." Several young women in short dresses and long legs, champagne flutes in hand, ogled its charms and giggled over the prospects of a bachelorette party cruise around the city in a star-speckled white Cadillac Brougham hearse with a pink-and-white interior.

Gotta love being part of a city where weird as a way of life meets geek computer culture, creating our own brand of Northwest nerd cool.

But I don't love prowling for parking. I turned left, made another left, and another, back to where we'd started. Nothing. I drove south another block and went left again, wondering if I should go back home. I get nervous leaving the Mustang too far from my destination.

"What say we cross our fingers and double back?" I glanced in my rearview mirror as if expecting Arf to reply.

And that's when I saw it. Wedged between a red Camry and a dented blue pickup sat Bonnie Clay's van.

I found an alley to pull into and made a call. "I ought to have you on speed dial," I told Detective Spencer.

"You're sure it's hers?"

"Yep." I hadn't paid much attention to the van when we dropped Bonnie off Friday night, but the bumper sticker removed any doubt. Next to an earthy brown handprint were the words "I make art from mud." I read Spencer the van's New Mexico plate number and waited while she ran it.

"Hmm," she said. "Then why is it registered to Elena Sophia Istvanffy?"

I inhaled sharply.

What the fennel . . .

Changing your name when you marry, fine. Picking your own first name or shedding an outgrown nickname, good on you. I understand cultural traditions, like when a law firm employee changed her name in accordance with her Cheyenne heritage, though it did create a record-keeping challenge.

But stealing a name? From a woman who'd been your friend?

"Detective, if you're thinking my mother bought the van for Bonnie, or registered it for her, using her maiden name, think again. Not a snowball's chance. I'm unsure about a lot of things right now, but I am positive those two women hadn't exchanged a word in thirty years."

"I'll send a patrol car," she replied. "And we'll be there in twenty minutes."

"I'll wait for you in the bakery."

Across from Wedding Row, a gaggle of future brides and attendants piled into two BMWs—one black, one white—and I zoomed into the parking spot they left. "You're my lucky charm, dog."

I'd bought cookies twice today but had gotten nothing more than one nibble of a sugar cookie boat, long sacrificed to the pigeons. I wrapped Arf's leash around a chair leg and popped inside where I ordered a double latte, iced, and half a dozen gingersnaps. No sign of Josh.

"The Airedale outside is yours, right?" the barista asked. "Can he have a cookie? Pumpkin and almond flour, all organic, made for dogs."

I said yes, then took our treats to the sidewalk table, in the partial shade of a red umbrella. Quizzing the neighbors no longer seemed like a bright idea. Not with cops nearby, and detectives about to descend.

I sipped my coffee and bit into a cookie. A peppery bite took me by surprise. Arf sat up abruptly, facing the street.

Across the street, framed by the overgrown yews flanking his steps, Mr. Adams waved his golf club at me.

"Come in, come in," he said when we approached, swinging his three-iron like a machete.

Age and arthritis may have slowed him down, but the rhodies and azaleas had been deadheaded, and the junipers and forsythia neatly trimmed. Coleus in their flamboyant reds, pinks, and greens burst out of the brick planters beside the front steps, set off by the three-lobed chartreuse leaves of sweet potato vine.

Surprisingly cool for the warm day, the house was tidy, a hint of yeast and cinnamon in the air.

"I brought cookies." I held out the bag. "But you bake."

He settled into a deep maroon recliner next to the big front window. A lace-covered table held a lamp, his reading glasses, and the TV remote. He set my gift next to his coffee mug. I sat on a green ottoman, Arf at my feet.

"My daughter takes care of me every Sunday. Big family do, like when my wife was alive. She runs the curry—what do you call it? The program that says what teachers gotta teach? Curriculum office, that's it. And my granddaughter, she coulda been a chef."

Family photos covered the walnut sideboard. In the center stood a portrait of a young man in navy dress whites, unsmiling, hair cropped close. A shadow box held ribbons and medals; a triangular box held a folded flag.

"Vietnam?"

His eyes glistened. "My boy."

I stood and picked up the gold frame, my throat aching for his loss. Next to it, a black-and-white photo showed a barefoot boy sitting on a dock, cypress trees behind him—Mr. Adams as a child. A wedding portrait, circa 1950. His wife could have stepped off the cover of *Ebony* magazine. He looked like the class nerd who'd caught the brass ring. A photo a few years later, of the couple with two girls and a boy. More recent shots of his daughters and their families.

I picked up a photo of a shining girl in cap and gown. I shouldn't have been surprised. "Mr. Adams, I've never properly introduced myself. I'm Pepper Reece. I own Seattle Spice. Your granddaughter Cayenne works for me."

"I know who you are. You were in the paper, right before she hired on. You and your dog." A wicked grin spread across his wrinkled face. "You think I let just anybody into my house?"

I smiled and glanced out the window, hoping to see the detectives. The break in the yew hedge, where the crumbling steps led to the sidewalk, gave him a clear view of the tables outside the bakery.

"Mr. Adams, you remember anything more about the night Bonnie Clay was killed? You saw a car speed away."

"Like I said, one of them hot new SUV things. My other daughter drives one. She's a school principal, over near Spokane. They both started out as teachers, same as their mother." His gaze flicked back to the sideboard, first to the portrait of his wife, then to the image of that beautiful young man. His jaw quivered, and he picked up his coffee cup.

A cup in the blue and brown glazes I'd come to recognize as Bonnie's signature.

"She gave me this, Bonnie did. She was a tough broad. Didn't say much about herself. But when she saw that picture . . ."

Out on the street, a police tow truck passed by, pulling Bonnie's van, the detectives following. I desperately wanted to talk to them, desperately hoped they'd found something in the van that pointed to the killer.

I turned back to Mr. Adams. "I'm so sorry about your son. I know it's been a long time, but I imagine it never stops hurting."

"You get a pain in your ankle, it doesn't stop you from walking. It's a pain in your heart, but you keep living. You got to."

"If your daughters and your other grandchildren are as lovely as Cayenne . . ."

"They are." He ran his gnarled fingers over Arf's ears. "Now that we're all friends, don't be strangers."

Twenty-two

Avoid traffic problems. Move to Albuquerque.

        —Emmett Watson, legendary Seattle reporter
        and curmudgeon

OH, TO HOP A FERRY AND SAIL AWAY, GLIDING ACROSS Puget Sound to the Olympic Peninsula. Take my dog for a drive in the ancient rain forest. Browse the lavender farms at Sequim. Ogle the historic homes of Port Townsend. Stroll along the Strait of Juan de Fuca, gaze across the waters to Canada, and pretend I was a sea captain, exploring the New World.

Oh, brave new world!

Fat chance.

Nobody tells you when you buy a shop that you can never take a vacation. That you're on, even on your days off. You feel like you've married a building and an inventory and your staff, not to mention your vendors and your customers and your neighbors and Market management.

I'd waited for the detectives to stop and share their secrets with me over cookies and cappuccino, but they'd sped on by without so much as a wave. I sat in the Mustang and glared at my phone. Three texts from the staff, all semi-urgent. Two from Tag, which I ignored.

A text from Ben saying he finally had some time between meetings to research Russell and would e-mail me the results later today. *Good. Maybe then I can get somewhere.* I tossed the phone in my bag and stuck the key in the ignition. Time to get back to work. I didn't really want to indulge my running-away-from-it-all fantasy. I am reminded daily that chucking the corporate world for a life of spice is a very special kind of living the dream.

Besides, the shop needed me. Customers and employees needed me. I had pounds of hibiscus on its way and no plan.

All that, I could handle. What gave me the fire-alarm-from-a-dead-sleep-at-two-A.M. willies was the thought of telling Kristen the true history of her stolen bracelet.

And of forcing her to admit she knew more about the past—and Bonnie-Peggy's role in it—than she was telling me.

We crept up First Avenue South at a pace that would have bored a snail. When we finally reached Safeco Field, I saw that the Mariners were home, playing an afternoon game. Once we cleared the stadium traffic hangover, I zoomed up to the loft to park, then headed to the Market. Along the way, Arf and I stopped to visit a few vendors. I wasn't procrastinating; I was being social.

At least, that's what I told myself.

"Boss, this registry—"

"Sandra, no. Don't tell me the computer's on the blink or we have another Momzilla on our hands." I was barely in the door when my second-in-command charged me.

"No. That's what I wanted to tell you. The registry is a hit. Wherever you got that idea, go back and get more brilliant ideas."

I kissed her.

I set my sights on Kristen. My BFF and most congenial employee had given me the slip all day, but her time was up.

"I need to make a delivery and wet my whistle. Walk with me."

Her chin dipped, and she gave me a hard look. "Don't suppose I have a choice."

"Nope." I faked a sunny smile and picked up a bag of spices Sandra had packed.

Part of the Market's charm is its history. Another is the nooks and crannies, the half-hidden places. My mission was Emmett Watson's Oyster Bar, a nook and cranny if there ever was one. The late founder and namesake had been a notorious grouch who'd used his newspaper column to advocate for Lesser Seattle. Tongue-in-cheek or not, he'd made an art of urban skepticism.

I handed the bartender his order—a black pepper he favored for his Bloody Marys, and dried chiles to flavor his vodka. He grunted his thanks. Kristen turned to leave, but I steered her toward a booth, and we squeezed in. Too grouchy to enjoy real food, I ordered a beer and deep-fried zucchini.

"Just iced tea," Kristen said, her mouth tight, expression wary.

I'd learned, in fifteen years of solving personnel problems, that no matter what approach you take—and the options are legion—always, always leave out the emotion.

Trouble was, this problem wasn't personnel—it was personal. And I didn't know whether I was confronting Kristen, or protecting her.

The waiter slid our drinks onto the table.

"It's time to stop hiding the truth. Tell me everything you know about Bonnie. Peggy. Roger Russell." I gripped the frosty glass and took a tiny, careful sip.

Her head jerked as if on a string, and her eyes narrowed. "Don't you push me."

I leaned in, both hands and forearms on the table. "I need to know. What happened in June of 1985? We got to St. Louis, and my mother got a call. She flew home alone." We made the long, sweaty trip to my grandparents' house every summer, hitting the road the day after school let out.

Kristen stared into the past. From the TV above the bar came the crack of a bat, followed by an anxious silence, then the staff and patrons cheered.

"And when Dad and Carl and I got home two weeks later," I continued, "my mother had found the house in Ravenna and we moved."

Kristen clenched her icy glass. The waiter set the fritters between us without a word.

I pressed on. "My parents always said we moved because it was time, we needed more space, especially with a growing boy. But it was more than that, wasn't it?"

A tear formed on the inner corner of her eye. "I couldn't tell you. I wasn't supposed to know. They argued and argued. They couldn't agree on what to do."

I reached for her cold, damp fingers. "It had to do with Peggy, didn't it? And the tragedy."

She looked up, baffled. "How did you find out?"

Suddenly I felt colder than the beer, than her iced tea. "They didn't know, did they? Your parents and mine? Tell me they didn't know what Roger and Peggy were planning."

Tell me, I meant, *that our entire childhood wasn't a lie. That our parents really did work and pray for peace and justice.*

Tell me we were who I thought we were.

She shook her head slightly. "No. They didn't know until afterward. And I'm not sure they ever learned everything." Her fingers tightened on mine. "Aja had a nightmare and woke up crying. She'd left her doll in the playroom, so I crept down to get it, and I hid behind the door to listen. Terry told the group what had happened. Roger had been killed. Peggy had disappeared. They thought . . . That's when my mother called yours."

That's what my mother meant, last week in the Market. "They thought she'd been part of the attack at the Strasburgs' house. They thought she'd been killed, too."

"I'm certain none of them—your parents or mine—knew about the plan. The police came—several times—but the adults were careful to get the kids out of the house. I never did find out exactly what happened, or what Roger and Peggy expected to accomplish. But—but—" Her voice grew urgent. "Our house was the focal point of the community. Meetings, dinners. Everyone shared the van, the garden, the meditation room."

"They crashed in the guest room and stored their stuff in your basement."

"Right. So I always thought they—we—were the center of the community. In charge."

"There were a lot of people doing a lot of projects in the name of Grace House. By then, it had lost its cohesiveness." Not that I'd realized any of that as a kid. Not until now, when I could see that our parents had still been young themselves. Trying to figure out a new way to live, and raise their kids, and change the world.

But when it comes to people, some things never change.

"Right. And I think our parents were badly hurt when people started projects on their own, without consulting the others."

"Without consensus." Part of their credo.

"So when your mom came back, there were all these hush-hush meetings. Everything changed. When your family moved out, that was the beginning of the end for the whole community."

With the self-centeredness of a twelve-year-old, I had not given much thought to the changes in our mothers' friendship.

But now that I saw that time through older eyes—we were older than they had been then—I could see the rift that never healed.

"All these years and you never said a word."

"Nothing to say." Kristen swished a zucchini fritter through the cucumber sauce. "Our lives didn't change much.

We were still friends. We were still in the same class and activities."

"But the truth," I said. "I would have known the truth."

"Do any of us know the truth? I just knew a few more details."

When I discovered that Tag had betrayed me with another woman, the details of our lives had realigned themselves. Shirts that came back from the cleaners that I didn't remember taking in, his last-minute schedule changes—they made a different picture. I questioned every good thing he'd ever done, every declaration of love, the essence of our lives together. The essence of my own life.

Details lose their power to hurt us over time, but like Mr. Adams had said, you don't forget the pain.

Something like that had happened to my mother in 1985. Part of me thought I should spare Kristen those details now, but this was no time for holding back.

Trust her strength. Trust your own.

"Peggy wasn't killed. Obviously. She took off, but first she came back to the house. For how long, or who knew, I don't know. But long enough to hide the bracelet in your basement."

Kristen's hand flew to her mouth, her barely pink nail polish the same shade as her cheeks.

I told her about my visit to Detective Washington and the picture he'd shown me. "No question. It's the same bracelet."

She pressed her hands together, thumbs beneath her jaw, steepled fingers against her lips.

I did the same. When it comes to justice, I believe in work. But praying never hurts.

Twenty-three

*Bitter though it may be to many, Cadfael concluded,
there is no substitute for truth, in this or any case.*

—Ellis Peters, *The Raven in the Foregate*

"DO YOU KNOW HOW MUCH I LOVE WORKING DOWN
here?" Kristen said as we strolled out of the Soames-Dunn
Building, arm in arm, as much to stick together on the
crowded sidewalk as to reaffirm our best-friendship. "It's
like, in the Market, anything can happen."

"And does." Across Pike Place, in the craft stalls, Bonnie's absence created no visible gap.

But those invisible gaps are a whole other story.

A familiar figure wearing Seahawks number 12—the
fans' number—sauntered out of Starbucks. The staff know
Hot Dog's love of cappuccino and occasionally buy him one
from the tip jar.

"Summon your persuasive powers," I told Kristen.

She gave me a conspiratorial wink, and we flanked him.

"Uh-oh. Two pretty women picking up a dude like me,
somethin' ain't right."

"Ah, Mr. Dog, a man of great taste," Kristen said. "Not
to mention talent and wisdom. You know, there's an espresso

bar at Changing Courses. And when you graduate, you can find a job with all the cappuccino you want, all day long."

"Yes, ma'am." The three of us sidestepped a couple, the woman using a motorized scooter.

"Now if you're worried about not being able to do the work—" Kristen said.

"Oh no, ma'am. I want to do it, real bad, but—"

"Is it your health?" I asked. "That new medication—"

We'd reached the corner across from the Spice Shop, and he stopped. It was impossible to tell from his face whether he was worried about the program or about disappointing us.

"Been a long time since I've spent the day inside. And I'd miss"—he waved a hand—"all this."

From where we stood, I could see half a dozen takeout spots and smell a dozen more. Then there were the butchers and bakers and specialty grocers who open every morning by rolling up giant aluminum doors or pushing collapsible gates aside. Not to mention the food trucks and street vendors that dot the city much of the year, places of business not marked by four walls.

"Then you, my friend, have identified your first job requirement. That gives you a leg up."

"Make that two job requirements," Kristen said. "Fresh air and fresh coffee."

Hot Dog's laugh rumbled up from the soles of his faded black Converse sneakers, a caffeinated burst that enveloped us all. After we'd stopped howling, and he'd promised to fill out an application the next day, Kristen and I headed for the shop.

"I'm gonna run down to the PDA," I said at our door. The Public Development Authority, our landlord. "See if they'll tell me when Bonnie applied for a permit and when she started selling here."

"Pepper." Kristen grabbed my arm, her face serious. "Thank you for being a nosy, pushy, naggy little you-know-what. I hated feeling a wall between us. I don't ever want to not be best friends with you."

We hugged, and as I wove my way down the cobbled street, my throat felt full and the day looked a little brighter.

"He drove out to Carnation to see a flower grower," the Market Master's assistant told me five minutes later. "I'm not sure I can give you vendor information. Since she's—dead."

Exactly. She's dead—what difference does it make to you? "Could you call him? Since I'm here?"

"If he's in the car or with a potential vendor, he won't answer," she warned. "You know what a stickler he is about the rules."

Sure enough, no answer. The assistant left a message, and I left irritated. Didn't help that the busker plying the customers near Rachel the Pig, at the Market's main entrance, was an elderly man playing a Chinese instrument that Ben—a font of arcane musical knowledge—had called an *urhu*. A small barrel-shaped body with a stringed neck, played with a bow, its sound was both haunting and irritating, depending on my mood.

Two feet inside the Spice Shop, my irritation turned to puzzlement. To perplexion, if that's a word—or even if it isn't. Hands clasped behind her back, Detective Spencer studied the wall map, pins marking the origins of our spices. (The map also hides a crack in the plaster that no amount of spackle or paint had covered. I am a practical decorator.)

And in the nook, Detective Tracy studied his phone.

"You never read my texts," Sandra muttered between clenched teeth.

Guilty.

"What happened?" Spencer missed nothing. "Are you limping? Your elbow's all scraped."

I'd changed my torn pants earlier, but after all the

running around, my bruised knee had begun to act up. I should have changed into my lucky pink shoes. "Nothing. Not watching where I was going."

Spencer scowled.

"We actually came to speak with Mrs. Gardiner," Detective Tracy said. "But she insisted on waiting for you."

Kristen had taken refuge behind the front counter, arms crossed.

"Ready if you are," I said.

The nook got mighty tight mighty quick, and not from the head count. Unspoken tensions and unanswered questions take up a lot of room.

Spencer spoke first. "We're grateful to you for finding Ms. Clay's van."

"Ms. Clay. Ms. Manning." I snorted. "Or whoever the heck she was. Why was she using my mother's name?" My sympathy for Bonnie-Peggy dwindled as I saw the ripple effect of her actions.

"Without you, we might not have found her van for weeks, until someone in the neighborhood got suspicious."

"Or tired of seeing it never move," I said.

"And we would never have found this." The detective drew a plastic evidence bag out of her pocket and set it on the butcher-block work top.

Nothing in the tales of Brother Cadfael and Sister Frevisse, or in *The Complete Idiot's Guide to Private Investigating*, prepared me for the sight of the Strasburg family jewels.

Kristen spoke first, in disbelief. "She stole the bracelet in 1985. And then, last week, she stole it back."

"Looks that way," Spencer said. "We found it hidden in a rusty metal toolbox under the floorboards of her van."

Tracy opened a slim leather folder and pulled out the 1985 photo Detective Washington had shown me that morning. He placed Kristen's photo next to it on the table. Between it lay the diamond and sapphire MacGuffin, wrapped in plastic.

There was no question, no doubt. The lost had been found.

Kristen's hooded glance did not escape our detectives' notice.

"Care to share those thoughts?" Spencer said.

Kristen let out a noisy breath. "I thought Bonnie—Peggy, or whoever—was killed because someone wanted the bracelet. But now that we know she stole it—"

"Twice," Tracy interjected.

"The question is, who else wanted it? Who else knew about it?"

Brian Strasburg. Though I couldn't work out why he'd steal it. Or kill for it, thirty years later.

"Somehow, she was able to hide the bracelet in the basement of Grace House without being seen," I said.

"Place like that," Tracy said, "anybody could have wandered in and out."

No one ever seemed to get that our lives as kids had not been an undisciplined free-for-all. But he was right. In those simpler, trusting times, Grace House had rarely been locked. Peggy could easily have slipped in, hidden the bracelet, and vanished.

"What about Hannah Hart? Isn't it just as likely that the killer is someone from the present as the past? Hannah wanted Bonnie out of the studio and apartment. And Bonnie didn't want to leave."

"Too soon to close any doors," Tracy said. "But it would all be a lot easier if your mother would open up."

"Is that why you're here?" I leaned forward, hands on the table. "To guilt me to pressure her? To do what? You've interviewed her, more than once. She's told you all she knows."

Truth was, I didn't completely believe that. Why wasn't she clamoring to find the killer?

"No," Spencer said. "No guilt, no pressure. But time has a way of highlighting one's priorities. I hear your mother was a fierce advocate for justice. What's changed?"

Good question. I wished I knew the answer.

KRISTEN and I walked the detectives outside, then watched their unmarked car creep down the cobbled street. We made an odd pair, I knew, the fine-boned blonde and the spiky brunette, both dressed in black, arms crossed, faces guarded.

"They still think we know more about the 1985 incident than we're admitting," she said.

"All we have is conjecture. Theories aren't evidence, especially since we haven't actually got one that works."

Kristen scooped a discarded sample cup out of the gutter. "True. I always knew there had been an upheaval and that it involved Roger and Peggy. But the bracelet—that's a shocker. I wonder why she didn't take it with her."

"She intended to come back."

Terry Stinson had said Peggy finally understood they were no threat to each other. If Kristen remembered right who was involved in all the discussions, then he had known about Peggy's role in the Strasburg incident. So had my mother. Neither had known she survived.

Why did Peggy no longer fear him? What had changed?

"My dad wouldn't be any help," Kristen said. "He stayed out of it. When tempers flared, he took the dog for a walk."

"And all my dad knows is what my mother told him." Not that Detective Tracy believed our dads' absence anything but a convenient coincidence.

Now there was a man who didn't trust the Universe.

"Do you work here?" a thin woman in a sleeveless red

blouse asked. "Where's the best place for a late lunch? With a view?"

"And a bar," her husband added.

"The deck at the Pink Door," I said at the same moment as Kristen said "outside at Maximilien." I slipped an arm around her waist. We were back in sync, but that didn't mean we agreed on everything.

Kristen took off early to pick up the girls for a special last-day-of-school outing. The boxes of books she'd been unpacking when first I, then the detectives, had interrupted her blocked one narrow aisle.

Never the same day twice, in retail.

"Oh, good. We've been waiting for this one." I shelved two copies of *World Spice at Home*, featuring new flavors for classic dishes, then stacked the rest amid a display of spice blends. Maybe Laurel and I should write our own cookbook.

I slit open the next box and reconsidered my working theories about Bonnie's murder and the no-longer-missing bracelet. She had seized the opportunity, in Kristen's bedroom, to take the bracelet, but she had not dared leave it in her own apartment or studio.

She'd been afraid of someone connected to that bracelet.

But her apartment and studio had been undisturbed. The killer wasn't prowling for jewels.

The killer wasn't the person Bonnie had feared.

That gave me two mysteries to solve. And it put the elusive Hannah back on top of the list of suspects.

I made room for two of my favorite food memoirs— *Home Cooking: A Writer in the Kitchen*, by the late novelist Laurie Colwin, and *The Art of Eating*, by M. F. K. Fisher, which had the added advantage of being thick enough to crush a garlic clove. As I shuffled books, I decided Brian

Strasburg warranted a closer look. He had a powerful motive for wanting to know who else to blame for his father's murder. And if the bracelet had sentimental value—the insurance company would have paid its dollar value ages ago—he might have wanted it back, too.

I flattened an empty box—always satisfying—and slit open the next one. Had his mother kept a scrapbook of ancient clippings, like mine had? Had he asked Callie to do any unusual research recently, to use the people-finder databases that professional investigators—and lawyers— sometimes use to track down missing heirs and witnesses?

If Strasburg had found Bonnie, née Peggy, I had to believe he'd have told Detective Washington. He would not have gone rogue.

Hold on, Pepper. That day he'd come to the Market, in early May, he and his son had been searching for a Mother's Day gift for his ex-wife. They'd chosen a gift box—our Middle Eastern spice blends, if I remembered right. We'd chatted a bit. The boy had been polite and curious, our spice tea too strong for him.

If they had wandered through the craft stalls, they might have seen Bonnie-Peggy. Though whether either lawyer or potter would have recognized the other, I had no idea.

Wait. He'd been ten. He'd seen his father killed. Had he seen her?

He would not have forgotten those eyes.

I shivered and shelved a new foodie mystery by an author who wrote under both her own name, Daryl Wood Gerber, and a pen name, Avery Aames. What if Peggy Manning was itself a made-up name? Ever since its founding, folks had flocked to Seattle to escape the strictures of life elsewhere. No doubt more than a few had left their names behind, alongside their histories.

In mainstream culture, no one changes her name over and over without a darned good reason—like fear of being found. Of course, few people who'd circled through Grace House back then swam in the mainstream.

My frustration with the late Bonnie Clay turned darker, bitter. She'd been on the run. She'd come back to the place where it started. She'd been keeping an eye on me.

Why, why, why?

"Hey, boss. What about a hibiscus spice rub on ribs?" Cayenne's interruption brought me back to the present.

In the memoir section, I slid a copy of *Day of Honey* into the Cs, for Ciezadlo, and leaned against the shelves. "Sounds delish. Go for it. Hey, I saw your grandfather this morning. He's so proud of you."

"I was hoping the police would have good news. He's so stubborn. He and Grandmama bought that house when they moved here in 1950, and he insists he's going to die in his own home."

"Anybody tried to hurt him, he'd smack 'em with his three-iron. Why does he use a golf club instead of a cane?"

"He wanted to play, but most courses in Louisiana were whites-only back then. Black men could caddy, and he did. One of the members gave him that club—an old one of his, I suppose—and Pops hung on to it."

"Did he ever pick up the game? When they moved out here—"

"He was busy, working at Boeing, raising kids. Raising a garden. Pepper, do you think he's in danger? If Bonnie was killed by a gang or a burglar—he's up all hours of the night. But he's harmless. Just a neighborhood busybody."

Neighborhood busybodies. Me and Louis Adams.

Home. Was that why Bonnie had wanted to return to Seattle? To die in the city where she, a wandering soul, had most belonged?

Truth was, Mr. Adams had seen something, right out that window and through the opening in the hedge. Nothing useful—an unidentified car speeding away. But the killer might not know that. The killer might think the old man a threat.

"Don't worry about him," I said. "The police have pretty much ruled out a neighborhood criminal."

Truth was, I didn't have a clue. And until the killer was caught, we might all be in danger.

Twenty-four

Every 3.5 seconds, someone in America loses a cell phone—usually in a coffee shop. So, it makes sense that Seattle, first in the country for number of coffee shops, also ranks high for lost cell phones.

—NW Lawyer, the Washington State Bar Association blog

WHERE HAD SHE BEEN, ALL THOSE YEARS? THAT WAS THE question dogging me as Arf and I closed up the shop.

And another: What had Detective Washington told Brian Strasburg about the cold case and other suspects, besides the late and apparently not-much-lamented Roger Russell? You'd never think a grieving family member would take the info police gave him, to keep him informed, to keep him satisfied that they were doing their job, and use it for vigilante justice.

The average person wouldn't think that. A cold case detective, on the other hand . . .

I dropped Arf at the loft and took off.

And spotted my target just in time. The big man crossed Cherry, an after-work pick-me-up from Starbucks in one hand, a battered brown leather briefcase in the other, and started up the hill.

"*Come on, light.*" Not smart to tempt fate by jaywalking in front of police headquarters. Red became green, and I sprinted across Fifth.

"Detective," I called.

Washington stopped and turned toward me. "Ms. Reece. I'd say it's a pleasure, but I suspect I should reserve judgment on that."

"Working overtime on a cold case. Must mean you got a break." I paused to catch my breath. This block of Cherry might be flatter than the lower stretches, but that didn't say much, in this city of hills. "Did your office keep tabs on Bonnie Clay? Or Peggy Manning, or whoever she was?"

"Why would we do that, and why does it matter so much that you came all the way down here to ask me?"

"I want to know if she's been hiding behind my mother's name all these years. And I imagine you wanted to quiz her about the Strasburg incident. To find out if she knew who else was there, the night of the murder." *To get her to admit she was the one who got away.*

Washington set his briefcase on the sidewalk. "My office, as you generously put it, is me. Certainly we did quiz Mr. Russell's large circle of friends and associates. The detectives worked long, hard hours tracking down everyone they could, but mouths were pretty tight. And cold cases don't get the attention you might think from watching TV and reading books."

A dark sedan emerged from the police parking garage, and the driver rolled down the window, sizing up the situation. Washington raised a hand in an "it's okay" gesture, and the car turned up Cherry.

I folded my arms, feet wide. "You kept your suspicions about another person out of the news. Makes sense. But if you thought Roger Russell acted alone, you'd have closed the case way back when. So when you couldn't crack anyone at Grace House—and I know you tried—you concluded that the other person had disappeared." *You*—and I meant it in the generic sense, his bosses and predecessors—*had pushed my mother and her friends. You drove a wedge into the community that broke it apart.*

He peeled the lid off his coffee and blew on it, his gaze never leaving my face. "Certainly we wondered. Disappearing was easier back then. And once the trail grew cold, the resources got pretty slim."

"But if someone else had the resources . . ."

"What are you saying, Ms. Reece?" His tone got a notch gruffer and a hair demanding.

"Two things. The bracelet proves someone else was there. And you have an eyewitness. He was only ten, and he didn't know what he'd seen, let alone who." I stepped back to let a passerby through. "You never met Bonnie Clay, Detective. But no one who did, no matter what name she was using, ever forgot her eyes."

He said nothing.

"You knew she'd been close to Roger Russell. If there was a third person, who more likely than Peggy? And she'd gone missing. Then, thirty years later, Brian Strasburg is all grown up. He's raging and vengeful, and he has the money and the ability to track her down. Funny thing is, after all that effort, he ran into her right here in the Emerald City. Because, it turns out, there really is no place like home."

The detective's jaw rose slightly. I'd hit the mark. Brian Strasburg *had* seen Bonnie—Peggy Manning. He *had* seen those eyes. Sympathy pains for the boy whose family had been destroyed warred with my anger over what he might have done.

"We had no evidence directly linking her to the Strasburg tragedy. Not until today." He pulled keys from his jacket pocket, then picked up his briefcase and started down the ramp into the parking garage.

I trotted after him. "You can convict on circumstantial evidence." Not for nothing had I been a cop's wife and a veteran law firm staffer.

"We didn't even have that. She was a person of interest, nothing more."

"But her return to Seattle after all these years must have made her more interesting. Especially to Brian Strasburg."

He clicked his key chain, and a tan Camry blinked its lights. "To all of us. For years, Strasburg called me every three months. One day a month or two ago, I realized I hadn't heard from him in ages. So I called him." He slowed his steps and sipped his coffee. "That's when he told me he'd seen her selling pottery in the Market. He said seeing her changed everything. He realized his therapist was right: His obsession with his father's murder was killing him. His mother had died, and it was time to let it go."

"And you believed him?"

"I did. I do. But my job is to not let it go. I strolled through the Market, saw her myself. Tasked the patrol officers, including your ex, with keeping an eye on her."

Tag knew?

I swallowed that sharp surprise. "Not close enough, apparently, or she wouldn't be dead. So let me get this straight. Through a combination of therapy and a chance sighting, Brian Strasburg claims a change of heart and you let him off the hook?" Washington opened the back door and set his briefcase on the floor behind the driver's seat. "Maybe he stopped calling because he didn't need you anymore. He'd found her. He could get revenge on his own."

The detective opened the driver's door and took another sip of coffee. "And you wonder why I haven't been sleeping."

"Wait." I grabbed the edge of his door. "You went to the Market. You saw her. You bought a piece of her pottery, didn't you, for the fingerprints?"

His eyebrows rose. He slid into the car and reached for the door handle. "Detective Spencer is right. You have great instincts. But I wish you'd stay out of my case."

I let go of the door and stepped back, watching as he started the Camry and drove away.

I can't stay out of it. I'm too deep in it.

AH, home. Shoes off, I headed for the kitchen. Punched on the oven, put the butcher's gift in the fridge, and gave my ever-patient dog the bone. Changed my clothes and cued up my sit-stay-think-cook-pout playlist—Ani DiFranco, Emily Elbert, Madeleine Peyroux. And Brett Dennen, so I could dance while pouting. The oven beeped, and I popped in a pan of ziti with mushrooms and zucchini—a Ripe takeout special—and got out the big mixing bowl.

The first batch of gingersnaps was ready to go in when the ziti finished baking. I poured a glass of Chianti, and put my feet up.

As investigations go, this one was about as thick as cookie dough. Only two suspects had surfaced, and neither fully solved the mystery.

What was I missing?

Washington as much as admitted that Strasburg's connection to the old case made him a suspect in the current one. He claimed an alibi, but killers always do, don't they? I'd let Spencer and Tracy run that one down—they had those "resources."

If Callie were in town, I might be able to weasel a tidbit or two out of her. But over the phone or by text? No way. She would not disclose a boss's private project unless she were convinced it was absolutely necessary to avoid an injustice. Even for an old boss.

And while lawyers often rely on their assistants for research, I suspected that finding Peggy Manning would have been too important to delegate. The satisfaction would lie in the hunt, in knowing he was doing everything he could to track down everyone involved in his father's murder. That old wound, that old grudge, might have driven him to his profession in the first place. Tag had briefly worked with a woman bent on pursuing the man she believed had killed her sister. Too focused on the one crime, too bereft to serve and protect anyone else, she'd been unable to crack the case. She'd left the force after a few years, destroyed by grief and failure.

One more victim of the crime.

I could not see the hard-driving, hard-edged, hard-nosed Brian Strasburg as anyone's victim. But those hard shells, those tough crusts people put on can hide some awfully tender spots.

"What do you think, boy?" I stroked Arf's back. He needed a good commercial cleaning, and I made a mental note to call the groomer.

Why had Bonnie-Peggy taken the bracelet, that summer night so long ago? An impulse grab, or a means to finance other protests?

But this bracelet had not been sold. It had been stashed away and left behind.

The intercom interrupted my musings.

"Delivery, for Ms. Pepper Reece."

I buzzed Tag in and grabbed my phone. Sure enough, the first text I'd ignored had said he had a belated birthday gift from his mother. The second message said he'd swing by tonight.

Be nice, Pepper.

Minutes later, he set a large, bulky shape wrapped in a red-and-white checked picnic cloth on my dining room table. His mother's decorating style runs Danish modern with a hint of Frank Lloyd Wright, where mine tends toward midcentury Middle America, but Phyllis has a talent for finding the right gift.

"Happy Birthday. Sorry we're late." Arf padded over to join the fun, and Tag's fingers went automatically to the terrier's floppy ears. "Open it."

I untied the tablecloth to reveal a vintage picnic basket of woven maple. Inside the hinged lid, elastic bands held silverware, the plastic handles the same sunny yellow as the four plastic plates and cups stacked beside a red-and-yellow plaid thermos. The red-and-white gingham napkins looked new. The bottle of champagne was cold—Tag's contribution.

My thumb and forefinger pinched the skin of my throat, as if to loosen the emotions swelling there. "It's perfect. Tell her it's perfect. Dinner?"

I poured him a glass of Chianti. We put salad and ziti on the picnic plates and climbed out the window.

But the gift hadn't wiped away all my irritation. "I hear you've been on spy duty."

"Well, that's part of my job." He speared a cherry tomato with his yellow-handled fork. "Got anything particular in mind?"

"John Washington told me he asked you to keep an eye on Bonnie Clay."

"He wanted to know her routine, whether we saw anything unusual."

"Did he want you to find out whether she was in touch with me or Kristen?"

"Wha-a-at?" His eyebrows dipped, and his mouth hung open. "No. Detectives ask us to do stuff all the time. They don't bother telling us why. I didn't even know you knew her."

"Me, neither. Not until—" The oven timer went off, and I pushed back my willow green bistro chair and squeezed past him. The pungent scent of my secret ingredient made my mouth water. I slid in the second tray, reset the timer, and stepped back outside.

"Okay, so you brought your mother's gift, and that was sweet, but you're here about the murder, right?"

"Pepper." He reached over and grabbed my wrist. Not hard, but it was enough to stop me. To catch my attention.

I wrested my hand free, but he'd scooted his chair close to mine, trapping me on my own veranda. No choice but to stay and face the music.

At the moment the only music I could hear was an old Foreigner tune streaming out Glenn's open window, drowning out every sound except the blood pulsing in my brain.

"You want me to back off and leave the investigating to the professionals. Well, let me remind you, Mr. I-never-made-detective-and-it-still-pisses-me-off. I'm a pretty darned good investigator. I found two killers before Spencer and Tracy did, and uncovered a trail of identity theft and fraud that might never have surfaced if not for me. And before you go off on your rant about putting myself in danger, remember I managed to get myself out of danger just fine." With a sprained ankle and a few scrapes, and help from a dog. I ignored my stiff knee and resisted the urge to rub my skinned elbow. "Besides, if they think my mother had anything to do with Bonnie's death or what happened in 1985—"

"Pepper." He leaned forward. "I'm not telling you to stay out of this because I don't trust you. I'm not—"

"Everything okay out there, Pepperonella?" The music had stopped, and Glenn's voice filled the silence, an innocent question warning anyone who might be threatening me.

"All good, Glenn," I called out. "Thanks."

When I turned back to Tag, his lips had curved down, and his sky blue eyes had lost their verve, but not their look of concern.

"Pepper, this isn't about being smart or strong or brave.

You're all those things, and nobody knows it better than I do. You watch out for people. You fight for people." His breath had steadied. "I—"

Ohhhmygod. I did not want to hear this. Arguing with Tag was no fun, but if the alternative was hearing him declare his love and devotion and guilt and regret one more time . . . "Tag, don't—"

He held up a hand. "But if you uncover something that incriminates someone you love, can you live with that? Can you—what's that beeping?"

"The oven!" I jumped up and wriggled past him, then hopped inside. How long had it been screaming at me while I'd been caught up in drama? I grabbed a pot holder and the oven door, and slid out the baking sheet. Miraculously, I detected no telltale odor of scorched sugar or burnt molasses.

The cookies looked exactly as they should.

Thank goodness something did.

I grabbed a spatula and slid them onto a cooling rack. Wondered what Tag had meant about evidence incriminating someone I loved.

My mother? Kristen?

Ridiculous.

Another buzz sounded. I glanced at the oven, frowning, sure I'd turned it off. A second buzz, short and irritated. "Who's here now?" I said as Tag stepped through the window, our empty plates in hand.

Though the intercom distorted the voice, I could tell Tag recognized it, too. I bit my lip and pushed the button to open the door.

Who needs bad luck, when you have a mother?

Twenty-five

They say that timing's everything,
In stocks and crops and love.
They say that it's what matters most,
When push comes right down to shove.

—Don Beans, "Timing"

"YOU COULDN'T CALL?" I LOOKED PAST MY BROTHER TO my mother, who was now hugging Tag.

"She didn't give me time," Carl said, matching my low, exasperated tone as he set my mother's big black suitcase inside the door. "Besides, would you have answered?"

"Point taken. Sorry. What's this about?" I watched my mother step out the window to sniff the herbs and flowers. In the kitchen, Tag poured her a glass of wine.

"Plumber called. He's starting our job on Monday, so I need to pull the tub and toilet, patch the subfloor, and who knows what else."

"You know plumbers never start jobs on Monday. They start on Friday, so they can leave you all weekend with one toilet for the whole family. It's required. It's part of the building code."

"We've been waiting for months. If I put him off until

Mom's gone, Andrea will have my head on a platter. Mom said no woman should ever have to share her bathroom with her mother-in-law, and she'd come stay with you."

And she'd insist on sleeping on the futon, refusing to let me give up the bedroom. That, and the grandkids, were why she'd stayed with Carl in the first place.

"No. Why's she really here?" I recognize an ulterior motive when I smell one.

"Beats me, Sis. I never can figure her out." He sniffed. "Are those cookies?"

"Gingersnaps," I said, and he groaned. "I'll put on coffee."

"Ooh, I'd love a cup," Tag said.

I clenched my teeth and pointed to the door.

"Let him stay." Mom set three red tomatoes on the counter. "Pick these as soon as they ripen, or they get mealy. Maybe he can help us solve our predicament."

"He's a cop. And you're a witness." To what, I wasn't sure. An invisible ice pick stabbed my jaw, and I winced. I reached for the coffeemaker.

"Five minutes of meditation every morning, Pepper, and that jaw pain will never bother you again."

It's a basic principle of conflict resolution that telling someone to relax or calm down only jacks up the tension. My mother's words had the same effect. But before I could respond, Tag's hand warmed the small of my back, and he set a full glass of wine in front of me.

He knows me too well. "What you said outside," I whispered. "About fighting for people. Thanks. And thanks for staying."

I lowered the volume on my mood music, and we sat in the living room. My mother asked after Tag's parents and brothers. The rich aromas of the Costa Rican beans she'd brought almost tempted me away from the earthy, fruity wine, but not quite.

"Tag," she said, "tell me why those detectives think my

friendship with Peggy Manning—or Bonnie Clay—has anything to do with her murder."

Arf lay on the floor next to Tag. He'd always said no to a dog, pleading shift work, but whenever he came by the shop or loft, it was clear that they'd bonded. "Actually, Lena, Pepper knows way more about all this than I do."

I shot him a dirty look, but he was picking a crumb off the upholstery and feeding it to my dog.

"The police found the stolen bracelet this morning." I described spotting Bonnie's van while searching for a parking place. Tag's eyes darted between my mother and me, and I thought I saw him struggle between being a cop or a member of the family. Divorce doesn't always end relationships; sometimes it only complicates them.

Carl leaned forward, arms folded, elbows on his knees, coffee and cookies forgotten. "What took them so long to find her van?"

"Oh." Realization struck, and I sat up. "I'd assumed she'd had to park that far away, like I did, but that late on a Friday night, all the businesses on her block would have been closed. The street should have been half empty. She hid the van on purpose, so whoever—whomever—she was afraid of wouldn't find it."

"She was afraid someone would link her to the past, right?" Carl asked. "And kill her for it. But why?"

Underneath her year-round tan, my mother had gone pale as any Pacific Northwesterner in winter.

"Mom, the van was registered in New Mexico. In your name."

My brother doesn't much resemble my mother, but at the moment, their faces were twin pictures of horror.

The only sound in the room was Arf padding across the floor, returning to his bed and bone.

"I—have never—been—to New Mexico. That is not my van."

"I know that, Mom, and I think the police do, too. It was clearly hers. What we don't know yet is whether she'd been using your name for other purposes, or just for the vehicle registration." After fortifying myself with a long sip of wine, I told them what I'd learned about the twice-stolen bracelet's link to the incident in 1985. About the deaths of Walter Strasburg and Roger Russell. About the ten-year-old who'd watched his father die, and the detectives' belief, because of the missing bracelet, that another person had been present.

"That's why you thought she was dead, isn't it? That day in the Market, when we took the salt pigs and cellars back to the potter, and you recognized her. The police never mentioned that missing bracelet, so you didn't know the police suspected she had survived."

After a long silence, my mother stood and went to the kitchen, returning with the wine bottle. She refilled our glasses and sat back in the corner of my couch, her bare feet tucked beneath her on the golden brown chenille.

We'd waited thirty years. Another thirty seconds wouldn't hurt.

"After all this time," she finally said. "She called herself Peggy Manning when she moved in, sophomore year. Three girls in a funky one-bedroom apartment on the Ave, an old yellow brick building. It's still there."

University Way, always called "the Ave."

"I can't honestly remember—and believe me, I've asked myself—whether she said she was a student or we made that assumption. You wouldn't guess, seeing her now, but all the men in our crowd were crazy about her. Not your father—we met later. She had a waifish appeal, thin and blond. Like Twiggy, the model. Not to mention those eyes."

I could picture that Peggy in the photo from the pantry opening fifteen years later, still attractive, though no longer young and fresh. Harder to see her in the Bonnie I'd met last week.

"She kept them all at a distance," my mother continued. "Except Roger and Terry."

"Terry we know." Carl plucked two cookies off the plate, his diet temporarily free from Andrea's scrutiny. "Seriously good cookies, Sis. But who was Roger? You mentioned him the other night, but I can't place him."

"Roger Russell. Short, dark haired, bearded. Intense. Adjunct faculty at U Dub, in the poli-sci department," I said, courtesy of the brief dossier Ben had sent this afternoon, and which I'd barely had time to skim.

"That's right." My mother sounded surprised at what I knew. "He was a serious rabble-rouser, constantly challenging the administration. He led the campaign to divest the university from military spending and other investments. Of course, he wasn't alone, and some of the older faculty joined in, but he became the public face of dissent."

Ben had dug up a history of the antiwar movement in Seattle, written by an ex–journalism student. Roger Russell was all over it. "He was older than the rest of you."

"A few years." My mother sipped her wine. "Peggy never got any phone calls or mail. She had no friends outside the movement. One night, she took a shower and left her bag in the living room. A hobo bag made from upholstery samples, all the rage, and I rummaged through it. I suppose I shouldn't have, but she was so darned secretive. She had three driver's licenses, in three different names."

"So the name changes were a pattern," I said.

"Was she an informer? Hoover and the FBI claimed they had spies in the SDL and Weather Underground all over the country," Tag said.

"SDL?" Carl asked at the same time as I said, "What do you know about that?"

"I read," Tag said, with a touch of indignance. "I'm not just a pretty face."

Jen at the Mystery Bookshop says men read more

nonfiction than women, and Tag had shelves full of books on history. Last winter over dinner, he'd raved about a book on the famous U Dub rowing team that won Olympic gold in Germany in 1936. I'd never heard him talk about the Vietnam War, but he could have read an entire encyclopedia since our divorce. If encyclopedias still existed.

One more pair of opposites that we personify.

"Student Democratic League," my mother said. "We all belonged at first, until it got too crazy. So we did wonder about a plant. But they both seemed to be the real deal. They stuck around after the major protests in Seattle ended. Roger got kicked off the faculty—"

"No shock there," Carl said. He gestured with his cell phone and ducked into my bedroom to call his wife.

I took a moment to refill the cookie plate and hoped Arf's bladder held.

"So, back to Roger," I prompted when we were all back in place. "Oh, and what about Terry?"

My mother reached for a cookie. "We called them the Unholy Trinity. At first, Roger and Peggy were an item, then they became a threesome. I don't mean anything kinky—"

"The '60s have their reputation for a reason," Carl said, earning a motherly glare in return.

"People in the neighborhood called us a commune, said the adults all slept around and the kids ran wild, but that was before they got to know us. You two know"—she looked from me to Carl—"there was no hanky-panky, and plenty of parental discipline. We were two families who shared a house and a philosophy, and tried always to live consciously and consistently. But some of our friends . . ." She let the words trail off.

"Roger would blow up," she continued, "and Peggy would seek refuge with Terry. But it never lasted. Some couples seem to thrive on that sort of intensity, mistaking it for love."

That had not been Tag's and my pattern, but I knew what

she meant. Ben had confessed to an emotional roller-coaster ride in his last relationship. And Josh had described a text-book case with Hannah.

Arf snored softly in his bed, but my own patience was running thin. "Fast forward to 1985, Mom."

She sighed and twirled her nearly empty wineglass. I threw Carl a meaningful look, and he went to the kitchen to open another bottle. She and I weren't driving anywhere tonight.

"Peggy helped out in the day care. When she started learning pottery, she had everyone in the house working clay. Do you remember making those little animals?"

I slid to the floor and rooted around in the wicker trunk for the shoe boxes I'd seen last Sunday. Blew the dust off the one bearing my initials and lifted the lid.

Inside lay a lumpy ladybug, recognizable mainly by the black spots on her red back, and an exquisite emerald green turtle. I didn't have to turn over the ladybug to know I'd find a childish PR carved on the belly. But the turtle . . .

On the bottom of one foot was a pair of neatly carved diamonds. Bonnie's mark. And Peggy's, too—one identifier that hadn't changed. I cradled the gem-like memento, finally knowing where the memories had come from.

"Roger was chief gleaner. He and your father convinced the grocery stores on Capitol Hill and in the U District to donate produce and baked goods to the Pantry. Your dad taught all day, so Roger made most of the pickups. He also got restaurants and caterers on board. I'll never forget the day we got twelve dozen deviled eggs from a canceled wedding. The clients thought they'd gone to heaven."

The clients were the men, women, and children we'd fed. "I remember that. We had half days the last week of school, and I was helping out. Was that 1985?"

She bit her lower lip. "After the—*incident*, they traced the van to Grace House. That was the first inkling we had that Roger still believed in bringing the war home."

"A Weather Underground slogan," Tag said.

"We'd all protested the nuclear buildup. We supported Bishop Hunthausen's stance against the nuclear subs in Puget Sound. We stood on street corners with signs and petitions. We wrote letters and organized boycotts. And we kept on teaching children, and advocating for the homeless, and feeding the hungry." She paused, sipping, reflecting.

"So what happened while we were in St. Louis?" Carl said.

"Ellen called—the police were at the house. The shooting and explosion were all over the news. Roger was dead—they found his body. The community van was found abandoned near the Strasburgs' home, in an exclusive neighborhood. It was registered to Ellen and Greg." Kristen's parents. "No one kept tabs on it."

"But Roger was doing more than picking up overripe bananas and day-old maple bars," Carl said.

"He'd been scoping the neighborhood for days, weeks, figuring out the Strasburgs' schedule. Neighbors had seen him, but they saw our logo on the van so they trusted him. That may have been the worst betrayal—hiding behind a program that fed hungry kids, and all the while, he was plotting violence."

"What if he didn't mean it to turn violent?" I said. "He broke in while the house was empty. He attacked the computers Walter Strasburg used to create code for the nuclear subs. Not that the vandalism wasn't criminal, but he didn't plan on attacking the family."

"He had a gun and explosives," my mother said flatly. "And when the family surprised him, he shot the father in front of his son. Yes, Walter Strasburg got out his own gun, and yes, that was wrong. But Roger created the danger. He was responsible for everything that happened after that."

"What triggered the explosion?" Carl asked.

"According to Detective Washington," I said, "a simple device anyone could have made, with the right materials."

"No one in our group ever got involved with bombings," my mother said. "We eschewed violence. We had no reason to think Roger had explosives." She raised her glass, but her hand shook badly and she set the glass on the crate.

"A few months before the shooting, Greg Hoffman—Kristen's father—" she said to Tag, "cleaned out the garage behind the house. It was ancient and half falling down—it hadn't housed a car since the days of the Model A." She reached out a hand and wiggled her fingers. I found a clean tissue and laid it in her palm. "He found . . . We assumed it was left over from when old Mr. Hoffman set off fireworks displays for the neighborhood."

"Mom, what did they find?"

"Blasting caps. Detonator cords. Everything you need to make a starburst in the sky."

"Either he didn't find it all, or Roger had a secret stash," I said, my voice shaking. "And he used it at the Strasburg house."

"So that's why you flew home, and we stayed," Carl said. "I remember Dad called you a lot, and Grandpa got all riled up about the phone bill, even after Dad said he was good for it."

I might bemoan the cost of my cell package, but I didn't miss the days of overpriced long distance. But I knew Grandpa's heart. His irritation over the phone bill was a cover-up for his worries about his family.

"Tension gripped all of us," my mother said. She untucked her legs and propped her feet on the coffee crate. "The police made noises about shutting down the clinic and the pantry. It was a pressure tactic, and it scared us, but the truth was, none of us had known what they were up to. We couldn't believe that two of our own were involved. We were so angry, we couldn't mourn the deaths properly. And that poor family . . ."

Tag had been quiet during Mom's revelations. "Lena, any idea why Peggy took the bracelet, then left it behind?"

She frowned. "Peggy never showed any interest in

jewelry. Ellen had a diamond that had been her mother's reset in an engagement ring. A simple setting, but pretty. I remember all of us trying it on, except Peggy. She said diamonds were ostentatious. Symbols of greed and vanity, and exploitation in the mines. Tact was not among her gifts."

"What did Peggy want, Mom?" I said.

"What we all wanted, I thought. Peace, justice, a home, and friends. But every chance she got, she chose something else."

Choices. A cramp bit my side, and I massaged it. "Mom, last week at the Market, you went back to her stall. There was shouting. Everyone heard you."

"I could not believe she'd been alive all those years and never told us. Not a word. And then she just turns up again, as if nothing had happened."

"Who do you think killed her?"

My mother had always looked like she'd sipped from the fountain of youth. At the moment, the fountain had run dry. She answered my question. "I don't know."

Carl's pocket buzzed. He scanned the screen, sent a reply, and stood. "I gotta get the kids—school decorating party. Remember, Mom, school assembly tomorrow. I'll pick you up at noon."

"I'd better say good night, too." Tag stood and leaned down to kiss my mother's cheek. Then, sliding from former son-in-law back to the cop I'd almost forgotten he was, he added, "We'll do everything we can to catch her killer, Lena. I promise."

"I walk this dog alone every night. It's not even close to dark."

"You're not walking alone tonight." Arf peed in the storm grate—a habit I'd been unable to break—and we strolled on, Tag matching his stride to mine.

We walked the first block of Western in silence.

"Nobody thinks my mom killed Bonnie, do they? You heard her. Besides, she was home at Carl's, and how would she have known where to find the woman?" Carl did have a white SUV. And Mom did have the keys. And she could have taken Bonnie's business card with her studio address, like I had.

"When Washington heard that Peggy Manning—Bonnie Clay—was back and asked me to keep an eye on her, he hadn't yet refocused on the others in the community. Eventually, he realized I'm Chuck and Lena's son-in-law and officially put me out of the loop. Sorry."

His use of present tense caught my ear.

He went on. "But in cold cases, you go back and retrace all your steps. Reinterview the witnesses, reexamine the physical evidence. That means tracking down everyone who was part of that community. Your parents and Kristen's dad are the only ones left."

"From the house, yes. But there were others. Terry Stinson, Dave McNally and his wife, Tim McCarver and his ex. They were all at the party."

"So they all saw Bonnie," he said. "And the bracelet."

"Oh, she makes me so mad. My mom, I mean, but Bonnie, too. I thought I was investigating *for* them, but now I'm investigating *them*."

"How about them Mariners?" Tag said.

I laughed. "Don't you have to work at dark thirty? I haven't seen much of you lately. You seeing someone?"

Beside me, Tag stiffened. "I've been out a few times, but no one special."

Kristen always tells me not to get involved with Tag again, and I know she's right. But at times like tonight, when his presence was a help and a comfort, when we seemed to understand what hadn't been spoken, I wonder.

We rounded the corner and headed for Alaskan Way. He spoke quietly. "I've been too hard on you about Ben. About dating. I need to let you make your own choices."

I stumbled on a crack in the sidewalk, and Tag grabbed me before I fell. Arf glanced back at us, and for a brief moment, I thought that if Tag hadn't just mentioned Ben, he might have kissed me.

Ben might not be my Mr. Right.

But that didn't mean Tag was.

A group of thirtysomethings came out of a restaurant and swelled around us. "Good dog," one said, stopping to pet Arf, then sprinting after his friends.

"Your mom's a lot nicer to me now that we're divorced," he said. "She never liked me."

"That's not true. She never disliked you. She just didn't think we were a good match."

"Same thing," he said, "when it comes to your kids."

"Do you ever—" I stopped myself. No point asking if he ever regretted that we hadn't had kids. That by the time he was ready, something in me had said no.

"Yes," he said, in a tone that told me he'd read my mind.

The phone I'd slipped in my pocket buzzed. Since I'd actually bothered to bring it, I figured I'd better look.

And almost wished I hadn't.

Twenty-six

Love your enemies and pray for those who persecute you. . . . Because the Lord causes the sun to rise on the evil and the good, and the rain to fall on the just and the unjust.

—Matthew 5:44-45

A LIGHT RAIN FELL AS WE CAME OUT OF THE HARBOR-view ER a tick past midnight. Tag offered to bring his car around, but I didn't mind. After the shock of Cayenne's call and the hours of worry, the rain—not much more than a mist—had healing powers. I closed my eyes and raised my face, like a baby bird.

If it hadn't been for that cast-off three-iron, Mr. Adams might not have made it. But he'd given nearly as good as he got. Somewhere in the city, a hooligan—the ER doc's overly polite euphemism for a would-be killer—nursed a cracked shin, or worse.

"You have to work in three hours," I said. "You didn't have to stay."

"I called in. I'm taking second watch today."

Eleven thirty A.M. to eight P.M., much more reasonable hours. "Watch" for "shift" had an almost medieval sound that I found reassuring. It reminded me of Brother Cadfael, but I was too tired to wonder what the old monk would do.

I hadn't been surprised to see Spencer and Tracy arrive minutes after we did. A beating that sends an old man to the hospital is obviously going to summon the police, and some sort of cross-indexing would quickly flag the case for the dispatch supervisor, who would alert the detectives. They don't care for that attack-on-a-possible-witness thing.

Turned out that Cayenne had shortcut the system. After her mother had called to relay the news, Cayenne called me from the car while her husband raced to the hospital, then tracked down Detective Spencer herself. She didn't like that attack-on-a-witness thing, either.

Tag unlocked the black Saab, and I slid in. "I can't believe you're still driving this car. We bought it, what, fifteen years ago?"

He gave a halfhearted laugh. "Said by a woman who drives a car older than she is."

"The Mustang is a classic. Though if my parents move home, I'll have to give it back." I leaned against the headrest. "Thanks. You didn't have to take me up there, and you didn't have to stay."

He made a left on Madison and crossed the freeway. "Of course I stayed. I can't believe you said that."

"What happens next? With the investigation, I mean. All Mr. Adams saw the night of the murder was a car speeding away—at least, from what he told me."

"Someone thinks he saw more than that. They'll go over his statement with him. Put the bits and pieces of his recall tonight together with the Friday night incident and see if anything jumps out. He may remember more as time goes on, as the shock passes."

I bit my lip to keep from crying. "He was already so frail."

Tag reached across and squeezed my hand. He eased the Saab onto Western and stopped in front of my building.

No point telling him he didn't have to walk me up the stairs.

Inside the loft, my cheek warm from his lips, I set my tote gently on the bench beside the door and peeled off my shoes. In the glow of the light my mother had left on in the kitchen, I saw that she'd put away the pasta and cookies and washed the dishes.

On his bed by the window, Arf raised his head. I crouched beside him and whispered, "He's going to be okay." I buried my face in the terrier's thick black-and-tan fur and let him nuzzle me. "Tell me everything's going to be okay."

Minutes later, I climbed the iron staircase—barely more than a ladder—salvaged during the building's conversion and peeked into the mezzanine. "Meditation space," the builder had called the area above my bedroom, obviously on my mother's wavelength. She'd fallen asleep on the futon—it pulled out into a double bed, but she hadn't bothered. A paperback from my collection lay on the floor—Margaret Frazer's *The Traitor's Tale*.

Back in the kitchen, I poured a glass of a dry Washington Sauvignon Blanc that Laurel calls "loft white" because I drink so much of it. (Turnabout being fair play, she's got her own "houseboat red.") Sank into the paisley chair where Tag had sat hours ago, found on closeout at an import store.

We'd reached the hospital minutes after the family. In the ER waiting room, Cayenne had introduced her mother, a regal woman easy to picture controlling a rowdy classroom with the flick of an eyelash, and her father, the source of her height. I already knew Cayenne's husband and her sister, who'd seen the HIRING sign in our front window and sent her to me last spring.

"A concussion," Cayenne told us. "And a broken arm—a compound fracture. They're taking him to surgery as soon as an anesthesiologist is free."

With her and her mother as our escorts, Tag and I had been

allowed to visit Mr. Adams for a few minutes. He'd been ashen, in pain, but called me by name without prompting.

He'd heard a noise outside the back door and opened it to investigate.

"Did you turn a light on?" Tag asked.

"'Course I did. I'm a fool, but not that big a fool." Mr. Adams winced as he tried to sit up. His daughter's hand on his shoulder stopped that nonsense. "Yard's all fenced. I thought it musta been a stray dog, dug his way in, ripped up my shrubs. But then I saw him, the thug that hit me. I hit him back, I did."

"Did he say anything?" And to think I'd dismissed the thug theory of murder as an old man's delusions.

"He yowled up a storm when my three-iron hit his leg, I'll tell you that for nothing."

"What about before that, Pops?" Cayenne gripped the rail at the foot of the bed.

"'Keep your mouth shut, old man, if you know what's good for you.'"

"Shut about what?" Cayenne's mother asked.

Tag spoke quietly. "Did you get a decent look at him?"

"It happened so fast. White guy, short hair. Tattoos all down his arms." He tried to raise his left arm, but the IV tube got in the way. "Used to be a nice neighborhood, when we raised our kids there. Then a killing and this."

"Maybe it's time to think again about coming to live with us," his daughter had said. He did not protest. His eyelids fluttered shut, and I'd been about to suggest we go when Tag reached out and touched the old man's hand.

"Patrol officers are checking around your house, and they'll interview the neighbors. We'll do everything we can to make your neighborhood safe again."

Safe in my loft, I stared at the Viaduct, the lights racing past. The cool wine could not quench my guilt. Louis

Adams, patriarch, had been attacked because someone thought he'd seen something the night of Bonnie's murder.

But no one would have ever made that connection, if not for me. If they hadn't seen me chatting with him on the steps last Saturday. Or they'd seen me this morning, when I stopped to visit after finding Bonnie's van.

I'd led the attacker to him.

Maybe the police didn't need my insight, my knowledge of the people involved, my willingness to ask any questions that occurred to me, not bound by protocols or procedures or preconceived ideas.

Maybe I needed to spend more time in my shop. More time with customers, preventing Bridezilla repeats. More time building relationships with the food press, so I didn't have to bite my nails, worrying that one wrong word from Nancy Adolfo could destroy us.

More time calling on commercial accounts, so we could avoid situations like the one Sandra had reported at the staff meeting. If he wasn't important enough to get a call from the "boss lady," a chef had told her, then he saw no reason to give us his business.

Maybe I needed to focus on my sorry love life. All week, Ben had ignored me while he chased a story. But I'd been equally bad, more interested in what he dug up than in him. The feelings I still had for Tag had been enough to remind me of the feelings we'd once shared and make me long to feel that way again.

I didn't know what my mother saw in Ben's stars, but I knew what was in my heart.

I picked up the glass float the gillnetter had given me last Sunday at Fisherman's Terminal and cradled it in both hands. It had traveled a long way, caught for who knew how long in an abandoned net, then hauled to the surface. *In a ghost net,* the fisherman had said. *You never know what you'll find.*

Was I messing up what mattered most because I was too

busy pretending to be Nancy Drew or Dame Frevisse? My shop was suffering. My love life was plummeting. My relationship with my mother was in turmoil. My best friend had withheld the truth from me, for thirty years. My assistant manager was stressed beyond belief, and the employee I had such hopes for might never forgive me for what had happened to her grandfather.

It isn't quitting to realize you're in over your head.

I wanted to pace, to work out the problem on my feet, but not with a sleeping dog across the room and a sleeping mother upstairs.

As a kid, I'd thought that once you got to be twenty-five, you had your life all figured out and you lived it. Then I turned twenty-five and there went that illusion. So then I hit forty and it finally seemed, in the year or two after, after everything fell apart, that I had put my life back together the way it was supposed to be.

And now it was falling apart again.

If Laurel were here, she'd tell me I was churning, letting one negative thought spiral and drag me down.

But Laurel was home asleep, as I ought to be. I carried my wineglass to the kitchen.

Maybe the Universe needed to stop dragging me into these situations. Because I was not about to close my eyes and ears to the troubles around me. I'd been given a talent and a natural curiosity, and I had an obligation to follow through.

It wasn't just curiosity or nosiness, though I'll never believe those aren't good traits. Useful traits.

The success of a life depends on the choices we make.

And I was never going to choose to turn my back on people in need.

THE Wednesday night mist had left a Thursday morning shine on the world outside my loft. The Sound—what little

I could see of it—sparkled. Outside, water glistened where it had pooled on the mint leaves and in the cupped petals of my zinnias.

Inside, all was quiet. My mother and the dog were gone.

I tugged at my rat's nest of hair and took a shower. The moment I toweled off, the smell of coffee enveloped me. I pulled on a robe and checked my phone, then poured a cup and joined my mother on the veranda.

"How is Cayenne's grandfather?" she said.

"Surprisingly good." I took the empty bistro chair, the bright green of spring pea shoots. "She texted this morning to say the surgery to repair his broken arm went fine, but they're going to keep him a couple of days, to make sure that knock on his noggin isn't causing any internal bleeding."

"I thought I might fill in for her this morning, until Carl picks me up." She sipped her coffee, eyes averted.

"Sure. If there's time after you talk with the detectives."

She let out a long sigh. "Why is it we put off doing what we know we need to do? We only make it harder on ourselves, churning things over in our minds."

Churning. The same word I had used in my internal rant last night. I knew with the next sip of dark roast that I would call it quits with Ben today. Or whenever we managed to get together.

And in the sip after that, I realized how pissed I was at her. Not sure I trusted her to reveal all the gory details. "And I'm going with you, like it or not."

She reached out and gripped my hand. "I wouldn't have it any other way."

I texted Sandra to ask if she could come in early and open the shop. You can't hear grumbling in text messages—one of their advantages—but I knew that despite her stress over Mr. Right's condition, she'd do everything she could for me.

And as soon as this is over, I vowed, *I'm doing everything I can for her.*

*   *   *

"WE understand Mr. Adams is expected to make a full recovery," Detective Spencer said an hour later as we took seats around the small conference table. Behind her, Detective Washington closed the door. "He gave us a good description, and we're interviewing all the neighbors. But if you've got any leads, please, fill us in."

"Wish I did," I said. "Obviously someone thinks he saw something important. Or—"

"Or what?" Tracy looked his rumpled self, but I knew he'd been at the hospital or down on Beacon Hill much of the night. He'd earned the wrinkles in his jacket and the bags under his eyes.

"Or maybe someone saw him with me, someone who knows I've been investigating, and thinks he must have given me the critical details. But no one's come after me—"

Or had they?

They all stared.

"I was sure it was just an accident." I dug in my tote while telling them about the white SUV that had nearly struck me in Pioneer Square after I'd gone to meet Hannah Hart at the gallery. I held up the parking stub. "Eureka! Partial plate number, from a witness."

"White SUV," Tracy said, taking the ticket. "That narrows it down."

"It actually might," Spencer said. "The vehicle Mr. Adams saw hit the street sign was a white SUV. I'll see if CSU can get a paint sample." She picked up her cell and stepped to the corner of the room.

I wondered what Hannah drove.

"So many threads here," Tracy said, "I hardly know where to start. You do weave a tangled web, Ms. Reece."

My mother had insisted we bring a box of baby cinnamon

rolls. I pushed them closer to him. A combination peace offering and sabotage for his diet.

"Start by explaining how you tracked down the elusive Hannah Hart," Spencer said.

"Used the artists' grapevine." The cinnamon and sugar scent got to me, and I took a napkin and a roll from the box. "You remember my former employee Tory Finch. She has a friend who has a friend who knew—but Hannah blew us off."

Their faces told me they hadn't been able to catch up with her, either.

"In this business," Detective Washington said, his tone level, his gaze locked on my mother, "you learn fast that when people avoid you, it usually means they have something to hide."

"We told you everything we knew—the detectives on the case, I mean. It was long before any of you were on the force," my mother said.

"Not true, ma'am," Washington said. "I was a young patrol officer. I responded to the scene at the Strasburg home, and I assisted the detectives with their inquiries."

"It was a tragedy. And I have always regretted"—she took my hand and squeezed it, then focused on the big detective—"that we were not able to prevent it. That's the real reason the Grace House community fell apart. We did not know what Roger and Peggy were planning. We thought she'd been killed in the explosion. We—" She broke off, her cheekbones damp.

She told them what she'd told us last night, how the rest of the group had been kept in the dark. How angry they'd been at their friends for the murderous betrayal, for killing in the name of justice. "By that point, Roger and Peggy were on the periphery. He still worked in the Pantry, and she worked in the day care, but they rarely came to community dinners or meetings. I don't remember where they lived—"

"In a basement apartment in Ballard," Washington said.

"—or what other jobs they held. We broke up the household—Ellen and Greg, and Chuck and I—not because of any disagreement between the four of us, but because we realized it had become a lie. We started with good intentions, and I think we truly did share the same values and philosophy. But over time, we grew apart. We lost focus. Too many people came and went, working on a pet project for a few months, but never committing. We weren't a community anymore."

"Ms. Manning never contacted you? None of you ever suspected she'd survived?" Washington pressed harder.

"I can only speak for Chuck—my husband—and me. We had no idea. But I don't believe the others knew, either."

"And yet, apparently, she snuck back into the house and hid the bracelet," Tracy said. "Before she took off for parts unknown."

Mom's chair squeaked as she rocked, her lips tight. "I never had any reason to tell anyone this until last night, when I told my children." She told them about the driver's licenses and the explosives, the anger and suspicion. It was a long story, and an emotional one, but she powered through, determined to end the lies and the secrets.

You could have heard a pin drop.

She gripped the arms of her chair and sat up straight. "What else did she do in my name? Who else did she harm?"

So much for trusting the Universe.

Detective Washington set his coffee on the table and broke the silence. "If you truly didn't know she'd survived, then you have no reason to feel guilty for anything she did."

My mother leaned forward. "Do not mistake my anger for guilt, Detective. I am no guiltier than anyone in this room. We were betrayed. We built a community based on trust, on good works, on radical hospitality, and we were betrayed. There has never been a day in my life since June of 1985 that I have not grieved for the Strasburgs, and for all of us, for what we lost. But I have never felt guilty."

I had never heard such steel in her voice. *Go, Mom.*

From her seat at the end of the table, Detective Spencer

spoke. "You won't be surprised to know that Peggy Manning was also a pseudonym. And we confirmed your suspicion— she never did officially enroll at the University. The lab ran the prints from the vase Detective Washington bought." She pointed at a vase, ten inches high, sitting in the middle of the table, in its plastic evidence bag. The same pale green as the porcelain piece I'd seen at her stall in the Market, the same simple flute shape as the one on Sharon Stinson's desk. "And we took more prints, from her apartment, the studio, and the van. Unfortunately, as you know, prints can't give us a name unless they're already in the system."

"Meaning—?" My mother drew out the word, sentence unfinished.

"Meaning," I said, "that we might never know who she really was."

"We do have a couple of leads, from the FBI," Spencer continued. "The most promising is an heiress from Connecticut who went missing in 1968. She'd been involved in the antiwar movement, with a group best known for a series of bombings. After an accidental explosion that killed two of their members, the group splintered. One faction continued setting bombs but focused on property damage. They even sent out warnings, to limit the risk of injury."

My mother's mouth fell open, her posture rigid. "So it was Peggy who took the explosives. Not Roger." She spoke slowly, deliberately, the gaps between her words filled with pain. "Detectives, you have to believe—we never had any idea that she knew the first thing about explosives."

Washington broke the silence. "The explosion was so loud, it rocked houses on the other side of the lake. It flattened two-thirds of the Strasburg house, took out half the house to the north, and knocked down the garage on the south side."

And yet, a woman and two young boys had survived. Miracles do happen.

Beside me, my mother breathed in large gulps of air.

"Some people"—Spencer opened a folder—"are too extreme for the extremists." She laid a photograph from the FBI files in front of us.

Déjà vu all over again. Beside me, at the sight of young Peggy—or whoever she was—my mother breathed in sharply.

"Whoever she was," Tracy said, "that bracelet pretty much proves her involvement in the Strasburg murder. What puzzles me is why take it, then stash it in the house?"

My mother shook her head, baffled. "No idea."

"One of the quirks of the community," I said, "was a fervid antimaterialism. As if the older our couch and the more secondhand clothing we wore, the better. Style was too—I don't know, middle class. Sorry, Mom."

She smiled wryly, no humor in it. "The simple life, gone too far. It sounds so judgmental now."

"And it backfired. Five kids in the house, and we're all chronic collectors and remodelers. Oh. You said she was an heiress." I reached for the vase, the plastic crinkling as I turned it over to point to the double diamonds on the bottom. "Jewelry, wasn't it?"

Spencer nodded.

I remembered my first thought when I saw her work and read her name. I remembered my mother's comment that Peggy always seemed to want one thing and choose another. "She wanted a simpler beauty. Her name betrays her. Bonnie Clay. Pretty Pots."

A wave of sadness rippled through me, to think that her true name and fate might never be known.

Who were you, Bonnie Pretty Pots? Why did you always need to leave?

And why did you come back to us?

Twenty-seven

You owe it to us all to get on with what you're good at.

—W. H. Auden and Christopher Isherwood, *The Ascent of F6: A Tragedy in Two Acts*

"PEPPER, SLOW DOWN."

Hard to do with a full head of steam. And I was steamed. Ticked. Mad as a wet hen. Pick your metaphor, it fit.

I stopped in the middle of the sidewalk. "Secrets, Mom. I am so sick of secrets. I've done little but deal with all this the last twenty-four hours, and I can't hold it in anymore."

"So much about parenting is a judgment call. You do your best, and then you wonder, and worry."

"Don't play the parent card, Mom. That was a long time ago. You never thought, in all those years, that maybe you should tell us? It changed our lives, too." Even though we didn't know all the details or remember all the players. It's emotional memory—you remember that something went wrong, that you were hurt, and if you don't know why, you try to work out the reason. As often as not, you're wrong.

"It never came up, until last night."

"It came up last week."

We were standing on one of the patches of purple glass

prism lights that dot the sidewalks near Pioneer Square, skylights for the basements that had been street level before the regrade after the Great Fire of 1889. We were standing on the sidewalk barking at each other.

"Pepper, I'm sorry. This whole thing is a mess that won't go away. I'm sorry we didn't tell you sooner, and I'm sorry I disappointed you. I need to be alone for a while. Go back to your shop and do what you do well."

Ah, but what was that?

I watched her walk away, feeling lower than a toadstool's back end, to quote my grandfather Reece. I hated arguing with my mother even more than I hated behaving badly in public. More than I hated being kept in the dark.

Her small figure got smaller in the distance. I understood she hadn't wanted to think about the past. It was a troubling time. She wasn't proud of it. Who among us doesn't have a moment—or several—like that?

I aimed north, hugging myself as I walked. The problem— the reason I was having trouble forgiving both myself and her—was that when facts are doled out piecemeal, one at a time, you form an impression, and in two shakes, you have to change it. Like putting together a puzzle of a cat, then getting a piece that convinces you it's a dog. Or an umbrella.

It seemed probable that Bonnie—Peggy, or whatever her name was—had gathered the explosives and hidden them in the garage. But while my mother was adamant that they had been disposed of—legally, she insisted—it was obvious that Bonnie had kept another stash. A small one, but big enough to do serious damage.

Big enough, my mother had believed all these years, to have killed her.

"You thought they were fireworks?" I'd said, in the detectives' conference room. "And then, you think your friend is killed in an explosion and you never make the connection?"

"We had no reason," she insisted. "It was months earlier.

There were ancient sparklers and smoke bombs and all kinds of fireworks, from when they were legal. Why would we have thought Bonnie had a private stash? Or kept it at Grace House, where she never lived?"

And, in fact, Bonnie had not been killed. Now she was dead, and we didn't know why. Finding out mattered more than my childish pout over truth withheld. Although that mattered, too—because it forced me to rethink who I was, and where I'd come from.

But then, that's how we figure out who we are, and where we're going.

THE shop was buzzing.

Actually, it was the phone in my pocket. Lesson learned, I pulled it out and read Tory's text: *Call me X2.*

Meaning call me on the double, or that she had two things to tell me?

A low moan came from behind the front counter. I circled around and crouched to pet my sweet dog. "Sorry, buddy. Some places, you can't go." Police headquarters chief among them.

Then why would you want to go there? his soft brown eyes said.

Good question.

Cayenne had only worked here two months, but the place felt empty without her. It was not empty, thank goodness. Sandra and Reed worked behind the counter, he taking orders and ringing them up, she weighing and bagging. Matt had the day off, and Kristen worked the floor, answering questions, making suggestions. She appeared to be back in full form, if a little less sparkly than usual, and tossed me a tired but friendly smile. "We'll talk," I mouthed, and she nodded.

In my office, I tossed my tote under the desk and dug out

my phone. It doesn't do any good to read texts when they come in if you ignore them.

Tory's message begged for voice-to-voice contact.

"Jade ran into a friend at the art supply," Tory told me. "He said Hannah is house-sitting near Seward Park. Water views and room to paint. What's not to love?"

"So why'd she blow us off? What's she afraid of?"

"Don't know. That's your job, Ms. Detective. Speaking of detectives, Spencer came by and quizzed me this morning, when I was out on the sidewalk painting. Can you believe, she bought one of my abstract oils? From the Spice Shop series."

"She's got good taste."

"Yeah. Thanks. Anyway, she wanted to know everything I knew about Hannah Hart, which wouldn't fill a saltshaker. But that was before Jade texted, so I didn't know where Hannah was then. I should call and tell her, shouldn't I?"

"'Fraid so. But I wouldn't mind if you got tied up for a while."

A pregnant pause. "Well, it is tourist season. The gallery's busy, and I'm here alone today."

But before I took my dog and went prowling around Seward Park, I had another stop to make.

No fancy art cars out front this time, and no baby ballerinas. The noon rush had ended, and I parked in front of the bakery. Across the street, Mr. Adams's house stood silent behind the yew hedge. Arf and I climbed the broken steps. ("He won't let us fix them," Cayenne had told me at the hospital, "so no one will think he has anything to steal. Funny thing is, he doesn't.")

It all looked so *normal.*

Arf and I walked through a gate in the weathered wooden fence closed by a simple finger latch. The backyard was a haven. On one side of the steps, fragrant tea roses hid the house's foundation. On the other side grew hydrangeas, their flowers giant blue puffballs. Along the back fence, black-berry blossoms promised jam. A strawberry bed nearly drew me off course.

The light over the door still burned, a clear glass fixture accented by copper bands. The line between vintage and dated can be subjective, but I put the fixture on the far side of desirable. Still, it cast enough light for Mr. Adams to tee off on his attacker.

Torn leaves and petunia blossoms lay on the back steps, surrounded by dark brown potting soil and shards from a deep red ceramic planter. The glass in the lower half of the back door had been spidered by the impact of the old man's skull as he went down.

I dropped Arf's leash and scooped up the remains with my bare hands, depositing the dirt in another planter and the broken bits in the trash bin near the back gate. The gray plastic hose reel had tipped over, probably in the tussle. I righted it, then hosed off the steps and watered the other planters and the vegetables.

The old man had lived. No reason his sweet corn should die while he recovered.

I rewound the hose. As I maneuvered the rig into place, a glint caught my eye. I bent down to pick it up, snatching my fingers back just in time.

"Sit," I told Arf. "Stay." I closed the gate and hustled across the street to the bakery, where I begged a clean, clear plastic bag. Back in the yard, I used the bag as a glove and picked up the brass round, about the size of a quarter, attached to a scrap of striped ribbon.

I sat on the concrete stoop and peered through the clear plastic. Curved letters beneath a figure and a pair of crossed swords read FOR SERVICE IN IRAQ. Dirt obscured the other side.

Not stolen from the shrine inside—too new. Had the

attacker lost this? How else could it have landed here, in this small, well-tended space?

Mr. Adams had been attacked because Bonnie's killer believed he'd seen something. The murder was connected to the bracelet theft.

Who was connected to all three crimes, who might have lost this memento?

We left the way we'd come. Arf kept his thoughts to himself, as usual, but mine were a mix of sadness that Mr. Adams's sweet oasis had been violated and determination that it not be in vain.

Revenge may be sweet, but violence is always in vain.

"HE just left," the counter girl told me. Today's musical selection had a Latin beat. "He's catering a bridal shower luncheon over by Lake Washington. He should be back by three. Unless he kills the bride and gets arrested." She blanched, then flushed. "I shouldn't joke like that."

"No problem. Hey, I've got some finishing salt he wanted—for this job, I think. I need to catch him."

"Hang on." She zipped to the kitchen window, consulted the schedule, and gave me the address. Not a sign of good retail training, but I wasn't going to complain.

"One more thing," I said. "Hannah been by lately?"

"Practically every day. Good thing he's out—last time she came in, he threatened to call the cops on her."

"Whoa! She's not getting the message."

"Some people can't let go, you know?"

"I guess. Thanks again. Hey, Sharon." I held the door, and Terry Stinson's wife stepped in, tugging at the tight, sleeveless dress that showed off her workouts, a smudge of dirt near the hem. After seeing a picture of the young Bonnie-Peggy-whoever, I was struck again by their resemblance, and wondered if Terry had been attracted to Sharon in part because she reminded him of his lost love.

"Uh, Pepper. Hi." She ran her fingers along her jaw, wiping off a bit of dirt. "Thought I'd grab a cup of coffee while my daughter's in class. Join me, if you'd like."

A polite invitation she didn't mean. "Thanks, but I gotta run. Another time?"

A few minutes later, Arf and I were zipping down Lake Washington Boulevard. The same shrubs dotted these lawns as in Mr. Adams's neighborhood—hydrangeas, syringa, and roses—but the lots were bigger, the cars newer, everything shinier. The address I'd been given had sounded familiar, but I could have sworn I didn't know anyone living down here. Too rich for my crowd.

Josh's van stood, doors open, in the driveway of a gray-brown shingle-style home from the early twentieth century, his white-clad assistant unloading trays of party fare. I parked the Mustang on the tree-lined street and trotted down the hill. Josh emerged from the side door of the home, in his usual white T-shirt and blue bandanna. Today's cotton pants looked like a cleanup rag from a paintball party. If the manicured lawns and scissored hedges were any indication of the bride's taste, he'd be changing clothes before serving lunch.

"Hey, Josh," I called.

He tossed his clipboard aside, a wry half smile on his face. "I don't know who's worse, the brides or their mothers."

"Hazard of the business, I'm learning. Sorry to interrupt, but I knew you'd want to know. Mr. Adams is going to be okay." I gave him the nickel version. "His granddaughter works for me, so we're practically family."

"Thank God." He cast his eyes toward the cloudless sky. Farther down the hill, a stone patio jutted out behind the house, and a carpet-like lawn sloped to the lake. I gathered this was an outdoor affair. "Lou's old-school. Happy to see retail back in the neighborhood, but not too sure about this wedding theme bit."

"His family's not convinced the neighborhood is safe."

"After the murder, and now this—" Josh shook his head. "I don't blame them. But shit—sorry, bad stuff happens in any part of the city."

As the Strasburg incident demonstrated.

"Hate to bring up a sore subject, but any chance you've heard from Hannah lately?"

"No, thank God. Maybe she finally gets it. Life's crazy enough without turning yourself upside down and inside out on purpose."

"Amen to that. I'll let you get back to work."

"Most days, I say work is my sanity, but this woman is driving me nuts." He gestured toward the house, then slid a tray out of the van and lifted one corner of the plastic covering. "Care for a cream puff?"

The chocolate-covered morsel was halfway to my mouth when the side door flew open and banged shut. A tall blonde shrink-wrapped in black spandex shorts and a violet halter stomped toward the van, and I knew why the address had looked familiar.

"You are not giving the help my food," she shrieked.

I raised a hand to Josh and slunk away before she could recognize me, leaving him to deal with Bridezilla.

I may not have learned much, but at least I'd scored a cream puff.

Twenty-eight

THE MUSTANG IS YOUR BASIC ELDERLY BUT WELL-LOVED sports car. No frills and no electronic gadgets. But who needs GPS when you've got a dog as your copilot and a phone that talks to you?

Still not sure whether I was an insightful, intrepid investigator or too stupid to live, I searched for the address Tory had given me, somewhere in the tangle of streets carved into the hillside a century ago, by developers determined to create as many lake view lots as possible and line their pockets with the cash.

I was convinced that Hannah Hart knew something I needed to know.

Bonnie—and the late, unlamented Roger—had destroyed our community.

The killer had deprived us of the chance to find out *why*.

And inspired by the terrier in the backseat, I had no intention of giving up until I figured it out.

A dark sedan streaked past me. Had I been daydream dawdling like the worst bad driver?

Then a blue SPD patrol car roared by. Two more approached from the opposite direction. I pulled to the curb and took the Mustang out of gear, watching the police cars converge on a sage green two-story, half a block away, a white SUV in the driveway.

The one that had nearly hit me the other day? Maybe. I hadn't seen car or driver up close. At the time, I'd blamed the incident on myself. But with all that I'd learned since, it looked like I'd been wrong.

More vehicles arrived. A bevy of uniforms jumped out and circled the house.

I glanced at the numbers on the nearest mailbox, then found a Google Earth view of my destination.

That was the one. Tory had waited, as promised, to alert Detective Spencer, who had called out the cavalry. I sucked in my breath and stayed put. I'd gone from investigator to observer in nothing flat.

Spencer and Tracy emerged from the sedan, each encased in bulky, official vests. The longer it takes to track a witness down, the more evasive the witness looks, and the higher the level of preparedness climbs. They approached the front door and knocked.

Why were they not pounding on the door?

Like so much of police work, this seemed to be a case of hurry up and wait. I switched off the engine and watched from my point of safety as the cops conferred, used their phones, conferred again, knocked again. Nothing happened.

Fifteen minutes later, we were all still waiting. My dog had to pee. So did I. I was about to back into the nearest driveway and head out the way I'd come when Spencer strode purposefully toward me.

"So, did Ms. Finch call you before or after she called me? Not that it matters. Helping us find Hannah does not give you permission to spy on a possible killer."

"So you think she could be the killer? But why? She's a spurned lover who just wanted to cause trouble."

Spencer's gaze met mine. "Sounds like reason enough to me."

Sitting here ruminating, too focused on the bracelet and my own family's role in this mess, I'd nearly talked myself out of thinking Hannah Hart a killer.

"We've put up barricades at both ends of the block. If she's holed up in there, we'll wait her out. I'll radio the officers to let you leave. Go home."

I put the Mustang in gear and wound through the idling patrol cars, then past the barricade. But I did not go home. After all the craziness, Arf and I deserved a walk in Seward Park, a forested peninsula jutting into Lake Washington.

At the bottom of the hill, I turned into the park's circular entrance, bright with early-summer blooms.

"C'mon, boy." Arf didn't have to be asked twice. He dashed over to the bushes and did his thing, then we found a restroom where I could do the same.

We strolled north on the main trail, past the old brick bathhouse, now a community art studio. This wasn't my part of the city, and I hadn't been down here since the torii, a ceremonial Japanese wooden gate, had been restored in time for cherry blossom season.

It felt good to move. Stretch my legs. Get the lead out, my dog trotting beside me.

Living where I do, it can be easy to forget that there are wild pockets in the heart of urbanity. That foxes and blue herons, bald eagles and itty bitty ferrets thrive a stone's throw from paved streets and parking lots.

We passed the swimming beach, and I unhooked Arf's leash. He leaped into the water. Two minutes later, he was back, showering me with droplets and that amazing terrier smile. I sometimes wonder if it's fair to keep a dog his size in an apartment, but I'd be lost without him.

And I like to think he's happy. Sure seems that way.

Back on the trail, we trotted onward. No doubt the police knew more about Hannah than I did. Let them decide whether she was merely a person of interest, or a murder suspect.

Regardless, I imagined that was why Bonnie had not wanted to take a piece as valuable as the Strasburg bracelet—a piece that linked her to a killing—into her studio or the apartment. Not after knowing that a woman with a grudge and a key might come at her anytime.

The past week had been hell on my friends and family. We'd been confronted with secrets and shame and dark corners in our lives. We'd been forced to reconsider relationships we'd never questioned, even our very identities.

A squirrel darted across the trail, and Arf tugged on the leash.

Beyond the tip of the peninsula, a handful of sailboats chased the wind. We followed the trail south, Mount Rainier's white slopes sparkling in the distance. On the water, a pair of red kayaks bobbed, the boaters' oars dipping in and out of the waves like a pair of birds used to flocking together.

In the classic movie *Gaslight*, Charles Boyer marries Ingrid Bergman so she will lead him to a hidden cache of jewels that had belonged to her murdered aunt. Jewels he had killed the aunt, years earlier, to find. The theory that the killer had counted on Bonnie to lead her—or him—to the bracelet raised other questions. Brian Strasburg suspected that Bonnie had a connection to his father's murder. Did he know—or suspect—that she had taken the bracelet? Had he been tracking her for that reason?

I wondered what the police had found when they dug into Strasburg's alibi. But even if it fell apart, I had no evidence putting him anywhere near Wedding Row on Friday night. And why on earth would Bonnie have buzzed him into the building, or opened her apartment to him?

Hannah, on the other hand, had a key. But she could only have known about Bonnie's search for the bracelet if Bonnie had told her.

And that made no sense.

But if Bonnie had come back to Seattle to get the jewels, why had she made no move? Track down Kristen, drop by the house to say hi, reconnect, blah blah blah.

A bicyclist whizzed around us, and it hit me. *Pepper, you're an idiot.* Ben's article had quoted both Sandra, my "estimable second-in-command," and Kristen, whom he'd termed my "loyal childhood pal."

Bonnie hadn't been watching me. She'd been watching Kristen.

What a boon, to find me on the front page of the paper and discover that my childhood friend was still by my side.

She'd scored an unexpected spot in the Market when a daystall opened up. It wasn't strictly first come, first served—management considered product mix, uniqueness, and quality.

The stars had aligned.

Bonnie's reluctance to go to Kristen's party had not been an act. She'd wanted very much to get into the old house— I'd misread the expression in her eyes as we'd climbed the broad steps. What she hadn't wanted was to be seen. To reconnect with any of us.

We were not her community anymore.

Life isn't a movie, Pepper. The story line doesn't have to make sense. And there may not be a happy ending—or justice.

A squirrel dashed across the trail, and Arf halted, hope drooling from the corner of his mouth as he peered through the dense underbrush on the hillside.

"Sorry, boy. He's too quick for you." We moved on, picking up the pace. The cobwebs in my brain and legs needed a good long stretch.

The kayakers had become specks in the distance. A seagull swooped low over the shoreline.

High atop a madrone, a bald eagle surveyed his kingdom. He ignored us, neither fish nor fowl. I drank in the warm sun, the fragrance of cedar and damp earth. *Oh, heaven.*

I'd hoped, when I first learned about Bonnie's role in the tragedy, that she'd come back to face it. To make amends. But if the need to atone had driven her back to the Emerald City, she would have declared her presence. At the very least, made an effort to contact my mother or Kristen, or even Brian Strasburg.

No. She'd had another plan.

Arf veered off the path, and I followed him a few feet uphill, where he squatted beside a wild rhododendron. Plastic bag in hand, I scooped the poop and took a step back to the trail.

Where a small, lithe redhead marched rapidly toward us. She slowed, then stopped to pet my dog.

"What a little gentleman," she said. "Airedales always look so courtly."

"I imagine if you walk this trail often enough, you'd see every breed of dog in the world." I let the leash go slack, but kept the loop in my hand.

"I wouldn't know yet," she said. "But it seems like a great park."

"New in the neighborhood?"

"Yeah. I'm an artist. A friend's parents lent me their guest apartment, above their garage, where I can live and paint."

Arf's hackles might not be up, but mine were. Could this really be Hannah Hart? Yes, there are plenty of small redheads in the world, but walking in the park midday barely a block from where the police surrounded her borrowed refuge?

Naturally, my phone was in my tote, locked in the trunk of the Mustang. I couldn't call the police.

How would Cadfael handle this? He would never dissemble; he would never be dishonest about his intentions. But he wouldn't volunteer them.

"That's rough," I said. "You know, I think you know a couple of friends of mine. Jade and Tory. They're part of an art gallery and co-op downtown. They said you were looking for space. I'm Pepper, and this is Arf."

For a moment, I couldn't tell whether she was going to run or stay. "I was supposed to meet them, to look at their studio space. But I've been so scared lately. I blew them off."

Careful, Pepper. Don't spook her. "Why were you scared?"

She sat on a flat gray rock and flexed her foot. "I did something I shouldn't have done, and I think my boyfriend— ex-boyfriend—reported me to the police."

"Wow. What happened?" I perched on a darker rock a foot or two away, summoning the listening skills honed in HR. A pair of joggers trundled by.

"I don't know what Jade told you. I met him when he bought the building where I rented. Gorgeous space. The studio has huge windows and tall ceilings, with an apartment upstairs. It has a pedestal sink and a claw-foot tub." Her wistful tone sounded genuine.

"Sounds perfect for an artist." Even Cadfael wasn't beyond guiding someone who wanted to talk.

"Our relationship got pretty crazy, and he threw me out. I didn't think he meant it." Her voice broke, and a tear rolled down her cheek. "But I was wrong."

"I don't understand. What would that have to do with the police?"

"I tried to help him out, by finding a new tenant. A potter." She stuck a finger inside her shoe and rubbed a spot below her ankle. "But that just made him mad. Then I tried to get her to leave, so he wouldn't be so mad, but she didn't want to move again."

A very different story from the one Josh told. The old medieval chants started playing. Every story has two sides. Sometimes more.

"But then Bonnie—the new tenant—got killed," Hannah continued. "I feel terrible, like I'm responsible for her being in harm's way. But relieved, too, that it wasn't me."

"I heard about that. It's awful. Do you know what happened?"

"No. But I keep wondering about this guy I saw." She paused. "I probably shouldn't be saying anything. I don't have any idea who he was."

When someone says they aren't sure they should say anything, and you desperately hope they will, keep your mouth shut.

"I dropped in one afternoon—I moved out so fast, I left some boxes behind," she continued, "and this guy was coming out of the studio. I'd seen him once before, having coffee upstairs. He was telling Bonnie not to worry, that no one would care what had happened all those years ago."

I stayed silent, though questions were pounding in my head.

"She said she wanted them to care, that it was time to confess to what they'd done. For the children. His face got all twisted, and he started to cry. Then she saw me, and I told her I needed to get a box I'd left, so she let me in and I didn't hear the rest."

"Wow." Arf lay down at my feet, and I silently promised him an extra-juicy bone tonight. "What do you think was going on?"

"I saw him again a few minutes later on my way out. His wife was giving him heck. I'd seen her before, too—she's one of the dance moms. A real witch." Hannah extended her leg and flexed the foot. "My impression? Bonnie's his ex-wife, and he left her for the younger wife, the dance mom.

You know how some men keep picking women who look alike? I don't see women doing that, do you?"

I pictured Tag and the men I'd dated in the last couple of years. "Now that you mention it, no."

"And Bonnie was back in town, and she wanted to tell their kids the truth about the new wife, and he didn't want her to."

"Makes sense," I said, and it did, though her story was completely off target. We're that way, we humans, standing on our heads to figure out the most logical explanation for something we don't understand, and convincing ourselves we're right.

When the real explanation is staring us in the face and we can't see it, until it clicks. But how I was going to prove what had just fallen into place, I didn't know.

"Hey, I'm sorry I gotta run. It's been really great to meet you, Hannah." I pushed myself up off the rock. "I don't know what happened to this Bonnie. But I am absolutely sure you have nothing to feel guilty about."

I wished I could say the same of myself.

Twenty-nine

I am a rock,
I am an island.
And a rock feels no pain;
And an island never cries.

—Paul Simon, "I Am a Rock"

PROBLEM WAS, I HAD NO PROOF. BUT I HAD A PLAN, AND I had allies.

I also had a deep heartache. The downside of community, as my mother had learned so long ago, is that you sometimes discover truths you'd rather not know.

Matt had once worked in a wine shop, so I sent him up to Vinny's for the afternoon, promising a bottle of his choice, up to fifty dollars, as a bonus. I hoped Vinny wouldn't hate me too much tomorrow to give me the employee discount.

The rest of us gathered in the Spice Shop. Kristen pulled up the collar of Vinny's navy blue Windbreaker and tugged the khaki hat down low. If he hunched, kept his back to the street, and leaned hard on that three-iron, a parent parked half a block away, waiting for a kid, might be fooled.

Cayenne was the key. I coached her carefully. "Park out front. Double-park if you have to. This only works if the driver of the white SUV with the front-end scraped from hitting the street sign sees you. When you help Vinny out of the car, keep your arm around him, so no one sees his face. Hustle him up the stairs and in the front door. Get him settled in the chair by the front window. Don't turn the light on—we need the shadows."

"Right. Then I'll come out," Cayenne said. "I'll stand by the car as long as I can, making sure I'm seen."

"I can't decide whether this is brilliant or crazy," Kristen said. "Vinny, watch where you swing that thing."

We were hoping to pass a short, fiftyish white man off as a short black man well past eighty. I'd briefly considered recruiting Detective Tracy, the only black man anywhere near the right size who knew anything about the case. Then I'd come to my senses. Sort of.

Laurel would think I'd gone off my rocker. Tag would be furious that I'd done something so stupid—and roped other people into it.

It *was* stupid, in a certain light. But not too stupid to work.

Though I was sure of the killer's identity, I had no proof to take to Spencer and Tracy. This was the only way to get it. I had accidentally led the killer to Bonnie, and to Mr. Adams. Bonnie might not have felt the need to atone for her sins, but I did.

And Vinny could defend himself. Plus, when the action happened, Cayenne, Kristen, and I would be hiding in the kitchen, cell phones and other weapons at the ready.

"And if you have even an inkling that something is going wrong, call the police," I told Vinny and Cayenne.

Mr. Adams himself was safely resting in his hospital room. If he ever found out what we'd done, I had to think he'd get a kick out of it.

And I was fairly sure Cadfael had set a trap or two, but at the moment, I couldn't remember in which tale.

The plan was for Vinny and Cayenne to drive to Beacon Hill and make the drop-off, as if Mr. Adams were returning home. I'd checked the dance studio schedule online, hoping I had this worked out right.

Then I got back to selling spice, trying not to think about the ruse and all that could go wrong.

During a lull, I flipped through the hibiscus recipes Cayenne had put together. They would need a thorough testing—no serious cook hasn't tried a recipe from a magazine, or even a cookbook, and wondered whether anyone ever actually attempted to make it. Any recipe that walks out of this shop with our logo on it has to be foolproof.

She was proving herself a great addition to the staff, aside from her willingness to help with the investigation. High hopes. I had high hopes.

"Stop watching the clock every two minutes," Kristen said. "They'll be fine."

I busied myself making another sample batch of the cocoa steak rub. It was nearly ready for production.

The door clanged opened, and my mother walked in, fresh from the school assembly. I composed my expression, sure she'd figured out I was up to something.

Instead, she took my face in her hands. "Pepper, I owe you an apology."

"I think I owe you one, too." When you're a kid, you think your parents have life all worked out. Then you become an adult and realize they were doing their best, struggling like you are. The trick is to shift your perspective, so you understand them through the eyes of an adult, not of a child. And sometimes that means reevaluating what you think you know about yourself.

"No. You were right. As soon as Peggy interjected herself into your life and Kristen's, I should have told you two everything I knew. I wanted to pretend it was all in the past."

"Even though you think about it every day?"

"Amazing how we fool ourselves, isn't it?" Her voice rose and fell as she studied me, and I had the sense, not for the first time in the last week, that I was looking in a mirror that showed me myself in twenty years.

I could live with that.

My pocket buzzed. I pulled out the phone. Kristen held up both hands, fingers crossed.

Mission accomplished, Cayenne's text read. *On my way home. Till 2nite!*

I let out a whoop. My mother's eyebrows rose.

"Trust me, Mom. You don't want to know."

THE sun sets late this time of year, so there was no question of sneaking in under the cover of darkness. Instead, we parked two streets over and ambled down the alley as if we had every good reason to be there.

"It's a working garden," Cayenne said to Kristen as she opened her grandfather's alley gate. "Not the fairytale paradise your backyard is."

"It's delightful." Kristen gazed at the fruit trees, the berry patches, the vegetable beds. "He takes care of all this himself?"

"We help. He says gardening keeps him young."

"Then I'm taking lessons from him."

We went in the back door. I left it unlocked, the porch light off.

"You bring me dinner?" Vinny called. "I'm sitting here starving."

"In the kitchen," I replied. "Don't forget to bend over and walk with the cane."

The kitchen window looked over the sink to the backyard. The four of us ate at Mr. Adams's table, well out of sight, then we sent Vinny back to the living room, lace curtains drawn, a single lamp lit, the TV broadcasting its blue glare.

Cayenne scrounged up a battered deck of cards, and she and Kristen played gin rummy. I was too nervous—plus it's a game for two.

This had to work.

At quarter to ten, I heard a sound and held out my hand. Nothing.

Kristen picked up her cards and opened her mouth to speak. Another sound stopped her—a metallic clang, followed by a creak.

"The gate latch," Cayenne mouthed. We picked up our makeshift weapons and I made sure my phone was at the ready.

If I was right, our intruder had long ago sworn off guns and explosives. Lost physical strength, too, to time and regret. We could handle this.

Through the open window, we heard a scraping—footsteps on concrete. Then, the crunch of steps on the broken gravel we'd hauled in from the alley and spread at the base of the stoop. A long silence. We exchanged looks, and over my thumping heartbeat, I half hoped we were wrong.

We were not wrong. The screen door hinges squeaked. The main door latch clicked open. If you shove your way through a balky door, it may be silent, but if you push it too slowly, too carefully, it may squeal.

This one did.

"That you, Cayenne?" Vinny called in his best old-man imitation. "I'm coming."

The end of the three-iron's handle made a soft thump on the thin living room carpet, growing louder when he reached the vinyl floor in the back hall. In the kitchen, Cayenne stood on one side of the door, ready to flick on the light as soon as we knew we had our man. I stood at the other, prepared to pounce.

"Say, you're not my granddaughter. Who are you?"

"You shut up, old man," the muffled voice said. "You shut up about what you saw that night."

"Saw what night?"

"That night the potter was killed. You told the police you saw me. Then you told that snoopy spice witch who won't give up."

And I wasn't giving up now.

"Didn't see nothing but a car. A white SUV. That what you mean?"

"And the license plate. The police were looking at my license plate," the voice said, rising in panic.

"You fool. I'm eighty-five. I can't read a license plate unless it's six inches from my nose. Now you get outta here before I make you regret it." Vinny's feet scuffled on the floor, and he barked the prearranged code word. "Go on. Scat!"

Cayenne threw on the lights, and I jumped into the hallway. Grabbed the intruder and pushed. Strong arms pushed me back, but Vinny went for the low head butt and slammed the figure into the wall, then aimed his three-iron at the knees.

"Owrrwww," the intruder yelled, dropping a small garden trowel and sliding to the floor.

I kicked the trowel aside. Kristen slammed a bowl over the intruder's head. Josh's roasted veggie salad slid over the intruder's head and chest, and filled the air with rosemary and thyme.

This person was way too short. I reached over and yanked the black ski mask off.

Revealing not the bearded figure I had expected, but his wife. The once-fierce blond dance mom now a whimpering puddle of veggies and vinaigrette: Sharon Stinson.

HALF an hour later, the suspect whisked away by uniformed officers of the South Precinct, Detective Michael Tracy closed his eyes and pinched the bridge of his nose. "And you didn't tell us who you suspected *why*?"

"You wouldn't have believed me if I'd said Terry Stinson was the killer," I said from my post by the kitchen sink. My three pals and Tracy were sitting at Mr. Adams's table. Spencer leaned against the doorway, arms crossed, her expression one of peeved amusement. I'd helped myself to a bottle of beer from the fridge. The detectives had declined, though Tracy looked longingly at the plate of gingersnaps.

"No," he admitted. "And besides, you were wrong."

I wasn't sure whether to be shocked or relieved that our attacker—Bonnie's killer—was Sharon. She'd been a blubbering wreck by the time we unmasked her, but I'd gotten her to admit this much: She'd been terrified that Bonnie would expose Terry's involvement in an old trouble, destroying the family that meant so much to them both.

"His involvement in what?" I'd needed her to say it. Vinny had wrapped his belt around her waist, cinching her into a kitchen chair, and Kristen and Cayenne used extension cords to tie her hands and feet.

"In the shooting over the computers," she'd said, and then I knew I'd been right—and wrong. What my parents and Kristen's—the entire Grace House community—had believed in 1985 was wrong. And it was Terry who'd misled them.

Roger Russell's sidekick in the deadly vandalism that killed Walter Strasburg and Roger himself had been not Bonnie-Peggy, but Terry. She'd fled, horrified by what the two men she'd loved had done. He'd stayed and let everyone believe her guilty.

Had he truly believed in the cause, or gone along with the whole terrible scheme to impress her?

That, I didn't ask Sharon. She'd suffered enough, keeping her husband's secret all these years. I was suddenly, irrationally, furious with him for making her carry that burden.

After my talk with Hannah, I'd concluded that Terry killed Bonnie because he feared she would reveal that he had known of her involvement all along. That in coming home to atone, to make amends, she would reveal his obstruction of justice. Her crime was far worse than his—in my version of the past—but he had more to lose.

It was a logical mistake, over a series of illogical crimes.

Either way, it delivered a shockeroo to my belief system. To my certainty that Terry was one of the good guys, the unflappable one who had continued rousing rabble and walking the talk. When he said, "Support the troops," he meant it—and when they came home, he took care of them.

Atonement. Dressing as Uncle Sam, drawing attention to the lingering impact of war, while serving the men and women who bore its scars.

Hannah had misunderstood Terry's plea to Bonnie about the children; another logical mistake. He'd been warning Bonnie to keep quiet to protect his own children, the late-in-life family he cherished.

And then I'd remembered the Iraqi campaign medal. I'd bagged it for evidence but forgotten to turn it in. I hadn't looked closely at the pin that had stabbed me in Terry's office, the one lost in the couch, but odds were they'd belonged to the same man.

"The man who attacked Mr. Adams the other night. He's one of Terry's clients, isn't he?" I'd asked her. "He came to your office last week, with a man in a wheelchair. Short blond hair, tattoos, baggy fatigues. He's been down here before—you were the dance mom who hired him to build new shelves in the studio. You came back to finish the job he started on Mr. Adams. When I saw you at the bakery this morning, you were a mess. You'd been searching for the medal he lost."

"You found it first," she said. "You're as snoopy as that old man. He stood in the bakery and defamed an honorable veteran, calling him a gang member and would-be thief, when he was only a vet trying to drum up odd jobs." She shot Vinny a dirty look, not seeming to realize he was a ringer. A live one, but a ringer nonetheless. "He saw everything. I had to stop him."

I'd wondered how Bonnie's killer knew Mr. Adams had seen him—or her. But it was my fault. I'd said so, in Terry's office, in front of Sharon.

"I'd been wondering how Terry knew Bonnie was back before the party last Friday night. If she meant to confess, she wouldn't have called him first, after all these years. Seattle's a big city; you don't just run into people. But sometimes you do. He saw her, when he was picking up your kids. They talked. She gave him the vase that sits on your desk."

"But why'd you have to kill her?" Vinny said. "That doesn't make sense."

"I wouldn't have done it if it wasn't for that stupid bracelet," she said, slumping down as far as Vinny's belt allowed.

"You knew she meant to give it back to the Strasburg family," I said. "But how did you know she took it? Did you see her, on the house tour?"

"What? No. Bonnie didn't take the bracelet." She wriggled her shoulders, her hands tied behind the chair back. "Terry did. He stole it for her thirty years ago, and he stole it for her again. I saw him slip it in his pocket, but I didn't say a word. When he went off to find her, I knew."

She's the kind of woman a man gives jewelry to, he'd said when I complimented his wife's diamonds. The diamond earrings she wore every time I'd seen her, even now. *That's because you're the kind of man who gives a woman jewelry*, she'd replied. I'd misinterpreted Bonnie's squirm as a remnant of that old antimaterialism.

After all these years, he'd still wanted her to have that diamond and sapphire bracelet. He'd never understood that she'd honestly meant to leave all that behind.

The flashing police lights had reflected off the front window and the TV screen at that moment, and Cayenne had let the officers in. Spencer and Tracy had been minutes behind.

"And she talked her way into Bonnie's studio that night," I told them now. "They fought. Sharon grabbed a platter—she works out, she's strong—"

"You're telling me," Vinny said, rubbing a sore spot on his arm.

"I can't believe you did that," Tracy said.

I slid the plate of cookies closer and touched his arm, the medieval harmonies playing in my head, not in warning but in celestial revelry. "Sometimes, Detective, you have to trust the Universe. And have a cookie."

Thirty

The Tao that can be told is not the true Tao.
The name that can be named is not the true name.

—Lao Tsu, *Tao Te Ching*

"WE'VE CONFIRMED WITH THE POLICE IN NEW HAVEN
and her one surviving sibling. Bonnie-Peggy is the missing
jewelry heir." Detectives Washington and Spencer met me
at the shop Friday morning. Tracy, they said, was running
down a few last details. They'd taken Terry Stinson into
custody last night. The girls were with relatives.

Between them, Sharon and Terry had done the very thing
they'd intended to prevent: In attempting to silence Bonnie
and protect their family, they'd torn their family apart.

"So all the names we knew were false. I wonder which
one felt most real to her." I hadn't started brewing our tea
yet, but the detectives had brought me coffee. And cinnamon
rolls.

When I'd returned to the loft last night and confessed the
whole crazy incident to my mother, she'd gotten right to
the heart, and I shared her observation now. "Ultimately,
Bonnie did honor her commitment to the community. She
came back, to confess her part in the murder and explosion,

and make up for the past. When she told Terry they had to tell the children the truth, she meant Walter Strasburg's children." And Kristen and me, as the representatives of our families.

Sharon acknowledged that she'd wanted to go after my mother, but Terry had been certain that Lena never knew his part in the deadly fiasco. He'd wanted to persuade Bonnie-Peggy that he was a true revolutionary. Instead two men were dead, and he'd lost her. He'd rebuilt his life, but her plans to confess threatened to destroy it all. She was destroying him—again.

"We're meeting with Brian Strasburg and his brother later this morning," Washington said. He looked mighty comfortable in my nook. "We can finally give them back that bracelet."

The irony was, Bonnie hadn't actually been there. She'd known the plan. She hadn't told the other community members, knowing they'd oppose it and go to the police. Terry insisted Roger had taken the explosives months earlier, without Bonnie's knowledge, that she'd had a change of heart about violence. She'd seen Roger and Terry off and waited for them to return.

But only one of them did. And when it wasn't the right one, she took off.

I knew how the rest of the community felt, their anger and sense of betrayal. But I could only imagine hers.

I had suspected Brian Strasburg because the son of a dead man makes a great suspect—especially a man with a volatile personality, the means and ability to conduct a private search, and a chip on his shoulder the size of Mount Rainier. When I thought Bonnie had participated in the attack at his childhood home, I'd assumed he'd seen her eyes and burned the image into his heart. Learning that Roger's accomplice had been Terry, not Bonnie-Peggy, destroyed that theory. But Brian had seen Bonnie in the Market and undergone a transformation. Had Washington revealed her name, to Brian or to his now-deceased mother? Had he tracked her down, following the same path as Ben and I had? Had he seen Bonnie-Peggy's eyes on a casual encounter, while she and Roger cased his neighborhood?

Perhaps I'd ask him one day. Or maybe not. It didn't matter.

Noticing eyes—my own personal superpower—was not always an asset, it seemed.

"While you were setting your trap, we were finishing the inventory of her locker in the Market, and her studio and apartment," Spencer said. "Besides the newspaper story on your shop, she had a stack of clippings on the Strasburg brothers—Brian's new law firm, his brother's tech company. Even their mother's obituary. She was planning to make contact."

I cradled my coffee, seeking warmth it couldn't give. "But my mother's arrival and the party invitation lured her back into the community too soon, before she could work out her plan. Why now, after all these years?"

"Stinson told us she'd gotten tired of living under a cloud. She was nearly seventy, and she didn't feel she could go back to Connecticut. Her family had disowned her ages ago. Seattle was her chosen home."

"It could have worked," I said. In getting justice for her, we'd also gotten a late, strange sort of justice for the Strasburg family. "Seattle, and the Market, are pretty forgiving places. What's going to happen to all that pottery, and her kiln?"

"I talked to the sister this morning," Spencer said. "She's in shock, but she thinks she'll want to donate the equipment and supplies. You might have some suggestions."

The community art studio at Seward Park. Continuing the legacy.

"Oh, hey, one more thing," I said. "How did Sharon Stinson

know you were checking her license plate?" Turned out Sharon had tried to run me over, on the spur of the moment, when she saw me crossing the street in Pioneer Square. But the witness had only gotten two letters and a number, one wrong, so the police had not been able to trace the car.

"Complete coincidence," Spencer said. "Their office isn't far from the police station, and a uniformed officer spotted her vehicle, parked in a 'no parking' zone. She saw him and jumped to the wrong conclusion."

Washington finished his cinnamon roll and licked his sugared fingers. "She was already on edge, believing the woman her husband had loved thirty years ago had the power to destroy everything that mattered to her."

"And yet, he cared as deeply as she did about protecting their family."

"He's ill, you know. Lung trouble of some kind. That's no excuse, of course. When it comes to love and passion, you never know what people will get up to," the big detective said.

Isn't that the truth?

THE hibiscus arrived sooner than I'd expected—you drop a ton of money, sometimes the seller upgrades the shipping as a bonus—and I took a bag down to Mary Jean. Josh had already called her about selling truffles and bars at Beacon Hill Bakery, and no walls could contain her excitement.

"Boss, you gotta see this." I'd barely set foot back in the shop when Sandra pulled a rolled-up magazine out of her apron pocket and laid it in my hand.

Northwest Cuisine. I'd forgotten today was publication day. My breath stopped momentarily. Sandra kept her face somber, but the twinkle in her eye gave the secret away.

Nancy Adolfo's review took up two pages, coupled with scrumptious photos. Her comments were begrudgingly good, starting with "a diamond in the rough." "The staff is knowledgeable, if prickly"—referring to Sandra, no doubt. Adolfo pronounced our blends "surprisingly tasty," another backhanded endorsement, and termed our packaging "a look that's both vintage and up-to-date, evoking the Market's special place in Seattle's past and present."

Exactly the image I'd hoped to convey.

"Your reviewer found the Spice Shop's Herbes de Provence beautifully captured both the tang and the romance of that region," I read out loud. "And the Backyard Rub will add the right mix of flavor and heat to your summer grilling, whether you've got two feet of deck or half an acre in the suburbs."

"Where do they come up with this stuff?" I said, then explained to the customer who gave me a quizzical look. "A review of our shop. We're thrilled, but food writers do sometimes wax a bit too poetic."

She laughed and took a magazine from the stack piled next to the cash register.

"She tested our recipes, too," Reed said. "Raves about the potato-broccoli frittata and the salty oat cookies."

The frittata had been my creation, the cookies Laurel's— both customer faves.

"She nixed the parchment-baked salmon, though," Sandra added. "She thinks cilantro should be treated like a weed and eradicated."

"Oh, I don't care for it, either," the customer said as Reed returned her credit card. "Tastes like soap."

"You're not alone. About fifteen percent of people can't eat the stuff. It may have to do with your sense of smell or your ability to tolerate bitter tastes." I handed her a copy of our popular salmon recipe. "Substitute parsley for the cilantro in the pumpkin seed pesto. You'll love it, and there's no cleanup, which is nice with fish."

She studied the recipe. "All I need is salmon, and I can make this tonight. Thank you."

I love my job.

A few minutes before noon, I snuck into the nook for a little experimentation. I ground a cup of hibiscus flowers and strained them into a bowl. Added small crystals of sea salt. My goal was a well-rounded blend, not a salt bomb.

"Mmm. Try this," I told Sandra.

A look of bliss crossed her cherubic face. "What about a little black pepper?"

"Good idea." I added a few twists of my favorite black pepper, a Tellicherry from India that we import by the ton, almost literally. "How did Paul's tests go?"

"Turns out, it's a blown disk. He's going to get acupuncture from Reed's dad."

She'd said she hates women who bawl at work, but that apparently doesn't matter when the news is good. Or when the boss cries with you. We sat in the nook, my arms around her, not caring who saw us. Or if they thought we were crying because the peppers were too hot.

"Give me a hand," I said, when the tears had stopped. Together, we created a new display featuring Bonnie's salt pigs and cellars. They weren't for sale, but they deserved to be seen.

She nudged me with her elbow. "Man at the door for you."

I girded myself for the sight of a certain tall, handsome police officer. Instead, it was a certain man of the streets, wearing the familiar blue jersey. I stepped outside.

"Miz Pepper, I wanted you to know I'm all signed up. Ready to go. Changing course."

The kitchen training program. "Hot Dog, that makes me so happy."

"Me, too. But you know, I had to give 'em my real name. Even if that baseball player is the famous one." He yanked the football jersey over his head to reveal a baseball jersey, then twisted his shoulders to let me read his back. "Reynolds."

"Seriously? You've got the same name as the best-known

ex-Mariner?" I threw my arm around his shoulder in a side hug. "Harold, this is the beginning of a beautiful friendship."

MIDDAY, my mother arrived, bearing lunch for the entire staff from the Italian deli. "Your father called this morning, after you left for work. They're in harbor for the day, picking up supplies."

I picked up half a grilled turkey sandwich. "You tell him everything?"

She nodded. "He's furious with you. And proud of you. We both are."

I swallowed, not sure if this was the time to ask, but pushing on anyway. "Mom, are you two moving back to Seattle?"

She exhaled. "I don't understand anything Peggy—I still can't think of her as Bonnie—did. But I do understand that longing for home. It's primal. We're thinking six months here, six months there. Costa Rica is an adventure, and your father loves it. But home can be kind of an adventure, too, can't it?"

We laughed so hard I nearly fell out of the nook.

I sobered up in a hurry when the door opened and a tall blonde marched in, a brunette trailing behind her.

"We're here to pick up my spice rack," Bridezilla announced.

"Ah-h-h," Sandra said. "We may have a problem. It was—"

"Nope. Got it." I slid out of the nook and darted behind the front counter. Arf, on his bed, opened one eye, then closed it and returned to his nap. I lifted a large, light-weight box onto the counter and slid out a chrome spice rack, complete with forty metal-topped glass jars.

"It was this shop?" the brunette said, her high-pitched voice rising. "You said you were registered at that other one." She poked a thumb over her shoulder, gesturing.

"No," Bridezilla said. "It was *this* one. *This* is the best spice shop in town."

My staff and I managed to contain ourselves long enough for Sandra to gift wrap the box—no matter that the bride knew what was in it—and for the two women to leave, the maid of honor bearing the precious package.

Sandra held one arm around her stomach, holding it in, the other hand to her mouth. "I was sure we didn't get the rack. When she walked in, I wanted to disappear."

"I saw it on the back-order list," I said, "so I started calling our competitors to find one. That's when I discovered she'd sent her maid of honor here by mistake. She'd registered at two shops, and made herself a pest at both. The owner of the other shop sold me the rack at cost."

Sandra gaped, eyes wide. "You are brilliant."

I glanced down at my pink shoes. "And lucky."

I did not feel so lucky that evening. Ben had called late afternoon and asked if he could come up for a drink. Even though my mother was out, inviting him to my place didn't feel right.

He'd already claimed a booth, and drunk half a beer, when I got to the blues club, a couple of blocks from the loft on Alaskan Way. The live show hadn't started yet, but I swayed to the recorded rhythm of a seriously rockin' guitarist.

I slid in. "How was Portland? How's the story coming?"

"Uh, good. We should be ready to run the piece next week, part of a series on infrastructure problems throughout the Northwest."

I ordered a BB King Manhattan—Crown Royal and Grand Marnier with a cherry. "So it's not just earthquake concerns about the Viaduct and that I-5 bridge collapse?"

"Uh, no." Alternately spinning and gripping his half-empty beer glass, he talked about bridges, highways, and resurfacing. About functional obsolescence, bottleneck, and gridlock. It should have been fascinating. It wasn't. He broke off in the middle of a sentence about the gas tax trust fund. "Pepper, we need to talk."

I set my drink down. "You're right. I've been thinking, and—"

"I haven't been completely honest with you." He stared into his beer and licked his lips. "I haven't been honest at all."

This wasn't going where I expected.

"I didn't mean to lie to you, I swear. But it's been clear for a while that you're just not that into me, and . . ."

The ex-girlfriend in Austin, the one he'd moved to Seattle to get away from, had taken a job with the Portland daily paper. There was a slot open on a regional weekly, and after the hearing in Olympia Monday, he'd gone down to Portland to interview. He'd been there all week. She'd found a great apartment in the very hip Pearl District, roomy enough for two. He'd given notice and intended to move by the end of the month.

It's disconcerting to plan to break up with someone and find yourself dumped instead.

"If this is what you want, then I'm happy for you. If you two have worked things out—"

"Yeah." His head bobbed. "Yeah, I think we have. You're okay with this? Really?"

"Yeah. Really." No point telling him what I'd planned to say. I'd made my choice, and it didn't matter whether he knew. I knew what I wanted in a relationship, and that I hadn't found it yet. Kristen had been right last spring when she said there was nothing wrong with my judgment. I'd known this wasn't the relationship for me; I'd known something was missing. It had been fun, and fun had been what I needed. Faulty judgment would have been to try to make it more than it was.

The music changed, classic U2. "I still haven't found what I'm looking for," Bono sang, and I agreed.

I leaned across the table to kiss his cheek one last time. Then I slid out of the booth and walked out into the night.

It's a big sea, and it's full of fish.

Thirty-one

There is a taste of thyme-sweetened honey
Down the Seven Bridges Road.

—Steve Young, "Seven Bridges Road"

"WELCOME HOME!" WE SHOUTED AS CAYENNE AND HER husband led the real Mr. Adams into his house Saturday morning. The doctors had pronounced him likely to outlive them, although he was going to need the help of his family, in the garden and elsewhere.

"We bought you a present." The old man sat in his throne by the living room window, and Cayenne handed him a cane tied with a big blue bow. "See, Pops? The handle is shaped like the head of a golf club, but the shaft is strong enough to support you. Unlike the three-iron."

"Humph. As long as I can fight off intruders." He gave it a test swing, and we all stepped back.

In the kitchen, I unwrapped my offering, a bowl of herbed black bean pasta salad. "I've got to get back to the shop," I told Cayenne. "Enjoy your day off with the family."

"Not so fast," she said. "There's still one mystery to solve."

I tilted my head, puzzled.

She waggled her brows. "Your real name."

"You remember who signs your paychecks, right? Not Reed or Matt, and most definitely not Sandra."

She crossed her heart with one burgundy-tipped forefinger.

"I suppose you have earned the right to know. Persephone." She frowned, and I explained. "My mother was in her Greek goddess phase. Persephone was the maiden of spring, the daughter of Demeter, the Goddess of Corn, also called the Goddess of the Earth."

"Is she the one who was kidnapped by what's-his-name?"

"Hades, the King of the Dead. He took Persephone to the underworld and made her queen. Her mother was so distraught that all the crops died, and the people began to starve. Eventually, Zeus sent a messenger to Hades, and they worked out a deal. Persephone spent half the year in the underworld, with Hades, and half the year above, with her mother. And that is why we have the seasons, both spring and harvest. Joy and sadness."

And why mother and daughter, even when they are close and the daughter is grown, always fear that they don't measure up to each other's expectations.

Cayenne stuck a serving spoon in my salad. "I thought *my* parents were crazy, naming me after an ingredient in Tabasco sauce."

After all we'd been through in the last ten days, there was nothing like a good, long, happy hug.

But before I headed back to the Market, I dashed across the street to see Josh. I found him at the far back table, sipping coffee and tapping his fingers to the reggae filling the airwaves.

"You here to check on my cinnamon supply or gloat about your great review?"

A copy of *Northwest Cuisine* lay on the table, open to a picture of his bakery, with the headline PLAIN, BUT TASTY.

Underneath, smaller type read "One bite and you'll forget the lack of atmosphere in this Beacon Hill treat house."

"Don't worry about her," I said. "She's the kind of critic who uses charm as a code word to suggest style over substance, but tourists won't understand, and locals know better."

He made a "you may be right" gesture. "She raved about our cream puffs—she calls them profiteroles—with coffee ice cream, but dismisses cupcakes as quaint. I'll have her know we sell dozens of cupcakes every day. And she called our interior 'bare bones' and 'yesteryear.'"

I surveyed the stark walls, the utilitarian furniture, the scuffed linoleum floor. "She's got a point. Though you'd think she'd save her barbs for the coffee shops that try to distance themselves from Starbucks while aping their decor. Or the opposite extreme—designers who mistake intentionally mismatched tables and cat knickknacks for style."

"So I shouldn't ask you to go shopping for cast-off tables and chairs with me? Hey, on a more serious note, thanks for the chocolates. And for finding Bonnie's killer. Not to mention underscoring my resolve to work less and make time for a relationship that actually works."

"All that? Wow. You're welcome. I've got a few friends in the artist community, including a couple who need a studio and apartment while they search for a building of their own."

He spread his hands. "Send 'em in. I'll give 'em a free month's rent if they'll paint this joint."

I left the bakery and walked down the block, past the wedding boutique. The green silk dress was gone.

Didn't matter. My destination was the gift shop. The owner listened to my pitch about custom herb blends as wedding favors while she wrapped up my prize: the vintage

Dr Pepper cooler. The perfect companion to the picnic basket. I didn't know when I'd use either one, but I trusted that the time would come.

In the car, I checked my phone for messages. *The car.* My mother hadn't said which six months of the year they might spend in Seattle, but I had little doubt it would be the driest six months. Mustang weather.

I patted the leather seat. All good things must end.

A text from Tag. *Drink that champagne this weekend? No strings attached.*

Seriously tempting. But I had another temptation in mind. Instead of hitting reply, I called the shop and said I'd be back later than planned.

Odd as it was to set out on an adventure without my dog, I drove with purpose. Found a parking spot up front. Passed by the patio full of Seattleites and tourists enjoying lunch in the sunshine, beside the pleasantly fish-scented waters, and strolled past the docks until I reached the right one.

The slip was empty. I set my calling card—a jar of the Spice Shop's new cocoa spice rub, with a hint of thyme—in the fisherman's creel tied to the dock post, a makeshift mail box accented with old rope and a glass float.

Because life is about the choices we make.

Recipes and Spice Notes

The Seattle Spice Shop recommends . . .

COCOA-PAPRIKA STEAK RUB

The combination of paprikas and a touch of cayenne makes for a great flavor that will enhance any cut of steak. If you have cocoa nibs, substitute them for half the cocoa—they add a darker note and a bit of texture. Ground thyme—not leaves—adds a mellow complement.

1 tablespoon unsweetened cocoa powder OR 1½
   teaspoons unsweetened cocoa powder and 1½
   teaspoons cocoa nibs
2 teaspoons sweet (standard) paprika
¼ teaspoon smoked paprika
1 teaspoon packed light brown sugar or turbinado
   (raw) sugar
¼ teaspoon cayenne pepper

2 teaspoons kosher salt
¼ teaspoon ground thyme (optional)

Combine all ingredients. Spices can be stored and used within a week or two.

Makes about 3 tablespoons, enough for about 2 pounds of steak.

ITALIAN HERB BLEND

This is a good basic blend that you can adjust for your own taste. Remember that blends take a few hours for the flavors to meld; because of the mildness of these herbs, you can use the blend generously right away, and taste how the flavors improve over time.

  3 tablespoons dried basil
  2 tablespoons dried thyme
  4 teaspoons dried marjoram
  4 teaspoons dried oregano
  2 teaspoons dried sage
  2 teaspoons dried garlic flakes or garlic powder
  2 teaspoons dried rosemary (break the needles with a
      mortar and pestle or in a small bowl with the back
      of a sturdy spoon)

Mix herbs in a small bowl.

Fabulous in tomato sauce over pasta or on pizza, in a pasta salad with cooked or raw veggies, or in eggs. Try it in place of the red pepper flakes, fennel, and cayenne in Laurel's Spicy Morning Sausage in *Assault and Pepper*. Toss into a soup, stew, or casserole. Try the blend whenever a recipe calls for two or three of its ingredients.

Makes about 10 tablespoons, just over ½ cup.

Thyme for a backyard party

TEQUILA-THYME LEMONADE

Serve as a spiked lemonade, at cocktail strength, or allow guests to choose. Tequila adds a fun summer flavor, but gin, vodka, or white rum are also tasty—and it's equally delicious without alcohol.

1½ cups sugar
8 to 10 sprigs thyme or lemon thyme
Cold water
2 cups fresh lemon juice (about 10 lemons)
1 cup tequila (or other alcohol) for spiked lemonade;
    2 cups for cocktail strength
Thyme sprigs for garnish (optional)

In a small saucepan, bring sugar, thyme, and 1 cup cold water to a boil. Stir until the sugar is dissolved—about 3 to 5 minutes. Remove from heat and set aside to cool, allowing the thyme to continue infusing the syrup.

Juice the lemons.

Strain the syrup into a medium bowl, and discard the thyme sprigs. Strain the lemon juice into the bowl, and discard the pulp. Stir the mixture and pour it into a serving pitcher. Add 6 cups of cold water. Chill at least an hour before serving.

To serve, add the tequila to the pitcher, garnish, and serve over ice. Or set out a variety of spirits and a jigger, and allow guests to choose their own flavor and strength. In a standard highball or cocktail glass, ½ ounce of alcohol will "spike" the lemonade, while 1 ounce will make a standard-strength cocktail.

Makes 8 to 10 servings.

HERBED BLACK BEAN PASTA SALAD

This salad is terrific by itself or as a side dish, especially with chicken or salmon. Whole-grain pasta and beans make it an excellent source of protein for vegetarians—something Laurel keeps in mind when stocking Ripe's deli case. You'll love the color the turmeric and fresh herbs add—and the combination of fresh herbs in the salad and the dried herbs in the dressing gives an extra punch of flavor.

FOR THE SALAD:
  1 pound regular or whole-grain penne pasta
  1 15-ounce can black beans, drained and rinsed
  2 to 3 carrots, chopped
  1 red bell pepper, chopped
  1 yellow or green bell pepper, chopped
  1 small sweet onion, diced
  1 cup marinated artichoke hearts, drained and
    chopped
  ¼ to ½ cup fresh basil, chopped
  1 to 2 tablespoons chopped fresh oregano
  1 tablespoon chopped fresh sage
  2 tablespoons chopped fresh flat-leaf parsley

FOR THE DRESSING:
   ⅓ cup mayonnaise
   ¼ cup Dijon mustard
   1 heaping tablespoon brown sugar
   1 teaspoon Italian seasoning blend
   ½ teaspoon turmeric
   ½ teaspoon sea salt
   Freshly ground pepper

Cook the pasta until al dente. Drain and rinse in cool water to stop the cooking. Meanwhile, drain and rinse the beans and chop the vegetables and fresh herbs. Place the beans, veggies, and herbs in a large bowl. Add the pasta and stir to mix.

To make the dressing, place all the ingredients in a blender or a small food processor, or use an immersion blender, and mix until smooth. Add the dressing to the salad mixture and toss gently until well combined. (You may fear not having enough dressing, but don't worry—it will surprise you!)

Serve warm or chilled, by itself or over a bed of chilled hearty greens, such as a mixture of spinach, arugula, romaine, or other sturdy lettuces.

Makes 8 to 10 servings.

CUCUMBER CANTALOUPE SALAD

For Kristen and Eric's party, Laurel sliced the green onions on the bias in 2-inch lengths and threaded them on skewers with the cucumber slices and cantaloupe chunks. But she's a caterer, and they do things like that. Pepper just dumps it all in a bowl. If you're among the cilantro-averse, use mint.

¼ cup fresh lime juice
½ teaspoon sea salt
½ teaspoon freshly ground black pepper
1 English cucumber, peeled in alternating stripes and
    coarsely chopped
8 cups cantaloupe, cut in chunks (roughly one large or
    two small melons)
3 to 5 green onions, sliced
½ cup fresh cilantro or mint, chopped

In a bowl large enough to hold all the ingredients, whisk lime juice, salt, and pepper together. Add cucumber, cantaloupe, onions, and herbs. Stir to coat.

Makes about 10 cups.

LEMON THYME COOKIES

The herbs give these shortbread squares a light, summery touch that tastes terrific in any season. Serve with lemon sorbet for an elegant pairing.

½ cup butter, softened
¼ cup white sugar
1 tablespoon fresh thyme or lemon thyme leaves
2 teaspoons finely grated lemon zest
1 tablespoon fresh lemon juice
¼ teaspoon ground cardamom
1¼ cups all-purpose flour
Coarse white or granulated sugar, for topping

Preheat oven to 350 degrees.

Beat butter with an electric mixer on medium speed for 30 seconds. Add ¼ cup white sugar and mix until combined. Add thyme, lemon zest, lemon juice, and cardamom, scraping the sides of the bowl if necessary to get all ingredients combined. Gradually stir in the flour and mix.

Form the dough into a ball. To make it easier to work, divide dough into three equal portions. Roll each out on a floured surface into a 6-by-4½ inch rectangle, about ¼ inch thick. Cut into 1½ inch squares with a knife or a serrated pastry wheel. Sprinkle with coarse or granulated sugar. Place squares on ungreased cookie sheets.

Bake 12 to 15 minutes, until edges and bottom are golden. Cool on a wire rack.

Makes 36 small cookies.

At home with Pepper

STEAKS WITH COCOA-PAPRIKA RUB

Letting the rubbed steaks sit half an hour before grilling takes the peppery edge off.

Choose any cut of steak. Rub cocoa-paprika spice blend into all surfaces, including the sides, with your fingers. (You can also lay the steak in the spice mixture, as if you were breading it, then pat the spices into the surface of the meat.) Allow steaks to sit 30 minutes before grilling or pan-frying to your desired temperature.

HERBY-CHEESY SPREAD

This spread is even better the second or third day if you can keep yourself from eating it all at once. An easy flavor variation: substitute 2 tablespoons of the Italian blend for the herbs and spices listed below, and omit the ½ teaspoon salt.

4 to 5 ounces Parmesan or Parmesan-Reggiano, cut in small cubes
4 to 5 ounces Asiago, cut in small cubes
4 scallions or ¼ cup chives, roughly chopped
1 teaspoon fresh or 2 teaspoons dried oregano
1 teaspoon red pepper flakes
1½ teaspoons Aleppo pepper
1 clove garlic
½ teaspoon salt
1½ teaspoons black pepper
½ cup olive oil, more or less

Place the cheese cubes in the bowl of a large food processor and pulse or chop until coarse. Add the scallions or chives, and the oregano, red pepper flakes, Aleppo pepper, garlic, salt, and black pepper. Process until fully mixed. Pour in the olive oil and process until fully blended and smooth. Use less oil for a thicker spread, more oil for a thinner, smoother spread. Taste and adjust the seasonings to your palate.

Let the spread sit at room temperature until you're ready to serve it, to allow the flavors to develop. Store leftovers in the fridge, but let the spread return to room temperature before diving in again to get the fullest flavor. Serve with hearty crackers, crostini, or cut vegetables.

SUMMERTIME CHOPPED SALAD

Heavy on the oregano, not thyme—but this salad is too tasty to quibble over herbs! Buy the provolone and salami sliced for extra ease of prep. Serve with a crusty loaf of bread and a crisp white wine. (Pepper is partial to A to Z Pinot Gris from Oregon; Waterbrook Chardonnay, Pinot Gris, or Sauvignon Blanc, from Washington; or a French white Bordeaux.)

FOR THE OREGANO DRESSING:
   4 cloves garlic
   1 to 2 tablespoons dried oregano
   2 teaspoons kosher salt
   Freshly ground black pepper
   2 tablespoons lemon juice
   ¼ cup red wine vinegar
   ¼ cup olive oil

FOR THE SALAD:
   ¾ pound cherry tomatoes, cut in half
   Sea salt
   1 (15-ounce) can chickpeas or 1¾ cups cooked
      chickpeas, drained
   1 small red onion, peeled and sliced into paper-thin
      rings
   ½ pound provolone, sliced ⅛-inch thick and cut into
      ¼-inch ribbons
   ½ pound hard or Genoa salami, or ¼ pound of each,
      sliced ⅛-inch thick and cut into ¼-inch ribbons
   4 medium or 8 small pickled pepperoncini, sliced into
      rings (with seeds and juice)
   1 head romaine, cored and cut in ½-inch ribbons

1 head radicchio, halved, cored and cut in ¼-inch
   ribbons
Fresh oregano stems for garnish (optional)
2 hard-boiled eggs, peeled and sliced (optional)

Make the dressing: Use either a mortar and pestle or a small bowl and a sturdy wooden spoon. Chop the garlic and place in the mortar or bowl. Add the dried oregano, salt, and teaspoon ground pepper. Use the pestle or the back of your spoon to make a grainy herb paste. Transfer the paste to a large salad bowl, and add the lemon juice and vinegar. Mix with a fork or a small whisk until the salt dissolves, then pour in the oil and whisk until well combined. The dressing should be thick with garlic and oregano.

Assemble the salad: Cut the tomatoes in half, season with 1½ teaspoons sea salt, and set aside until ready to serve. Add the chickpeas, red onion, provolone, salami, pepperoncini (including seeds and juice) to the large bowl, one at a time, and gently stir to coat.

To serve: When you're ready to serve, gently add the tomatoes, romaine, and radicchio to the salad bowl, and toss to combine with the dressing. Garnish with fresh oregano and sliced hard-boiled egg, if you'd like. Serve immediately. (Once mixed, the romaine and radicchio will hold up for a day or so, although the other ingredients will keep for several days. So if you don't anticipate eating it all within 24 hours, mix half the romaine and radicchio with half of the other ingredients, and mix the rest up in a day or two when you're ready for more.)

Makes 6 servings as a main course and 12 servings as a side salad.

PEPPER'S GINGERSNAPS

The classic, with a bite of a little something extra. Call it Pepper's personal touch.

2¼ cups all-purpose flour
2 teaspoons baking soda
1 teaspoon ground ginger
1 teaspoon ground cinnamon
½ teaspoon ground cloves
½ teaspoon finely ground black pepper
¼ teaspoon salt
1 cup packed brown sugar
¾ cup vegetable oil, such as corn or canola
¼ cup molasses
1 egg
¼ to ½ cup white sugar for topping (optional)

Preheat oven to 375 degrees.

In a large mixing bowl, stir together flour, baking soda, ginger, cinnamon, cloves, black pepper, and salt. In a small mixing bowl, combine brown sugar, oil, molasses, and egg. Beat well. (No need to dirty your mixer and clean the beaters—the oil makes this dough easy to mix by hand.) Add flour mixture and stir until well mixed.

Shape the dough into 1-inch balls. If you'd like to top the cookies with sugar, pour the white sugar into a small soup or pasta bowl or on a small plate. Roll cookie balls in the sugar. Place 2 inches apart on an ungreased cookie sheet or a cookie sheet lined with parchment paper or a silicon sheet. Bake about 10 minutes, until bottoms have darkened slightly and tops begin to crack.

Makes about 4 dozen. These cookies will be soft at first, but crisp up nicely. They freeze well.

Spice up your life
with Pepper and the Flick Chicks

RASPBERRY LIMONCELLO SPARKLERS

A marvelous drink for a celebration, or whenever champagne is called for.

FOR EACH DRINK:

   ½ teaspoon sugar
   ¼ teaspoon grated lemon zest
   A few drops of fresh lemon juice
   4 to 5 raspberries
   2 tablespoons limoncello
   Crushed ice
   ½ cup sparkling wine
   A strip of lemon peel, for garnish

On a small plate, stir together the sugar and grated lemon zest. Dip a clean finger in the lemon juice and moisten the rim of a champagne flute. Dip the rim in the sugar mixture to coat.

Place the raspberries in a small bowl with the limoncello. Use a cocktail muddler if you're lucky enough to have one, or a wooden spoon, to crush the berries and make a limoncello-berry puree. Pour the puree into the sugar-rimmed flute. Add a spoonful of crushed ice, and pour in the sparkling wine. Garnish with the lemon strip and serve immediately.

Readers, it's a thrill to hear from you. Drop me a line at Leslie@ LeslieBudewitz.com, connect with me on Facebook at LeslieBudewitzAuthor, or join my seasonal mailing list for book news and more. (Sign up on my website, www.LeslieBudewitz .com.) Reader reviews and recommendations are a big boost to authors; if you've enjoyed my books, please write a review and tell your friends. A book is but marks on paper until you read the pages and make the story yours. *Thank you.*

They sat in silence for a minute or two. Finally Althea said, "Maura, I'm really here to apologize. You've been great about trying to help me, and all I've done is complain and make demands. You and Gillian both—you tried to tell me to dial it back, and I didn't want to hear it."

"You had a lot at stake," Maura said carefully.

"Sure, I thought finding that painting was important, but I've realized I was only thinking of myself. I never stopped to think that looking for it and finding it would involve so many other people's lives. I never thought anyone would die because of it."

Maura sneaked a glance at her. Were those tears in Althea's eyes? "What are you going to do now?"

"I . . . don't know. I mean, I—no, *we* found the painting and it's everything I hoped it would be, and it's a terrific story, but . . ."

"What?"

"I don't feel right using that for my own ends. Not after all that's happened."

"You go public with the story, and it's worth more. You told me that," Maura pointed out.

"I know. But . . . I guess it's not as important to me to get it into that exhibit and to have my moment of glory as it was when I started. I can still work to get the word out, so that Eveline and Harry will benefit. Somebody in the world—and I'd like to hope it's a museum rather than a private collector who'll hide it away for another century—will get an incredible painting. But I don't want to profit from something that caused someone's death."

"Why, Althea, I do believe you've grown a conscience!" Maura said, smiling.

Althea looked at her then and returned the smile. "Ya think?" They clinked glasses. Then Althea went on, "You know, I should spend more time talking with you. I mean, you've got to have a story, right? You can't have had an easy life, growing up in South Boston, losing your family, not a lot of opportunities. And here you are, where you never expected to be, and it looks to me like you're doing just fine. How did that happen?"

"Ireland happened. I think you've seen some of that. Time seems slower here. People are willing to help you, if you'll give them a chance. I've got deep roots here, ones I never knew I had. I'm still trying to figure out how and where I fit, but it's a good place to be."

"Maybe I should stick around a while longer, or come back after the exhibit opens. I wonder if Harry would let me inventory his collection of paintings. At least then he'd know what he's got. Maybe I could bring Dorothy and her father over and introduce them to the rest of the family. And I could still help Gillian place some of her paintings where they'll get more attention. She really does have talent."

"All good ideas, but it's up to you. I've got enough on my hands here without trying to manage *your* life."

"You couldn't do worse than I have lately!" Althea laughed. "Anyway, I just wanted to thank you for everything. I guess I'd better get back to the hotel—I'm exhausted."

"Slán abhaile," Maura said. When Althea looked blankly at her she said, "That means 'safe home' in Irish."

"Ah. Well, thanks again."

Maura watched her go, to make sure she got safely to her car. She did and drove off, leaving Maura alone in Sullivan's.

Chalk up one more victory for Ireland, Maura thought. Funny how the place changed people.

The Spice Shop Mysteries by
National Bestselling Author

Leslie Budewitz

ASSAULT AND PEPPER

GUILTY AS CINNAMON

KILLING THYME

Praise for the national bestselling
Spice Shop Mysteries

"A dash of humor and a half-turn of charm
that will leave readers smiling."
—J.J. Cook, national bestselling author of
the Sweet Pepper Fire Brigade mysteries

"Pure enjoyment."
—*Suspense Magazine*

"A tantalizing mystery and a
fragrant treat for the senses."
—Connie Archer, national bestselling author
of the Soup Lover's Mysteries

lesliebudewitz.com
penguin.com